JUN 1 7 2021

Also by Melissa Savage

Lemons

The Truth About Martians

Nessie Quest

Melissa Savage

Crown Books for Young Readers
New York

Text and interior illustrations copyright © 2021 by Melissa Savage
Jacket art copyright © 2021 by Aleksandar Zolotić

All rights reserved. Published in the United States by
Crown Books for Young Readers,
an imprint of Random House Children's Books,
a division of Penguin Random House LLC, New York.

Crown and the colophon are registered trademarks of
Penguin Random House LLC.

Visit us on the Web! rhcbooks.com

Educators and librarians, for a variety of teaching tools, visit us at
RHTeachersLibrarians.com

Library of Congress Cataloging-in-Publication Data
Names: Savage, Melissa (Melissa D.), author.
Title: Karma Moon—Ghost hunter / Melissa Savage.
Description: First edition. | New York : Crown Books for Young Readers, [2021] |
Audience: Ages 8–12. | Audience: Grades 4–6. | Summary: "While in a haunted
Colorado hotel for her father's ghost-hunting television series, Karma Moon
must battle her anxiety, interpret the signs of the universe, and get footage
of a real ghost—you know, the usual" —Provided by publisher.
Identifiers: LCCN 2020010727 (print) | LCCN 2020010728 (ebook) |
ISBN 978-0-593-30279-8 (hardcover) | ISBN 978-0-593-30280-4 (library
binding) | ISBN 978-0-593-30281-1 (ebook)
Subjects: CYAC: Haunted places—Fiction. | Ghosts—Fiction. |
Anxiety—Fiction. | Television—Production and direction—Fiction. |
Fathers and daughters—Fiction.
Classification: LCC PZ7.1.S2713 Kar 2021 (print) | LCC PZ7.1.S2713 (ebook) |
DDC [Fic]—dc23

The text of this book is set in 10.625-point Gabriela.
Interior design by Andrea Lau

Printed in the United States of America
10 9 8 7 6 5 4 3 2 1
First Edition

For Tobin,
the littlest light that shines the brightest

Contents

The King of All Noodles

The Netflix people call on a Tuesday after school, and I know it's all because of the moo goo gai pan.

Every Monday night we get takeout from Noodle King of New York in the West Village. It's exactly ten blocks from apartment 4B. That's home for me and Dad, a two-bedroom fourth-floor walk-up on Charles Street.

Not to brag or anything, but it *is* my fortune cookie that predicts it. And everyone who's anyone knows that the almighty fortune cookie is *never* wrong.

FORTUNE COOKIE
A heavy burden will be lifted with a single phone call.

And that cookie is dead-on, too.

The call comes in the very next day, and I'm the one who answers it.

Me and Dad are just sitting there, eating Monday night's cold moo goo leftovers in front of the television like it's any other Tuesday afternoon.

It's my job to answer the phone after school and on weekends at the headquarters office for Dad's documentary film company, Totally Rad Productions.

But let me decode.

By company I mean me, Dad and his two best friends from high school—Big John and The Faz. And by headquarters, I mean apartment 4B's living room on Charles Street, which is littered with empty Noodle King cartons and film editing equipment. At least that's the way it looks since Mom packed five suitcases last summer on a quest to follow the signs to her new life.

A life without us.

And one thing I know is that when someone packs five suitcases . . . it's not a good sign they're coming back. The fortune cookie totally missed that one, but that's a whole other story.

So, this is how the Netflix call goes.

"Totally Rad Productions, where rad is our name and film is our game. How may I direct your call?" I say in my very best grown-up voice.

I've been practicing in the mirror.

Dad gives me a wink while he leans over the coffee

table, taking another giant bite from his wooden chopsticks and giving me an approving nod with a mouth full of moo goo.

He always says answering the phone like that makes it seem like we're bigger than just me, him, Big John and The Faz. After that, I'm supposed to cover the receiver with my hand. Dad says that makes it seem like I put them on hold—as if we have this very official, multiple-line phone instead of the ancient yellow wall phone with the old-fashioned dial on the front.

I finally had to draw the line when he asked me to hum hold music into the mouthpiece while the caller waited.

That's just weird. Plus, I don't even know who Barry Manilow is.

← Not even Wi-Fi compatible

"Please hold and I will see if Mr. Vallenari is available to take your call," I tell the woman on the other end of the line.

That's when I shove the receiver in my armpit and eyeball Dad hard.

"Dad," I whisper. "It's . . . *Netflix.*"

First he stops chewing his moo goo.

Then his eyes go wide.

He points a single chopstick in my direction.

"Karma," he warns me. "If this is some kind of joke . . . it's not funny."

3

"I'm not even joking right now," I tell him. "It's really them. It's Netflix calling *you.*"

He eyeballs me for a few more seconds and then jumps up from his seat on the couch while his chopsticks go flying.

Our extra-round pug, Alfred Hitchcock, is already crouched in ready position for such an event. He gobbles a piece of sauced-up bok choy and a few noodles before they even hit the shag carpet.

When it comes to flying food, he's a rocket. But ask him to do his business out front on the sidewalk in below-zero cold, the kind of freezing cold where your nose hairs fuse together, and he takes his sweet old time.

"Hitchy," I tell him, giving his low belly a scratch. "Dr. Portokalos says you're too big as it is."

Hitchy stretches his fat neck up to sniff at my plate on the coffee table before waddling back down under the glass to await the next flying morsel.

I keep eating, watching Dad pace the kitchen floor while he listens on the yellow phone. He's talking and waving his hands in that upbeat way he does when he's doing business. Up until now, business has consisted mostly of booking weddings and bat mitzvahs, with only the occasional documentary in between.

"Yes, of course," he says, stopping to scribble a note on the back of an unopened bill he's pulled from the messy pile on the folding table in the kitchen.

Dad's so psyched after he hangs up the phone, I'm almost positive I see his feet come off the ground.

"We did it, Karma!" he's shouting. "This is it. This is the call I've been waiting for my whole life. A contract with a major content provider for a docuseries! A *docuseries,* Snooks! And Netflix? Oh, man, they want an entire season, and this could be the beginning of even more. Do you know what that means?"

"That we can finally add egg rolls to our Noodle King order?" I ask.

Grumpy Mr. Drago, the building manager, bangs a broom handle on the ceiling of 3B right below us to say we're making too much noise. Four o'clock to four-thirty is an especially important time for grumpy Mr. Drago.

Judge Judy is on.

I asked the Grump if he has a crush on Judge Judy when I saw him out on the front stoop one morning in his bathrobe, sitting on a ratty lawn chair while he drank his morning coffee. But he just shook his head, waved a hand at me and said, *"Poof."*

But if you ask me, I think it's true love.

"Yeah, yeah, I mean sure, egg rolls . . . but it also means a *house,*" Dad tells me. "Finally. A house, Snooks. Somewhere across the river in Jersey or Staten Island or maybe even Connecticut. Someplace where we'll have an actual strip of grass. A yard for you and for Alfred Hitchcock. It's what Mom always wanted. We can even have a barbecue. A *barbecue,* of all things! Mom loves them."

"I've never heard her say anything about a barbecue," I tell him. "Or grass, either."

He's already dialing the yellow phone.

"Well, she's always wanted that," he says, slipping his finger in the dial and pushing it around.

I wonder if Mom would actually bring her suitcases back if he got her a house with a barbecue and a strip of grass. Obviously, he thinks so, but I'm not so sure.

"Wouldn't you like to barbecue out in a backyard?" he goes on.

I shrug. "Can you barbecue moo goo leftovers?"

"You can barbecue anything," he tells me, pushing the dial around again.

"Are you sure Connecticut has moo goo?"

"Everyone has moo goo," he tells me.

"But I bet Connecticut doesn't have a Toby's," I say.

Me and Dad go to Toby's Estate Coffee every single morning before school. It's our favorite place in the Village. A couple of years ago they changed the name to Partners, but we still call it Toby's because it will always be Toby's to us. It has old brick walls and brightly colored stools, and Ajit, who still wears his Toby's T-shirt and works the morning shift, knows our order by heart. Dad's order is Avocado Toast with a

Decaf Ghost Town Coffee and mine is Egg on a Roll with a hot Apple Betty.

Ajit's name means "unbeatable."

He told me so.

And it fits him too, just like Karma fits me. Ajit is going to college to be a lawyer. He wants to put criminals in jail to keep our streets safer. And I know he will, too.

His very name announces his future success, guaranteed.

Nothing beats unbeatable.

I'm a firm believer that names are very important in the universe.

My mom named me Karma Moon because she believed the theory of karma wholeheartedly. The theory basically states that if you do bad things, bad things come back to you. And if you do good things, good things come back to you.

Dad calls that kind of stuff woo-woo, which is his word for "cuckoo." But the story goes that he agreed to the name Karma only after Mom agreed he could brand the next kid, which they never had. Lucky for that kid, because I think it's really wrong to actually name a child C-3PO.

That's seriously questionable adulting.

"I'm sure there'll be a place we like just as much as Toby's, wherever we land," Dad says.

But I'm not so sure.

I'm used to Egg on a Roll. I love Egg on a Roll. Why would I want to eat anything but Egg on a Roll?

Dad is *still* dialing.

Because that's how it goes with an old-fashioned phone.

"Man, the guys are going to flip when I tell them we've got an actual documentary with Netflix," Dad goes on while he calls the guys. "Do you understand how big this is, Snooks? I think you need to come over here and pinch me. Just so I know this isn't a dream."

I can't help but smile. It's nice to see Dad so happy. To be honest, it's been a while.

"What's the show about?" I ask him.

He doesn't answer me this time.

"Dad," I say louder. "What is the documentary about?"

"Oh, some haunted-hotel mystery up in the mountains of Colorado."

I choke on my moo goo.

"Dude! We got it!" he shouts into the mouthpiece.

"I hate to be the one to tell you this," I call to him, pushing my horn-rimmed glasses up at the bridge. "The last I checked, you weren't a ghost hunter."

But he just waves my words away like that tiny fact doesn't matter.

Even though it seems like a pretty big fact to me.

"Big John! We got a docuseries!" he's shouting into the receiver.

I watch and chew as he listens and paces the floor.

"You'd better sit down for this one," Dad tells Big John. "An entire season with *Netflix*! *Netflix*, dude! Yeah, it's some ghost-hunting thing . . . they want a paranormal *series*!"

He listens.

I chew moo goo.

Alfred Hitchcock waits for flying shrapnel.

"Yeah, they said ten episodes to start and the possibility of extending to a season two. But they said we will definitely have to get an actual ghost on film for that to happen. Netflix is going to put Totally Rad on the map, man! After all these years! It's finally our turn."

I would never actually tell Dad that it was my cookie that predicted it. Because of his whole aversion-to-woo-woo thing. But he only thinks it's crazy because he doesn't really understand it. I knew something would come his way even if *he* isn't open to his woo-woo, because that's how it works with woo-woo and whatnot.

The truth is, the universe has a plan for us all. You just have to be open to reading the signs around you. I'm all about living by the rules of woo-woo.

Karma for sure because it's my namesake, but also the reading of any and all signs, keeping it real with my spirit guide, Crystal Mystic, tarot cards, past-life memories, the power of crystals, any and every Snapple lid fact and of course the almighty fortune cookie.

My personal mantra is and will always be: *Woo-woo isn't cuckoo and without it you'll have bad juju.*

And everyone who's anyone knows you don't want bad juju.

It's the *worst.*

A Bad Case of the What-Ifs

That whole night after Dad's Netflix call, he's far too busy walking around being happy to notice one very important thing.

I am *not.*

Far from it.

After Googling the Stanley Hotel, I learned that the place is so haunted, not one single, solitary guest will even stay there anymore.

Not one.

By bedtime, it's all I can do not to throw up my Noodle King order.

"Lights out, Snooks," Dad tells me from the doorway of my bedroom that night. "School tomorrow."

"Um . . . ," I say. "So, I—I've made a decision."

"Uh-huh," he says, coming in and sitting on the edge of my bed. "About what?" he asks, giving Alfred Hitchcock a pat on the head.

"Yeah, *soooo* . . . I think, I mean . . . I don't think . . . I mean, I c-can't go to Colorado with you guys," I tell him, staring down at my fingers while I fold and unfold them and then fold them again.

"Hmmm" is all he says while he takes in my words.

"What if we never come home?" I ask him.

Still nodding.

"It happens, you know."

"Uh-huh," he says.

"People go missing all the time, and if you want to know what I think about it," I say, "there's a definite possibility of paranormal disturbances behind some of those cases. I mean, unless it's an alien abduction, which is also a legit possibility. But you know, extraterrestrial doesn't really apply to *this* situation. But you never know."

"Hmmm," he says.

"So yeah, I guess I'm just saying, I—I can't go with you."

Here's the thing. Even though Dr. Finkelman, MD, PhD, LP, is supposed to be some kind of expert at getting rid of my bad case of the *what-ifs,* all we really do is talk about my feelings and play Uno during our Wednesday appointments. We meet every week for one hour while Dad waits in the lobby. And even though Dr. Finkelman has more letters behind his name than anyone I've ever met, playing Uno hasn't changed a single thing about my what-ifs.

They're always with me.

Always.

What-ifs may or may not be the technical term written in Dr. Finkelman's chart, but it explains it way better than anything else.

Simply said . . . I worry.

But not about weird things, like belly buttons.

That's an actual thing. The fear of belly buttons. It's called omphalophobia. I suppose I get it, in a way. Like all the lint and everything. But it's still a weird thing to worry about, if you ask me. Math, too; that's called arithmophobia. I totally get that one more than the belly button one, especially if you've ever had Mrs. Frickman for algebra.

There's arachnophobia, too. The fear of spiders. And I mean, that one just makes good sense.

My worries are way more normal than extra lint buildup or algebra.

To put it straight, I'm afraid of what *might* happen. And New York keeps me real busy.

WHAT IF

a nuclear bomb hits New York?

WHAT IF

*the next lockdown drill
at school isn't a drill at all?*

WHAT IF

Mom never comes home?

My worries run on a continuous loop.

And I don't know about the belly button kind, but mine invade my brain and my body, too. Every second of every day, but especially at night when the lights are out and it's quiet. On the inside of me, it sort of feels like jumping beans are jammed into every vein in my body and never let me be still.

And I know one thing is for sure, a ghost hotel isn't going to be good for my what-ifs.

Dad sighs and covers my fingers with his giant hand.

It's warm and heavy.

The special band is still there no matter how long Mom's been gone or how many suitcases she packed.

Mom taught me all about the woo-woo.

But I bet she doesn't know that my what-ifs went into overdrive after she left us alone here without her.

When I asked the greatest, almighty woo-woo source, aka Crystal Mystic, if what she did was totally messed up, it gave it to me straight.

CRYSTAL MYSTIC
YOU CAN THANK YOUR
LUCKY STARS!

Of all the woo-woo in this world and beyond, Crystal Mystic is my woo-woo surefire system.

Its awesomeness announces itself in its name.

Mystic.

With one solid shake, all your spiritual questions can be answered in one solitary second. The crystal globe awakens with a mystical flashing light, and through the magic of woo-woo and four double-A batteries (not included), it speaks its truth from beyond the stars, transmitting through the small speaker at the bottom.

The one and only problem with Crystal Mystic is it doesn't predict what *might* happen. Which can be a big problem when you have a bad case of the what-ifs.

Huge, actually.

If only I could find the perfect woo-woo that could help me predict the future, I wouldn't have to worry so much. Then the jumping beans would finally sleep.

And so would I.

Dad takes my hand in his.

"How can I possibly go a whole ten days without seeing this face?" he finally says with a grin. "I'm sorry, I can't do it."

"But, Dad," I say. "I feel like I'm having a heart attack even thinking about it."

"You're not having a heart attack," he assures me.

"You're right," I agree. "It might be a stroke."

He stares at me.

"Let's take a deep breath together," he says.

His voice is calm and his smile is that special one he gives me when I need it the most. A smile that says a lot without any words at all. It says I'm okay and he's okay and so is everything else in the world right this minute. And for a few seconds, while that smile is shining its light, a bright ray bursting through a worry storm, it actually feels true.

"Breathe in," he says.

We both take a deep breath, in through our noses and then out through our mouths the way Dr. Finkelman taught me to do.

"How's your heart?" Dad asks me.

I shrug.

"I think you'll live," he says.

"You don't know that," I tell him. "Kids have heart attacks, you know. It's a thing."

"Where did you get that?" he asks.

"Google," I tell him. "But Crystal Mystic confirmed it."

"Snooks, here's the thing," Dad says, inching closer to me and meeting my eyes. "We're a team. You and me. I can't do this without my partner."

"You have Big John and The Faz, though," I remind him.

He nods. "But they're not my Snooks. This is my big break," he tells me. "*Our* big break. This is going to change our life, and you're a part of that. You have to be there."

"But what if—"

"You're Research." He points to me. "We all have a different role. Who's going to do it if you're not there?"

I think about that.

"Big John?" I ask.

He shakes his head. "He's Video Editing and Sound—holding the boom."

15

"The Faz?" I try again.

"Directing."

That's when I point to Dad in one last-ditch effort.

He shakes his head. "I'm Cinematography. I'll be too busy shooting footage. We all have our role, Snooks. You can't let us down now."

"Fine," I mumble. "I'll go. But you better have a doctor on speed dial. I still may have a heart attack."

"I promise you'll be fine." He kisses me on the forehead and stands up to leave.

"Dad?" I say.

He turns around to face me again in the doorway.

"Yeah?"

"Tell me again why you call me Snooks."

He laughs. "Don't you ever get tired of that story?"

"Never," I say.

"When you were born and I saw you for the very first time," he says, "I knew you were the sweetest thing I'd ever seen. I couldn't decide if you were as sweet as a frosty snow cone on the hottest July day or as sweet as a home-baked cookie fresh out of the oven. So I called you Snookie. A combination of both."

He flips the light switch by the door. "See you in the morning. You know what? I think tomorrow I'm going to try something new at Toby's."

I laugh at that one. "No you won't," I tell him.

"No I won't," he agrees. "We're the same that way, aren't we? Creatures of habit."

"Definitely," I say.

"Night," he tells me, disappearing from the doorway.

Door open.

Hall light on.

He knows me better than anyone else in the whole world. Better than my best friend, Mags, even.

Better than Mom, for sure.

And I know him.

I listen to his bare feet slide across the old, creaky wooden floorboards on his way down the hall. He'll watch the news and then fall asleep on the couch during *Jimmy Kimmel*.

Just like he does every night.

"Dad?" I call out to him.

"Yeah?"

"I love you," I say.

"Love you more," he calls back.

And by the end of that week, it's set in stone. We'll go to Colorado over spring break. A ten-day assignment to search a haunted hotel for a paranormal life-force and hopefully even secure a season two.

This is Dad's dream.

His big break. The cookie even said so.

We just need one thing to actually make it happen.

A real live ghost.

My what-ifs are just going to have to suck it up.

The Arrival

Lucky for me, Dad lets me bring Alfred Hitchcock and my very best friend, Mags, along for our ten-day ghost adventure. Mags agrees, but only after she makes me promise one oddly specific, cross-my-heart-hope-to-die condition.

CONDITION: INFINITE DIBS ON EVERY BOY SHE SEES.

The thing is . . . I *need* my best friend for a haunted-hotel assignment, so I would have agreed to pretty much anything.

My very best friend in the entire world is Mags (Don't Call Me Margaret) Laverne Bogdonavich. She is twelve too and is more boy-crazy than anyone else I know. She loves eating breakfast for dinner, has a slight obsession with sea turtles and lives two buildings down from us on Charles Street. She pretty much sees herself as the Greta Thunberg of New York, which basically means she will call out anyone on the street who's using a plastic straw or a single-use water bottle. And if you're carrying a plastic bag—*look out.* Oh, and also she's hands down the best kicker on our Immaculate Heart of Mary K-8 after-school kickball team.

Mags isn't assigned to an actual job for the trip other than her usual policing of any and all plastic offenses, but I am. Before we left, Dad officially promoted me to Senior Researcher for Totally Rad Productions. He even said that with an official title like that, my name will appear in the credits.

My name on Netflix.

That's huge. My name scrolling across the actual television screen for all the world to see.

For the haunted-hotel project, it will be my job to help gather information for the narrative voice-over parts of the documentary that Big John will dub in later. It's my very first time doing something so important for Totally Rad, and I'm taking it very seriously.

Karma Moon's Official Ghost Log

I even have my very own ghost-sighting logbook to keep tabs on every single hint of paranormal activities I see.

The historic and stately Stanley Hotel

sits high on a hill overlooking the town of Estes Park way up in the mountains of Colorado. You can't miss it. It's stark white with a bright red roof and looks more like the White House in Washington, DC, than a Motel 6 or Holiday Inn.

On day one of our ghost adventure, Big John stops the rental van on the driveway in front of the matching red steps that lead to a front porch lined with tall white pillars.

"Let the ghostly mayhem begin," Mags says when the van comes to a stop, adding a *"Wooooooo"* to the mix. "I think I'm going to like it here," she adds, pointing her phone in the direction of some shirtless boy mowing the lawn out front.

"Mags Bogdonavich," Big John calls from the driver's seat. "I promised your father no boys on this trip."

"*Biiiiig* mistake," Mags says. "The picture is already on its way to the cloud to be saved for all eternity."

Big John pretends to try to snatch her phone away while she holds it high over her head. Everyone is laughing and joking and just . . . *being.*

Except me.

My jumping beans are already at it.

I couldn't even play I Spy with Mags and The Faz on the way up the mountain. I was too worried about being buried alive in an avalanche to spy anything but loose boulders.

Before we left for Colorado, Dr. Finkelman, MD, PhD, LP, gave me a prescription for the trip. Except this prescription wasn't the official kind you give to a pharmacist for hard-to-swallow pills or even a nasty-tasting syrup.

It was a Post-it.

The only problem is . . . my what-ifs have a *very* sophisticated GPS.

⭐

Inside the lobby of the Stanley there are two humongous wooden fireplaces with a main desk and a grand staircase in between. Behind the main desk are tiny wooden cubbies labeled with room numbers. Lining the grand staircase are ancient pictures of people dressed in fancy formal wear. Each picture is framed in ornate gold. To the right of the staircase is an old-fashioned golden elevator with a gated door. Taped to the front is a handwritten sign stuck on with yellowing Scotch tape.

I elbow Mags and point to the sign. "Do you think the risk is ghost-related or falling-to-your-death-related?"
She's not even listening.

"I'm definitely calling dibs on that one," she whispers back, still ogling the god of lawn mowing through the open double doors.

"I hate to be the one to tell you this," I inform her, "but you've already called infinite dibs for the whole trip. Calling it now is just plain redundant."

She doesn't take her eyes off the kid. "It's *what*?" she asks, fluffing up her blond curls.

"Redundant," I say. "It was one of our vocabulary words this year. Already stated. A duplicate. Totally unnecessary. Now shush, will you? Can't you see I'm working?" I wave my spiral-bound logbook at her.

"So work already," she says. "No one's stopping you. I've got a whole other thing going on here." She's still staring out the open double doors of the lobby.

"Who's supposed to be meeting us?" I ask Dad.

"Esmeralda Figueroa is the manager. She should be expecting us," Dad tells me, glancing at his watch and then calling out into the empty lobby, "Hello? Is there anyone here? Esmeralda? It's Vince Vallenari with Totally Rad Productions."

The glass door marked LETTIE'S GIFT SHOP opens with a high-pitched *ting*.

"Hello. Can I help you, sir?" A tiny old woman leans out the door, scanning us through a pair of cat-eye glasses she's holding up in front of her face.

"Yes, ma'am," Dad tells her, standing tall with a proud smile. "We are with Netflix and we are here to film."

It's nice seeing that grin again. It's been around a whole lot more since that Netflix call.

She starts toward Dad, eye-ing him suspiciously from be-hind the rhinestone-studded glasses before she speaks again. She's a thin woman, wearing a multicolored Western shirt  with leather fringe hanging on the front of it, with jeans and brown cowboy boots that have silver tips on the toes. Her grayish hair is swirled up in a giant puff on her head that's not quite as tall as Marge Simpson's, but it defi-nitely has a beanstalk quality to it. And not quite as blue as Marge's either, more like a light violet tinge.

"Film?" she asks.

"We are with Totally Rad Productions and are here to film a docuseries on the hauntings that are taking place . . . for Netflix?" Big John tells her.

Big John is a giant next to her tiny frame. He's got a bar-rel chest, wide shoulders and a large booming laugh too. The Faz is the opposite of Big John in every way. He's skin-nier, shorter and quieter. And he always, always wears a Totally Rad baseball cap no matter what. And even though his real name is Giuseppe Faziospoon, Dad and Big John call him The Faz because back in high school, he always wore a black leather jacket just like this guy The Fonz did in this old-time television show *Happy Days*.

He eventually lost the jacket, but the name stuck.

The tiny Colorado cowgirl scans us through her lenses again, her pinky pointed high in the air. "Oh, goodness," she sighs, clicking her tongue and shaking her head. "Not *another* group of ghost hunters."

"You've had them here before?" Big John asks.

"Many, *many* times," she tells him, raising her eyebrows on the second *many*. "So, what's a *Netflix*?"

"You've never heard of *Netflix*?" I ask her.

"Is it a television show?" she asks.

"Ah . . . not exactly," I say.

"Well, I don't own a TV myself," she tells me.

"No TV?" I say. "What do you watch while you eat your dinner—"

"I'm supposed to ask for Esmeralda," Dad interrupts. "The manager?"

"Ah, well, Esmeralda was three managers ago," she informs him. "We've had four since that one disappeared in the dead of night in February. Mr. Plum is the new manager. As of last Friday, anyway."

WHAT-IFS

Did she say disappeared in the dead of night*?*

I swallow. "Can you please define *disappeared*?" I ask her, my pen poised over my logbook.

"I don't understand," Dad says. "That can't be right. *Three* managers ago? I just spoke with her."

The cowgirl snorts. "I'm sure you did. It's nice to meet

you all. I'm Ms. Lettie and I have owned the gift shop since 1972. There are two of us who rent space in the hotel. Madame Drusilla, the house spiritualist, has an office down below the lobby off the back courtyard."

"Well, it's nice to meet you, but I mean, I made all the arrangements with Esmeralda like"—he counts on his fingers—"only six or seven weeks ago?"

She nods with a knowing smile. "Here at the Stanley, that's how it goes, but it keeps us on our toes. I'll ask Jack to fetch Mr. Plum for you. Last I saw him he was with Mr. Lozano, the new front desk clerk."

"That's Jack? Out there?" Mags points out the double doors. "The boy mowing the lawn?"

"It is indeed," Ms. Lettie tells her. "He's my grandson."

Mags is already scrambling out of the lobby and down the front steps. "I'll do it for you, Ms. Lettie!" she's hollering over her shoulder.

While Dad discusses the past managers with Ms. Lettie, I watch as Mags taps the sweaty boy on the shoulder and shouts words in his direction. The roaring drone of the mower comes to a stop, and he hops up the front steps with Mags following close behind.

"Yeah, Gran?" the boy says, giving me and Mags the once-over while he wipes sweaty drips off his forehead with the back of his hand.

"Would you mind running to fetch Mr. Plum, darling?" She motions at us. "There's yet another ghost group here looking to speak with him."

"Yes, ma'am," he tells her, giving Mags a white-toothed smile and running out the double doors.

"Bye, Jack," Mags hollers after him in a voice far too loud.

"Isn't Jack just marvelous?" Ms. Lettie says.

"He's mad marvelous," Mags agrees.

I roll my eyes and whisper to Mags, "You need to reel it in."

She gives me a smack on my arm.

"He's technically the busboy here," Ms. Lettie goes on, "but he also does backup. Any chores that need doing, Jack's your man."

Dad nods. "It was a pleasure meeting you, Miss . . . um . . . Mrs.—"

"Ms. Lettie," the woman says, turning toward the glass door of the gift shop. "If you need anything, you know where you can find me."

"Ah, excuse me, ma'am?" Dad calls after her. "We'd like to interview you for the series at some point as well, since you've been here so long. I'm guessing you have some wonderful stories to share. That is, if you don't mind."

She turns to face him again and takes a long, deep breath before speaking.

"Did you know that some cultures believe that when you photograph someone, you steal a little bit of their soul?" she asks.

"Ahhh . . . no," he says. "I d-didn't know that."

"I believe there is a lot of validity to that notion," she

tells him. "But I'd be happy to speak with you *off*-camera and answer any questions you may have."

Dad nods. "Yes, ma'am, understood. Whatever you prefer."

"Thank you," she says.

That's when I see a tall man with messy black hair and a matching bushy beard glaring at us from behind the glass door of the gift shop.

"Excuse me, Ms. Lettie." I hold up my hand. "But there's a strange man in a gray jumpsuit holding a plunger and staring at us."

She tilts her head to the side and smiles. "That's Ubbe Amblebee," she tells me. "He's the maintenance man here. He's a little skittish around new people."

When we all turn to look at him, his eyes widen and he darts away from the door.

"Well, good day, then," Ms. Lettie says.

"Good day, ma'am," Dad tells her.

Then we all stand in a line watching her tuck her mini-self away in the corner gift shop with another tiny *ting* of the bell. But not before she gives us one more peek from behind the glass door, where a hand-painted OPEN sign hangs from hooks suction-cupped to the glass.

I give Mags another poke. "What's with that?" I ask.

"What?"

"The filming-of-souls thing," I say.

She looks up at me. "So?" she asks.

I wide-eye her and lean in closer. *"So?"*

"Yeah, so?"

"You're not thinking what I'm thinking?" I ask her.

She stares at me. "I seriously doubt it."

"*Vampires,*" I whisper.

"Now *you*"—she points at me—"need to reel it in."

"No, *you* need to reel it out," I tell her.

"*Thaaaat's* not a saying."

"Vampires can't see their images, right?"

"Yeah, so?"

"Not in the mirror or on film, either," I go on.

"Except she's not pale *or* wearing a cape," Mags says. "And she's up in the daytime. Not undead. Just a plain little old lady with a mile-high hairdo."

"Capes are not standard issue for vampires anymore," I tell her. "Plus, the no-image thing totally supersedes the no-sun or the daytime-hours deal. Vampires have evolved, you know—plug in, why don't you."

Mags rolls her eyes in slow motion across the ceiling and back to me again. "It took you five minutes," she says.

I put my hands on my hips. "What is that supposed to mean?"

"It means your job is to do the research," she says.

"*This* is research."

"Vampires aren't research," she informs me.

That's when Dad says, "I have a feeling this isn't going to be the first interesting character we come across while we're here."

"You got that right," I tell him. "Do you want to know what your horoscope said today?"

"Nope—"

"Virgo," I recite by heart. *"New people are introduced into your life who will bring new adventures.* And you want to know what else?"

"Crystal Mystic confirmed it?" he asks.

"Exactly," I say.

"Hello!" A short, round, sweaty man with red cheeks and a too-tight blazer calls out to us as he hurries down the grand staircase separating the two lobby fireplaces. "I'm Mr. Plum, the manager. You must be the Netflix folks."

Standing next to him is a taller, skinnier man in cowboy boots with long white hair tied in a ponytail and the largest, whitest mustache I've ever seen grow under a nose.

Dad tried to grow a mustache once, and he looked more wolfman than man because it was wispy in places and bald in others. Thankfully, he finally shaved it off altogether and it's never made another appearance.

"Hello," Dad says, reaching out a hand for the man to shake. "I'm Vince Vallenari with Totally Rad Productions."

"Yes, yes," Mr. Plum says. "I was made aware of your arrival by the owners of the property when I took over this week. However, I didn't realize you were coming today. I was up on the fourth floor, and as you can see, it's hit or miss with the elevator. I'm so sorry to make you wait."

"Excuse me, Mr. Plum. Is *hit or miss* a ghost reference

or a guts-splattered-all-over-the-basement-floor reference?" I ask him, my pen poised over my ghost logbook.

"This is my daughter, Karma," Dad tells him.

"Ahhhh . . . well, let's just say, it's safer to take the stairs," Mr. Plum tells me.

"Noted." I nod once and scribble it down.

"This is Arlo Lozano." Mr. Plum waves a hand toward White Ponytail. "He's our new front desk clerk. Arlo, these folks will be checking in."

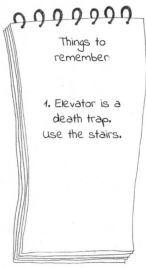

Things to remember:

1. Elevator is a death trap. Use the stairs.

"Overnight?" Mr. Lozano asks.

"That's right," Mr. Plum says.

Mr. Lozano gives Dad the once-over. "Are you sure you want to do that?"

Mr. Plum laughs off his questions with a loud, booming chuckle. "People make far too big a deal of this haunted-hotel business," he says to Dad, and then turns back to Mr. Lozano. "Please just radio Ruby Red to make sure the rooms are cleaned and ready. Rooms 332 to 335. We are going to need four, right?"

Mr. Lozano gives Dad one more good look and heads to the front desk.

"Ah, five, please," Dad calls after him. "We need one additional room for the paranormal consultants who are joining us later this afternoon. Actually"—he glances at his phone—"T. S. Phoenix and his wife, Tally, are on their way up the mountain now. They got lost outside Boulder."

"Ahhhh." Mr. Plum chuckles. "I see how it is . . . enough ESP for the ghosts but not so much for the directions, huh?"

Dad gives him a polite smile. "The last I heard, they had stopped for a piece of pie at the Colorado Cherry Company in Lyons, but like I said, they'll be here soon."

"Well, until then and while Ruby Red gets your rooms ready, let me show you around the grounds of the hotel."

"That would be wonderful," Dad says, securing a strap from the camera bag holding his fancy new Nikon D5600 inside it.

The one he bought using the money from the rent envelope in the kitchen drawer that he stuffed with the payment he got from the Rubensteins' bat mitzvah.

I'm not supposed to know the money is gone.

But I do.

Mr. Plum leads us out the double doors of the lobby and onto the crisp white wraparound porch.

"Mr. Plum," I call. "Are those old-fashioned portraits along the stairs of all the managers?"

"Ah, no," he says. "All these pictures show the different owners over time. The Jewel family opened the Stanley in 1909. Each of those portraits is a member of the Jewel family who has owned the hotel since that time. The current owners are Birdie and Happy Jewel. They live down in Denver."

"Oh," I say. "But what about the managers?"

"What about them?" he asks.

"Ms. Lettie told us there have been three managers since we made plans to come here."

Mr. Plum nods. "I'm afraid I don't have an answer to that. Scared off, I suppose," he tells me. "But it's hard to get anyone to talk about their experiences. You'll find that here. People stay pretty close to the vest about it. No offense to you and all that you, ah . . . do in your work, but I don't believe in the supernatural. It's all hooey, if you ask me. But I digress. My beliefs don't really make for very interesting television, now, do they?"

I look at Dad and Dad looks at me and I know exactly what he's thinking because he's gnawing on his bottom lip.

He has his own what-ifs. Even if he doesn't want to admit it.

I know what his worries are just by looking at him.

No house.

No strip of grass.

No barbecue.

And worst of all . . . no Mom.

But this is Dad's big break, no matter what Mr. Plum thinks. The fortune cookie even said so.

And one thing I know, the universe never gets it wrong.

Only people do.

Murder Is a Messy Business

By the time we make it to our room, a whole new missing manager theory is running through my brain.

One deranged hotel manager or Jewel family member serial killer, to be exact.

I eye Mr. Plum as he stands in front of room 332. On *Dateline,* they always say it's the ones you never expect.

"And finally, ladies, this will be your room," he says, slipping a key card in the slot and opening the door.

Inside the room is a tall, thin woman in a gray-and-white uniform with perfectly painted, bright red lips.

She's wearing earbuds and fluffing up a pillow on the bed. Her black hair is pulled tight to one side and tied into a twisted knot under her right ear.

"Oh!" She jumps, pulling out the earbuds. "I'm just finishing up your room now."

"This is Ruby Red, our new housekeeper," Mr. Plum tells us, propping the door for her.

"Good afternoon," the woman says, her eyes on the floor. "Please let me know if there's anything else you need to make your stay more comfortable."

"Thank you so much," Dad tells her, handing her a folded bill.

She takes it and quickly scurries past us, pushing her large, squeaky-wheeled cart down the long hall.

Mr. Plum hands us all tiny envelopes with key cards inside.

"Here are your room keys. I will leave you all to unpack and get settled in," he tells us. "We will all meet promptly at six for dinner in the MacGregor Dining Hall downstairs for one of Chef Raphaël's French masterpiece dinners. Tonight is coq au vin. You'll think you've died and gone to heaven."

From the floor up above, we hear racing footsteps.

Mr. Plum's cheeks redden, and he shakes his head and huffs, "Dag gum hooligans."

"Hooligans?" I ask.

"Oh, those local kids sneaking in here and racing up and down the fourth-floor hallway," he mutters. "But I'm never fast enough to catch them. Please . . . if you'll all excuse me."

We watch Mr. Plum hurry down the hall in the opposite direction, back toward the grand staircase, his blazer making a swishing sound as his arms rub against his round sides.

On our official tour of the grounds, we found out that there are exactly four buildings total. Two of them are permanently closed because of the lack of guests. That leaves two buildings still open—the main building, where we checked in and are staying, and the staff quarters across the flowered courtyard out back.

"I'm going in," Mags says, wheeling her suitcase through the doorway of our room to check things out.

"See you all at dinner," Big John tells us, unlocking a door across the hall.

"What time did he say?" The Faz asks, pushing his key card into the door next to Big John's.

"Six," Big John tells him.

Me and Dad watch them wheel their suitcases inside their rooms, and the doors close.

"You okay?" Dad asks me, putting a hand on my shoulder.

I swallow and let my head fall back against the doorframe.

"This place is mad creepy," I tell him.

"Sick!" Mags shouts from inside 332. "I can see the Rocky Mountains from our window! The only thing I can see from my window in the West Village is Mrs. Pickle's kitchen."

"This mad creepy business is what is going to put us on the map," Dad reminds me, his hand on my shoulder.

I nod.

"Right?" he says.

"Right," I say.

"We can put up with it for ten days, can't we?" He gives my shoulder a squeeze.

This time I don't say anything.

"I promise you, Snooks, that you can order as many egg rolls as you want once we get a ghost on film."

"Dad?"

"Yeah?"

I slip my hand in his. "Tell me again why you call me Snooks."

"We will make it out of here just fine," he says. "I promise you."

I shrug. "Okay," I say. "But I still want to hear it."

He smiles. "The minute I laid eyes on you, I knew you were the best thing that ever happened to me. And I still know it."

"As sweet as a frosty snow cone on the hottest July day and a home-baked cookie fresh hot out of the oven all in one?" I ask.

He nods. "Absolutely."

I sigh and he squeezes my hand.

"I'm right next door if you need me," he says.

"Oh, man! I can still see snow on the mountaintops!" Mags hollers from inside, and then I hear her body land on the mattress with a loud thud and she's all, "Dibs on the bed by the window!"

"You'll be fine," Dad tells me. "I'll see you in the dining hall at six?"

I sigh. "I sure hope so," I say.

"Hey," he says. "I'm glad you're here."

I give him a weak smile.

He gives me a kiss on the top of my head and I watch him fiddle with his own key card and disappear inside the room next to ours, letting the door swing closed behind him.

When I pick up my suitcase, I see Ruby Red with her cart stopped at the end of the hall watching me. She jumps when our eyes meet and lurches forward with her squeaky-wheeled cart again.

Squeak.

Squeak.

Squeak.

Mags is doing invisible snow angels on the brick-red velvet bedspread closest to the window when I finally wheel my suitcase inside our room.

There are two velvet-covered double beds, and the floor is covered in a dark green carpet with tiny white-flowered vines, and there's an ancient wooden wardrobe with large drawers in the corner of the room. The television is mounted on the wall. Near the door is a small desk with an old-fashioned typewriter with white paper wound inside, just waiting for someone to press the keys for an important message. I place my ghost logbook and Crystal Mystic next to the short, small glass vase filled with fresh-cut pink roses on the edge of the desk.

My what-ifs are kicked into overdrive and my jumping beans are set on high-velocity wiggle.

I lug my suitcase up on the bed closer to the bathroom and start to count and tap each finger to my thumb.

One. Two. Three. Four.

I sit down next to my suitcase and lean toward Mags. "Don't you think it's majorly weird that there have been three managers since my dad even got the contract?"

She's too busy taking pictures of the snowy mountaintops outside our window.

"I wonder if that Chef Raphaël does room service, too," she's rambling on, holding her phone out and snapping another shot. "I feel so grown-up. It's like this is our very own apartment, just like our plan for when we're adults. What do you think coq au vin is anyway? It sounds gross, whatever it is. I hope there's nothing green in it; you know how I feel about green foods. I mean, why not serve plain old chicken, *right*?"

One. Two. Three. Four.

"What if all the managers were whacked one by one

by some deranged hotel manager serial killer?" I swallow. "Each one of them . . . *dead.* And like he hid the corpses—"

She's still not listening.

"I suppose vegans don't like chicken." She takes another shot of the mountains.

"All of them taken in the dead of night," I go on. "And cut into small pieces."

"Or vegetarians in general," she says. "But you and I aren't vegan or vegetarian, so I'm just saying chicken would be good."

"And what if the body parts are stored in this very closet?" I say, standing in front of the wardrobe.

She stops then and her head snaps in my direction. "Wait . . . what are you talking about?"

I turn back to face her with wide eyes. "Ahh, only *a triple homicide?*"

"I thought we were talking about chicken."

"*You* were talking about chicken." I point a thumb at her. "I was talking about a deranged serial killer knocking off hotel managers in the dead of night. And now maybe the bloody demise of an entire docuseries film crew."

"That," she says, tossing her phone on the bed, "is messed up."

"Exactly what I'm saying," I tell her. "A bloody crime scene *would* be messy."

"Don't even," she warns me.

"What?"

"You know what. This is supposed to be a haunted

mystery," she says. "*Haunted.* No one has said a single word about serial killers or purple-haired old-lady vampires."

"What if all the haunted stuff is just some ruse for a vicious serial killer operation, conducting business under the cover of a haunted hotel? It's a brilliant diversion, if you ask me. You know, for serial killer motives, that is."

She blinks a bunch of blinks at me before she finally says, "You've been watching *Dateline* again, haven't you?"

I toe another carpet vine while she blows air out of her mouth and flops down on the bed.

"Dr. Finkelman said not to watch those shows," she tells me, aiming out the window again. "*Dateline* is definitely on the list. And *Scooby-Doo,* too . . ."

"I can so watch *Scooby-Doo,*" I insist.

"Uh-uh," she says without looking up. "I think it's on the list."

That's when I throw my hands out and go, "Mags, if I don't watch these shows, how am I supposed to know what to worry about?"

"You're so dramatic," she says.

"Managers are missing. No one knows anything about it. No guests in a hotel? I don't think I'm being dramatic to conclude there's a serial killer on the loose, bumping off managers in the dead of night and hiding their dead body parts in this very wardrobe."

"I thought your what-ifs were supposed to stay in New York," she says.

I shrug, my eyes on the carpet vines.

"You said Dr. Finkelman wrote a prescription to make them stay," she says.

"I know, but there was one big problem with that," I tell her.

"What?"

I toe another vine and mumble, "My worries didn't want to listen."

She raises her eyebrows at me and then puts her cheek in her hand. "I think Jack might like me," she says. "I get a vibe. I've got to get a picture of us together so I can show the girls at school. Darby Woods is going to be so jealous."

I sigh and flop down on my own bed and stare at the ceiling tiles while she swipes through her Rocky Mountain photos.

Dr. Finkelman, MD, PhD, LP, would tell me to breathe or meditate or write my feelings down and then throw them away.

Ghost Log Day 1

1. 2:12 p.m. arrival

2. Confirmed sightings? A big fat negative.

3. Hidden dead manager body parts a real possibility? Affirmative.

Jack + Mags

Mags wrote that! ←

But frankly, right this minute, my brain is way too busy for any of that monkey business.

WHAT-IFS

Isn't anyone *going to check the wardrobe for body parts?*

41

Ghostly Shenanigans

S o, it turns out that coq au vin is chicken after all. And lucky for Mags, there isn't one single green thing in it.

Even Hitchy likes it.

Chef Raphaël serves Hitchy's under our table on the same fancy china plates that he serves our chicken on. But I think Hitchy would have licked up every last drop of gravy on a plain old paper plate if he had to.

It's after dinner that we finally meet the paranormal ghost hunters from Denver, Lights Out! Paranormal Science and Research. It's a ghostly meet-and-greet with T. S. Phoenix and his wife, Tally, in the MacGregor Dining Hall.

That's when I find out that T. S. Phoenix is big-time in the paranormal world.

Google even confirmed it.

In fact, it turns out that the guy has more letters behind his name than Dr. Finkelman. And they don't give letters to just anyone.

The thing is, T. S. Phoenix, MscD, EVP, CPI, is not a doctor of feelings or even your garden-variety strep throat kind of doctor either.

He's a *doctor of ghosts.*

All those letters have nothing to do with feelings and everything to do with paranormal investigation.

MscD = Doctorate in Metaphysical Science (knower of all things ghost-related)

EVP = Electronic Voice Phenomena (catches ghost voices on recorder)

CPI = Certified Paranormal Investigator (official investigator of phantasms galore)

But he has something else that no other doctor I know has. Not even Dr. Finkelman.

A badge.

A *ghost* badge, to be exact.

That's certified big-time.
←

Dr. Finkelman doesn't have any badge on his front, just a disgusting handkerchief that hangs out of the pocket of his suit jacket.

As a general rule, I find people who keep their snot in a pocket highly suspicious.

And you want to know what Crystal Mystic said when I asked if this hanky philosophy is a funky business?

CRYSTAL MYSTIC
I'M PICKING UP
GOOD VIBRATIONS.

Aside from the snot-in-a-pocket thing, Dr. Finkelman has a framed diploma on the wall above his desk from Harvard University in Cambridge, Massachusetts. Apparently, Harvard isn't official enough to dole out badges, but the Institute of Paranormal Studies and Professional Ghost Investigation of Boulder, Colorado, is.

I bet Dr. Finkelman will be kicking himself that he didn't go there instead of Harvard when I tell him he could have had a badge too. Because everyone who's anyone knows there is nothing more official than a badge.

That's why they give them to police officers and health inspectors.

A badge can get you arrested, like the drug addict who robbed D'Agostino's on Greenwich Street last summer. Or a badge can shut you down, like with Chester's Deli around the corner from our walk-up on Charles Street.

And while we all knew Chester's would be shut down sooner or later, no one could deny Chester made the best Reuben sandwiches in New York.

"Hello!" T. S. Phoenix calls out to all of us seated at the small, square tables that are lined up diagonally throughout the dining hall, each one with a tall gold candlestick holding a single red candle. Me and Mags are sitting at a table up front. Dad, Big John, and The Faz are at the table next to ours. And the remaining hotel workers (the ones who haven't disappeared in the dead of night) are scattered throughout the hall.

There is Ms. Lettie (aka a tiny cowgirl vampire); Mr. Lozano, front desk clerk; Jack the busboy; Ubbe Amblebee (*and* his plunger); Ruby Red, housekeeper; Madame Drusilla, the Stanley Hotel's resident spiritualist; and, of course, Mr. Plum in his too-tight blazer.

T. S. Phoenix is standing on the stage at the front of the room with Tally by his side. He's a tall man with a thick head of curls tucked inside a backward baseball cap. Tally has a short black pixie haircut and a tie-dyed skirt and flat sandals. She jingles every time she moves on account of the gazillion metal bracelets that hang around her wrists.

"Thank you all for joining us this evening," T. S. Phoenix calls out to us. "Tally and I are thrilled to be here. I'm the science guy in our research team, and Tally is what we in the paranormal business call a *sensitive*. There are two approaches when it comes to paranormal investigation: through facts and through the metaphysic." He holds up two fingers. "Facts include tangible things that we can prove, and the metaphysic involves Tally's harnessed talents of clairvoyance and ESP. Tally?"

"Thank you." She clears her throat. "ESP stands for extrasensory perception, which means that I can oftentimes perceive things by methods other than physical experience."

My cell phone buzzes in my back pocket.

Mags.

> **MAGS:**
>> How much do you think she'd charge to tell me if Jack the busboy wants to be my boyfriend?

> **ME:**
>> Crystal Mystic will tell you for free.

Mags just gives me an eyes-to-the-sky roll.

She isn't quite as blocked against the woo-woo as Dad, but her channels definitely need a major cleansing.

Tally is still talking. "Oh, and Mr. Plum?" she calls out to the back of the hall. "Excuse me . . . Mr. Plum?"

We all turn to look at Mr. Plum. But he's busy scrolling through his phone and doesn't even notice.

"Excuse me . . . Mr. Plum," Tally calls again.

He jumps in his seat and peers over round reading glasses. "I'm sorry. Yes?"

"Driving directions aren't part of the ESP phenomenon. Unfortunately, I still have to consult my GPS."

Mr. Plum's mouth falls open.

Me and Mags wide-eye each other.

And a booming *"Ha!"* bursts out of Big John.

"Ah . . . yes . . . of course . . . ah . . . my apologies. Please continue," Mr. Plum bumbles out, his round cheeks shining like two bright red apples.

"We are here to learn about what is restless at the Stanley Hotel in Estes Park," T. S. Phoenix continues. "Paranormal disturbances are way more commonplace than people think. Many push aside the idea that something has been moved or misplaced in their home as an oversight. Or something like a flash of light is just a faulty bulb. The truth is it can actually be a paranormal disturbance. We must keep an open mind without getting pareidolic."

WHAT-IFS

Sounds contagious to me.

I raise my hand. "Excuse me, Dr. Phoenix," I call. "Is that catching?"

He laughs. "Ummm, kind of, but not by germs. *Pareidolic* means you find whatever you are searching for purely because you *want* to find it. I'm far from pareidolic. I'm a scientist first and foremost when it comes to my investigative process. I'm looking for facts that can be backed by evidence, using electronic equipment to substantiate those facts. We will be using cameras, Geiger counters, electromagnetic meters and more. Tally will enhance that search with information about any psychic energy in the anomalies we may find."

With my pen poised, I ask, "Can you spell *parei . . . parei*—"

"*P-A-R-E-I-D-O-L-I-C.*"

Dad scribbles it down in his logbook, and so do I.

"Think of it like this," T. S. Phoenix goes on. "If you are interested in UFOs, everything you see in the sky that you can't explain becomes an alien vehicle from a far-off planet. Or every log floating in Loch Ness becomes the Loch Ness Monster, because that's what you are looking for and that's what you want it to be. We want to have an open mind about what we might find, but also be objective. My first thought at the start of each investigation is, What earthly explanation can we attribute to this disturbance? Once I've exhausted all my options, that's when I examine the paranormal possibilities. Is that clear?"

I give him a thumbs-up and say, "Yes, sir, thank you."

"Does anyone here have a theory of their own about the Stanley Hotel or an experience they would like to share?"

Ghostly meet-and-greet silence.

That's when we hear racing footsteps somewhere high on the grand staircase.

Mr. Plum huffs out a "Dag gum hooligans" under his breath before excusing himself and stomping out of the dining hall.

After he's gone, T. S. Phoenix stretches his long arms toward all the Stanley Hotel employees like an invitation. "You are the experts," he tells them. "You work here. You live on the property. You've had your own sightings. Please share your experiences with us."

Ms. Lettie is the very first one to volunteer. She stands up, smooths out her cowgirl fringe and then clears her throat.

"I can tell you exactly who it is," she says.

"Yes, please share your thoughts, Ms. Lettie," T. S. Phoenix tells her.

"It's Mr. Ozgood Honeycutt, of course. I'm certain of it. He can tell you himself."

T. S. Phoenix looks at Tally and then back at Ms. Lettie. "How do you mean?" he asks.

And that's when the dining hall chandeliers all go out at the very same time.

Voices gasp.

Alfred Hitchcock woofs.

I grab Mags's knee under the table.

Someone screams (I think it's me).

And then as fast as the lights went off, they are on again.

Ms. Lettie gives us all a real big I-told-you-so grin. "He can be a real stinker when he wants to be," she snickers.

The chandeliers flicker again.

Dad's Nikon D5600 flashes three times.

"I'm afraid you'll have to be much quicker than that, Mr. Vallenari," Ms. Lettie tells him.

WHAT-IFS

I sure hope Dad put that heart attack
doctor on speed dial like we talked about.

I tap my fingers under the table on one hand and squeeze Mags's leg with the other.

One. Two. Three. Four.

"I think we should go back to our room," I whisper to her.

"You can't walk out now," she informs me, peeling my fingers from her leg. "You're Research."

"I quit," I tell her.

"You can't quit."

"Hold my hand," I say.

She reaches out and wraps her hand around mine. "It's just lights," she tells me.

"It's not just lights," I correct her.

"Yeah, I see that," she says, nodding her head up and down. "But that's what I'm going to keep telling myself."

"I think we need to hear more about this Ozgood Honeycutt," Dad says then.

Ms. Lettie nods. "Mr. Ozgood Honeycutt and his wife, Seraphina Jayne Honeycutt, came to the hotel to celebrate their honeymoon in 1909. On the third day of their vacation, they both died tragically. During a scenic horse-and-buggy ride, the buggy toppled over and they both tumbled down the mountain. I believe the haunting at the Stanley Hotel is Mr. Honeycutt looking for his bride and making it known that he is doing so. He lingers . . . wandering the halls . . . looking for his love . . . unable to move on without her."

"No disrespect to you, Ms. Lettie," Madame Drusilla says. "But my sensibilities tell me it's more of a haunting than just silly poltergeist shenanigans."

"What do you mean by that?" Dad asks her.

"So many outsiders have come. Like . . . you." She holds her nose up in Dad's direction. "Outsiders who don't belong here and claim to be investigating when they have no knowledge on the subject of the afterlife or how dangerous it can be—"

"Um, excuse me, Madame Drusilla," I interrupt. "Can you define *dangerous*?"

She turns to me. "Not safe," she says flatly.

My jumping beans lurch and my voice cracks. "Th-that's what I was afraid you meant."

Ubbe Amblebee shakes his plunger and says, "I agree with Ms. Lettie. It's definitely Ozgood, and Seraphina is here too. This hotel is a place of happiness. Of love. It's not evil. Those who stay here experience some of the best times of their lives. It just makes sense this is where they would choose to come in the afterlife. Especially in the case of the Honeycutts."

"Gran has even seen Mr. Honeycutt's image," Jack the busboy pipes up from the back.

"That's right," Ms. Lettie says. "It was in 2015. Mine was the very first sighting. I saw a man in a fancy tuxedo vest and top hat wandering the lobby, and then he just vanished as quickly as he appeared."

WHAT-IFS

Did she say . . . vanished?

Onetwothreefour.

Mr. Lozano raises his hand.

"Yes, Mr. Lozano," T. S. Phoenix says.

"Yeah, so . . . ah, I may be new here," Mr. Lozano says, shifting in his seat. "But I've done a lot of research on the history of this hotel. Ms. Lettie's was indeed the very first sighting here. And since that time, there have been more and more sightings. They've scared off all the guests. Mr. and Mrs. Jewel have had to put the hotel up for sale because of it, and no one wants to buy it because of all the paranormal activity. If things don't improve quickly, they will lose it altogether. I don't know what it is, but I know the problem needs to be fixed. Mr. Amblebee is right about this place. It's special. The Jewel family made it so for all these years. They don't deserve this—"

"I disagree," Madame Drusilla interrupts. "We can't disregard the fact that the outsiders who come here investigating, when they have no business being here, are unknowingly communing with evil spirits and drumming up chaos. And all I know is that once you let *them* in . . . well . . . that's when you have a real big problem."

I swallow hard and say, "Excuse me, Madame Drusilla. Can you define *problem*?"

She turns to face me again. "An evil spirit problem, of course," she says.

"Th-that's the kind of problem I was afraid you were talking about."

I knew this trip was going to be the worst mistake of my young life. And I know if Crystal Mystic were with me now, it would definitely confirm it.

As I sit there trying to calm my jumping beans while the others argue about which entity is haunting the Stanley, I notice one very important change to the MacGregor Dining Hall.

Ruby Red, who had been sitting alone at a back table near the door . . . is *gone.*

Television Fuzz and the In-Between

J ust in case my hotel-manager-serial-killer theory pans out, Mags agrees to check the wardrobe for missing manager body parts that night before bed.

"Make sure you check each and every drawer," I tell her, supervising from a safe distance.

"See?" She closes one drawer and then another. "Nothing."

WHAT-IFS

A pinky toe can easily hide in the crevices.

"See? Nothing," she says.

"Not even a pinky toe?" I ask.

"That"—she points at me—"is disturbing."

She proceeds to open all the remaining drawers and then close them again with a bang. "See? Nothing." Slam. Open. "Nope." Slam. Open. "Still nothing." Slam. "Can we go to bed now?" Open. "Wait . . . oh, no! Oh my God! The *horror*!" Slam.

While I'm hightailing it to the door, she's chucking out a big fat *"Ha!"*

"I'm kidding," she calls after me.

I turn around with my hand on the doorknob. "You're kidding?"

"I'm kidding."

I put two fists on my hips and give her a good glare. "Not funny."

She laughs. "You should have seen it from my angle."

"Still," I say.

"Are you finally satisfied?" she asks me. "No severed body parts equals no serial killer with *murderous intent*."

But I remain unconvinced.

When it comes to an empty hotel in the middle of nowhere, you have to be ready for anything.

After our ghostly meet-and-greet and Mags's official wardrobe check, we get ready for bed. Her in her regular nightgown and me in my mom's 1983 Journey concert tee, the *Frontiers* tour. I found it at the bottom of the hamper in the hall and started wearing it to bed after she left. I wore it Mom-stinky until the stink smelled more like my stink than hers. That's when Dad made me wash it.

Now it just smells Tide fresh.

But I still wear it.

We have a lot in common, me and the shirt.

We were important . . . once.

"Ready?" Mags asks.

"Ready," I say.

"Let the bargaining begin," she says.

I start the ante with the whole kit and caboodle.

Me: All lights on.

Her: Bathroom light only, door closed.

Me: I'll give you a bathroom light, but with open door, and raise you one desk light.

Her: Bathroom light only, door ajar, final offer.

Me: Bathroom light only, door ajar but wider, *final* final offer.

She taps her chin with her pointer finger, thinking.

Her: Deal.

We seal the deal with our typical fist bump, fanned fingers and a shimmy-shimmy to the floor before slipping under the covers.

It's funny that me and Mags ended up best friends since the third grade. We are as different as different can be. But we're the same, too.

She's outspoken and I'm the quiet one.

Her insides are bursting at the seams with confidence and I'm scared of everything.

She's always picked first in gym and I'm dead last.

She's blond and bubbly and I'm brown and brooding.

But we're the same in one very important way. We're both true blue.

I knew that in third grade when the bully of Immaculate Heart of Mary K-8, Darby Woods, shoved me in the girls' bathroom and told me I wasn't cool enough to be at that school.

Mags was the only one who would stand up for me.

That's how I knew I could trust her with anything. A person who does something like that is the truest of blue.

On the night my mom left and it felt like the world was ending, we binge-watched *Stranger Things* episodes on Netflix in Mags's bed and ate a whole bag of Chips Ahoy! cookies. And when I couldn't hold back the tears for another second, she held my hand until the tears finally stopped.

Mags is as true blue as they get.

And I know that's the real reason she's here. More so than infinite dibs.

True blue is everything.

We lay our heads on our pillows now and stare at each other over the nightstand between us in the light shining from our lights-on contract. Alfred Hitchcock is already fast asleep at the foot of my bed.

"You know what? I think maybe Ms. Lettie is right," Mags says, her cheek in her palm.

"You mean about Mr. Honeycutt?" I ask.

"Yeah," she says.

"Why do you think so?"

"Because of the poltergeist theory," she tells me. "I know all about them, you know."

"About what?"

"Poltergeists," she says. "I know all about them."

"Not since I've known you," I tell her.

"Uh-huh," she insists. "I saw this movie on it."

"When?"

"I don't know," she says. "A long time ago. It's on my dad's laptop."

"How come you've never told me about it until now?"

She makes a face. "One guess."

"Still," I say. "We don't keep secrets. It's the most important part of our best-friend pact. No secrets is our thing."

"Yeah, but if Dr. Finkelman doesn't want you watching *Scooby-Doo,* he certainly doesn't want you watching this."

"I can so watch *Scooby-Doo,*" I murmur.

"I don't think so," she says, slipping out from under the covers and sitting up with her pillow clutched tight in front of her.

"Just tell me."

"Fine, but don't blame me when you can't sleep tonight."

"Deal," I tell her.

"*Poltergeist* is this movie from the eighties. The actual word *poltergeist* is German for 'noisy ghost.' It's like the ghosts just want to cause problems for people because the spirits are unhappy being stuck in the middle between here and the afterlife. And in the movie, first that's all it is. Some ghost just throwing things around like a kid having a tantrum . . . until it's much more."

"And by *much more . . .* you meeeeean?"

"Something actually *snatches* the daughter in the middle of the night during a loud storm."

I sit straight up in my bed now too. "And by *snatch her . . .* you meeeeean?"

"It was kind of like a paranormal kidnapping. You know, like a ghost just took her."

"Took her where?" I ask.

Mags waves her hand through the space between us. "The in-between."

"How did it do that?"

"Through the television," she says. "Like it's some kind of portal to the beyond or something."

I stare at the television stuck to the wall of our room and tap my fingers under the covers.

One. Two. Three. Four.

"How does that work?" I ask Mags.

"What do you mean *how*?" she says. "Paranormal entities operate on a whole other set of rules of science. And in this case, their rules of science included a television, okay? You don't ask ghosts *how*. It just is."

I consider this.

"Was the television on or off?" I ask.

"It was on, but not like on a particular show. It was like, you know, fuzz."

I blink at her. *"Fuzz?"*

"Yeah, fuzz."

"You mean like no-picture-on-the-screen fuzz?" I ask.

"Right, like your-Wi-Fi-is-out fuzz," she says. "And then it just took her. Just like that." She snaps her fingers. *"Gone."*

"Gone?" I whisper.

"Gone," she tells me.

One. Two. Three. Four.

Onetwothreefour.

I try to swallow, but there's no spit left in my mouth to muster a gulp. My hands go cold and the centers of my palms start to sweat.

WHAT-IFS

What if the fuzz is watching you now?

"Wh-what happens to the girl?" I ask.

"In the movie they said there are two kinds of dead people. The ones that pass over the way they're supposed to after they die and the ones that get stuck."

"Stuck where?"

"You know, somewhere between living, and accepting that they've died and moving to the beyond. The light or heaven or whatever you believe. So, they're just hanging out on another plane of existence . . . out *there*." She waves her hands in the darkness. "Or in Mr. Honeycutt's case . . . in *here*—"

One. Two. Three. Four.

"And there's something else," Mags says. "I probably shouldn't even tell you."

"You should definitely tell me," I say.

"It's about this hotel."

"What about it?" I ask.

"This hotel is connected to *The Shining,* one of the scariest horror stories ever written," she tells me. "They made a movie of it too. My dad won't let me see that one because it's rated R. But I snuck it. I was going to watch the whole thing until I got to the eleven-minute, fifty-second mark. That's when I turned it off, and I'm not even going to tell you why. You'll never sleep again."

I swallow. "Worse than in-between fuzz?" I ask.

"Way worse. Like a million times worse," she tells me. "And you want to know what else—"

But before she even has the chance to finish, something horrible happens.

A *scream.*

A bloodcurdling, gut-wrenching, heart-stopping scream that seems to go on forever.

She wide-eyes me and I wide-eye her back.

Alfred Hitchcock hops to attention.

Footsteps pound the hall outside our door.

Voices shout.

Time stops.

Another scream pierces the air.

"Who is that?" I whisper to Mags.

"He's *heeeere*," Mags whispers.

Bang. Bang. Bang.

"Karma!" someone hollers from the other side of the door.

Mags jumps down from the bed and grabs both of my arms, giving me a shake. "How does Ozgood Honeycutt know your name?"

Bang. Bang. Bang.

Alfred Hitchcock jumps from the bed now and runs in circles on the viney carpet, barking whole-body barks at the ceiling.

"What do we do? What do we do?" Mags shouts, giving me another shake.

"Crystal Mystic will know," I tell her, grabbing it off the night table.

"Great." She throws her hands out. "Our very lives in the hands of a stupid, plastic ball. I knew you and your woo-woo would be the death of me one day, Karma Moon, and here we are!"

"Crystal Mystic, is that Ozgood Honeycutt here to snatch our souls to the in-between?" I give it a shake, and I wait for the voice from beyond the stars to guide us.

CRYSTAL MYSTIC

YOUR SPIRIT GUIDES ARE ON A
LUNCH BREAK. TRY AGAIN LATER.

"Great. Not helpful in an emergency? Check," Mags says. "I knew we shouldn't trust woo-woo."

Bang. Bang. Bang.

"Karma! Open this door!" the disembodied voice demands.

One. Two. Three. Four.

One two three four.

Onetwothreefour.

Another scream. This one turning into a wail and then . . . the knob on the door rattles.

"There's only one thing left to do," I tell her.

She nods and we both scurry under my velvet bedspread and hold hands while I shake Crystal Mystic over and over again under the covers, asking the same exact question.

Each time, the same stupid answer.

CRYSTAL MYSTIC

YOUR SPIRIT GUIDES ARE ON A
LUNCH BREAK. TRY AGAIN LATER.

"Maybe the evil spirits have clogged the channels."

"Or maybe it's a hunk of junk," Mags mumbles.

63

"Woo-woo isn't cuckoo and without it—"

"Don't even," she says, pointing a warning finger in my direction.

"But this is my surefire woo-woo system. It's usually right-on," I tell her.

"Usually isn't always, is it?"

Shake.

CRYSTAL MYSTIC

YOUR SPIRIT GUIDES ARE ON A LUNCH BREAK. TRY AGAIN LATER.

Shake.

CRYSTAL MYSTIC

YOUR SPIRIT GUIDES ARE ON A LUNCH BREAK. TRY AGAIN LATER.

"You need to rethink your surefire woo-woo system in emergency situations," Mags tells me. "What about your stupid crystals? Bring anything to ward off the evil spirits?"

"Oh, sure," I say. "They're stupid until you need them."

"Did you bring the ward-off-evil-spirit ones or didn't you?" she asks.

"I just brought your garden-variety courage ones." I pull the tiny leather sack of crystals that I wear around my neck out from under Mom's Journey T-shirt to show her.

She huffs air out and crosses herself. "We're doomed."

"I think you're right," I tell her.

"About being doomed? Or the fact that I knew one day your woo-woo would be the death of me?"

"About the fact that I definitely need a new surefire system for evil spirit emergencies."

Bang. Bang. Bang.

"I've got it," she says, grabbing her cell phone from her pocket. "911 will know what to do."

"You can't call 911 for a ghost emergency," I inform her.

"Watch me," she says, already dialing.

I wedge my ear next to hers and listen in.

911 Operator: This is 911, please state your emergency.

Mags: Ah, yeah . . . hello? We, um, would like to report a ghostly spirit attempting to snatch our souls to the in-between.

911 Operator: *Click.*

"Genius," I tell her.

"Hey, *you're* the one who left the antighost crystals at home."

Bang. Bang. Bang.

The knob on our room rattles again and we both scream.

Mags grabs my hand in hers. "You will always be my best friend, Karma Moon Vallenari." Her words tumble out at me, each one falling on top of the one before it. "And if Mr. Honeycutt is going to snatch us to the in-between, there's no one I'd rather be snatched with."

"Ditto," I tell her, squeezing her fingers.

And that's when I feel the courage crystals kick in, in a boost of bravery.

I stick my head out from under the covers and yell as loud as I can so the soulless entity hears me loud and clear, "If you are Mr. Honeycutt or even a hotel-manager-slash-film-crew serial murderer, you'd better keep walking!" I yell again. "'Cause you're not cutting anything off of us, got it? Not a finger or an ear or even a pinky toe!"

Suddenly the banging and the doorknob rattling stop.

We wait.

Then a voice.

But this time it sounds surprisingly familiar.

"Have you been watching *Dateline* again?"

"Oh my God!" Mags gasps. "Even Ozgood Honeycutt knows about Dr. Finkelman's list."

"That's not Mr. Honeycutt," I tell her, shoving the covers off me. "It's my dad."

She lets out a giant breath.

When I fling open the door, Dad is standing in bare feet and his gray sweatpants. The ones he always sleeps in, with a plain white T-shirt.

He grabs my shoulders and stretches his neck to scan our room. "Is everything okay in here? Mags, you good? You're both okay?"

He's all breathy, like he just got done running a marathon.

But before I can even answer him, we hear more loud voices floating up the giant staircase from the lobby downstairs.

"What is going on?" Mags asks Dad.

"I don't know," he says. "Come on, let's go find out. I want you girls to stay with me."

He grabs my hand and I grab Mags's and we all scramble toward the grand staircase with Alfred Hitchcock leading the way.

Polka-Dot Boxer Shorts

When we make it down to the lobby, everyone is there.

The double doors leading to the red front steps are wide open, letting the cool night breeze blow all the way up the giant staircase. Raindrops dot the sidewalk and the drive, and a slow rumble of thunder tells us a storm is brewing.

When I squeeze in between Ms. Lettie in her pink curlers and flowered pajamas and Ubbe Amblebee in his ratty blue bathrobe and hairy legs, I can see Mr. Plum standing on the very bottom red step outside the lobby doors.

In his *underwear.*

Polka-dot boxers, to be

← Ew

disturbingly specific. With a pair of matching socks, stretched all the way up to his knees.

T. S. Phoenix, with the worst case of bedhead on the face of the planet, is trying to coax Mr. Plum back inside like he's a lost cat and T.S. is afraid if he doesn't catch him, he'll run into the street and get hit by a car.

"I'm not going back in there," Mr. Plum is saying, shaking his head left and then right and then left and then right. "And you can't make me."

His eyes are wider than any eyes I've ever seen wide. Even the time when Mags punched Ollie Logan after he sang *Margaret Mags, you're a hag with bags that sag* in the third grade. I thought his eyes were going to pop right out of his head when he saw that bright red blood coming out of his nose.

"Just come on inside and tell us what happened, Mr. Plum," Chef Raphaël says, standing with his hands on his hips in perfectly pressed cotton pajamas, minus one chef hat. Who knew there wasn't a single lick of hair under there? His head glows like a glittering bowling ball. It sure is a good thing I don't have peladophobia. That's the fear of bald people. But it doesn't matter one whit to me that Chef Raphaël is a bowling ball.

Mr. Plum just keeps shaking his head. "First there was a breeze in my room and then someone was calling out to me and then I came down and I saw that." He points to the open doors.

We all turn and scan the lobby.

"You saw what, Mr. Plum?" Mr. Lozano asks him.

"D-don't you see it?" he asks.

"See what?" Madame Drusilla says.

"Th-the *furniture* in the d-dining hall. D-don't you see it?" Mr. Plum stutters.

I look again, but all I see is Alfred Hitchcock stretching and then jumping up on top of a comfy leather chair in front of one of the fireplaces. He scratches at the cushion until it's to his liking and then curls up in a ball, uninterested in Mr. Plum's sighting or anything else except a nighttime nap.

"What's wrong with the furniture?" I ask.

Mr. Plum takes five careful steps up the front stairs and then stretches his neck to peek inside the doorway and toward the dining hall.

"They're gone," he says.

"What is?" I ask.

"The dining hall chairs," he says.

I stretch my neck then too and see all the chairs tucked neatly in for the night, each one beneath its properly numbered table.

"They're still there," I tell him.

"They were stacked wonky-like all the way up to the ceiling," he says. "Completely defying gravity."

Mags gasps. "Completely defying gravity?" she says with wide eyes as she grabs my hand and holds it tight. Then she whispers to me, "That's exactly how it happened in the movie."

"*Poltergeist?*" I ask.

"Yes."

"Whoa," I say.

She nods. "This is getting real."

Ms. Lettie gives a chuckle and says, "Oh, that Mr. Honeycutt. He sure likes to cause mischief."

Mr. Amblebee nods in agreement.

"Well, they're all on the floor now," Dad tells Mr. Plum. "Come on back inside."

"No," Mr. Plum says, shaking his head again. "No, I'm not going back in there."

"Mr. Plum," T. S. Phoenix says, turning on the black machine with lighted dots in his hand, which he told me earlier is called a Geiger counter and measures ionizing radiation in the air. "What brought you down to the lobby in your underwear to begin with?"

"I don't remember everything except that there was a cold breeze inside my room and the window wasn't open. And then someone . . . someone was calling my name," Mr. Plum says, taking five backward red steps. "Calling me all the way down to the dining hall."

"Mr. Honeycutt knew your name?" Mags breathes.

"N-no," Mr. Plum stammers. "It . . . it w-was a woman. I—I saw her."

"What did she look like?" Dad asks him.

"I—I don't remember," Mr. Plum says.

"Come back in and we'll take some readings and check it out," T. S. Phoenix is saying.

"No, no, no," Mr. Plum tells him. "I can't do that."

"Mr. Plum," Tally says. "You can't just stand out here all night in your underwear."

At that exact moment, a rusted Toyota Camry with an Uber sticker in the window pulls to a stop right in front of the walkway.

"You're right about that," Mr. Plum says, opening the back door and sliding in.

"What about the hotel? Your clothes?" Ms. Lettie calls.

"Ah . . . dude?" the Uber driver asks. "Do you know you're missing your pants?"

"Just go," Mr. Plum informs him.

The driver hesitates and then says, "The thing is . . . I feel much more comfortable with passengers who have their pants *on*—"

"I said *go*!" Mr. Plum shouts.

The guy shifts it into drive. Mr. Plum slams the door and we all stand there watching the rusted Camry with a missing front hubcap lurch forward and fly down East Wonderview.

★

Once we get back to room 332, me and Mags are wide awake, holding hands underneath the covers of my bed.

Every single solitary light is on.

No negotiation needed.

Mags even pulled the chair out from under the desk and wedged it under the doorknob.

"Do ghosts come through the door?" I ask her. "I thought you said they come through the fuzz."

"You're right," she says, grabbing the TV remote from the night table between our beds, unwedging the chair from under the knob and throwing the remote into the hall before relocking everything and scrambling back for the bed.

"I'm starting to have second thoughts about agreeing to come out here," she tells me now, hunkered once again under the covers. "Infinite dibs is totally not worth this."

"Well, I'm glad you are here," I tell her. "I need my true blue."

"I know, but I said I'd come because I didn't really think the place was haunted," she goes on. "And now I'm totally freaked out."

"Tell me what happens at the eleven-minute, fifty-second mark in *The Shining*," I tell her.

"Never," Mags says. "And you can't make me."

"You want to know what?" I ask her.

"What?"

"I think there is something phony baloney going on here," I tell her.

"What does that mean?"

"I was thinking about it . . . not everyone was in the lobby after Mr. Plum screamed bloody murder," I say.

"Mmmm, no, I think everyone was there," she says,

starting to count on her fingers. "Mr. Lozano, Ms. Lettie, T. S. Phoenix, Tally, your dad, The Faz, Big John, Ubbe Amblebee, Madame Drusilla—Mr. Plum, of course. Polka-dot boxers and matching socks? Ew."

"Totally ew," I agree.

"Chef Raphaël was there . . . I've never seen a guy without a single hair on his head."

"What about the math teacher, Mr. Lund? He's pretty bald."

"Yeah, but he's still got that powdered-doughnut look around the back with a bite missing in the front. Chef Raphaël is bowling-ball bald."

"You know who wasn't there?" I say. "Jack the busboy."

"Yeah, but I found out he lives in town with his mom."

"So, that's everyone, then," I say.

"I think so."

"Wait, what about . . . *Ruby Red*," I whisper. "Where was she?"

"*Riiiight.*" Mags leans her head on her elbow. "Where *was* she?"

"That's the question," I say. "Not to mention, she just vanished from the dining hall during the ghostly meet-and-greet."

"Really?"

I nod.

"Well, maybe she doesn't live in the employee quarters and she went home early," Mags says. "That could be why she wasn't in the lobby just now."

"I'm pretty sure Jack the busboy is the only one who doesn't live on-site."

"Mmm," Mags says.

"So, why do you think she didn't show up when everyone else did?" I ask. "It's weird, right? Don't you think it's weird?"

"Maybe she didn't hear it because she was sleeping."

"Maybe," I say. "But he screamed pretty loud and everyone else seemed to hear it. Why not her? Could she really sleep through something like that?"

"Some people can," Mags says. "When we flew to Cleveland for my grandma's funeral last year, my dad wore earplugs on the plane while he was sleeping and he didn't hear a thing."

"I guess," I agree. "Did you notice that the employee dorms are directly across the courtyard from our window?"

"Who cares?"

"If there is something phony baloney going on in this hotel and a current employee is at the heart of it," I say, "we'll all care."

Mags snorts. "Don't you mean if there's a serial killer living across the courtyard?"

"Where do you think serial killers live?" I demand. "On Mars? No, they live here. Among us. Maybe even . . . *there*." I point toward the window.

"That's *Dateline* talking."

"Heed my warning, Mags Bogdonavich," I tell her.

"There is some funny business going on in this hotel as sure as I'm standing here, and I'm going to be the one to find out what it is."

"Uh-huh, and just how are you going to do that when you are afraid of the closet?"

"I'm not afraid of the closet," I tell her. "Just the missing body parts that might be hidden inside."

"Uh-huh," she says again.

WHAT-IFS

Are we sure she checked every *drawer?*

"Come on." I push the bedspread off me, feeling the bravery crystals kicking in again.

"Where are we going?" she asks.

"To do some investigating," I tell her, heading toward the window.

She scrambles in behind me and we peek outside between the crack in the heavy velvet curtains. The back courtyard below is completely dark except for one lone tall streetlamp with a dim umbrella of light shining down on the cobblestone patio. Across the paved courtyard are the employee quarters.

They're three stories tall and lined with four sets of windows on each floor. Every window is dark.

Except one.

Ruby Red's.

We watch through half-open curtains as she takes

off her black raincoat. Her wet hair is plastered to her head. She's no longer wearing her housekeeper uniform.

Official Phony Baloney List

1. 2:33 a.m. Ruby Red is phony baloney big-time.

Hitchy

"Look!" I point. "I told you, didn't I?"

I grab my ghost log and make a note.

"What is she doing?" Mags squints.

"I don't know," I say. "But why would she be out at two-thirty in the morning? Two-thirty-three, to be exact."

"In the pouring rain," Mags adds.

"Well, she must have heard Mr. Plum if she was awake."

"Then why didn't she come to the lobby with everyone else?" Mags wonders.

"Exactly."

"Maybe she was out on a date or something," she suggests.

"She's way too old to date," I say.

"I'm pretty sure old people date," Mags tells me.

"Mmmm . . . yeah, that doesn't sound right."

"Last year rumor had it that Ms. Morgan, the art teacher, was dating Principal Tannenbaum," she says.

"Yeah, I know, but I chose to suppress it," I say. "Ms. Morgan could do better. Plus . . . ew."

"Well, duh, but I'm just saying, it happens," Mags tells me. "Look at your mom and the creeper she's living with in Florida."

"That's *not* dating."

"Then what do you call it?"

"A nightmare."

"Wait." She points. "What's she doing? Is that a suitcase? Maybe she's quitting too. Maybe she freaked out at the lights in the dining hall and just bolted. And now she's packing to leave because she's too scared to stay, just like Mr. Plum and all the others. Except, you know . . . *dressed*."

We watch as Ruby Red shoves the suitcase with a brown leather handle under her bed before she moves to the window, looks outside left and right and then pulls the curtains closed, leaving only a crack of light showing between.

At precisely 2:38 a.m., her light goes off.

"She doesn't look scared to me," I say. "It looks like she's going to sleep."

We crawl back into my bed and lie under the velvet bedspread staring at each other.

"So, what do you think now?" I ask Mags.

"Phony baloney funny business supreme," she agrees. "But she couldn't possibly have done what Mr. Plum said he saw."

"Yeah," I say. "I definitely think there is something paranormal happening here too. I mean, how else could the dining hall chairs be completely defying gravity and then just not be?"

"Yeah," she agrees.

"What do you think it is?"

"You mean other than the obvious paranormal reason we came up here?"

"I don't know," I say. "We need to investigate what's going on."

"Agreed," she says. "But what if the funny business cancels out the haunted part?"

"But it's my job to do the research," I tell her.

"The thing is . . . if we prove this place is not haunted at all, your dad may lose his Netflix contract altogether."

WHAT-IFS

No barbecue = no Mom.

"And what if he never forgives you for that one?" Mags goes on.

"Right," I agree.

But my what-ifs take it one step further.

WHAT-IFS

What if he leaves you too?

Fun City

Once you see polka-dot boxers paired with matching socks on some old guy, you can't unsee it.

Add Mr. Plum's ghost sighting on the very first night to the mix?

Me and Mags already need a major mental health day. And it's only day two.

And lucky for us, Dad agrees. Probably more so because he wants us out of their way while they're busy setting up all T. S. Phoenix's scientific ghost equipment and Dad's film stuff for tonight's first big investigation.

T. S. Phoenix wanted to do their first official investigation in room 217.

The room.

T. S. Phoenix thinks it's probably *highly active,* which basically means it's a hot spot for ghosts. He thinks so especially after hearing Ms. Lettie's story about Mr. Honeycutt. Because room 217 is the room they stayed in on their honeymoon. But after Mr. Plum's sighting, the team thought it best to try to catch on film the ghostly woman who summoned him to the lobby.

Official Phony Baloney Suspect List

1. Ruby Red. Big-time.

Ms. Lettie might still be a big-haired vampire. More data needed to officially rule out the undead theory.

Over breakfast we give Dad, Big John and The Faz a whole briefing all about the phony baloney funny business we spotted going on across the courtyard. Dad says we do good work and to keep him updated on any new findings.

After breakfast, me and Mags decide our mental health day is best served at a place called Fun City. She found it on her Yelp app.

FUN CITY CLAIM: A FAMILY TRADITION SINCE 1969.

Its *whoopee* quality announces itself in its name.
Fun.
I don't even need to ask Crystal Mystic to confirm it because everyone who's anyone knows any place with

something called giant water walking balls *and* a rainbow slide *and* bumper boats is kid approved.

A perfect spot to spend a mental health day. Though Mags is more in it for the boys. Fine by me.

She had me at bumper boats.

While Mags is applying the contraband blush she's not supposed to have that she bought at JFK airport, my cell phone buzzes.

A text from Mom with a picture attached.

My heartbeat races.

It's been thirteen whole days since I've heard anything from her.

Thirteen.

Mags has been gone for a day and a half and her mom has texted her three times and called twice just to see how she is. She even asks Mags what she's eating and if she's taking her daily vitamin and going to the bathroom okay.

I open the text and see a too-tan Mom next to the ocean in a *far*-too-small bikini.

Having a great time at the beach.

Seven words in thirteen days.

And not one of them is about me.

Not my food intake *or* my vitamin regimen *or* even my daily trips to the bathroom.

Having. A. Great. Time. At. The. Beach.

I read the words over and over again while Mags puts on illegal blusher. Read them again. And then again. I squint at the picture of Mom posing on a brightly colored beach towel on the white sand.

Enlarge.

Reduce.

Enlarge.

Reduce.

If moms were like amusement park rides, Mags's mom would be like this slow-moving Ferris wheel mom. A predictable, steady ride that's always going in the same direction and you never once go upside down or feel out of control or like you're going to fall out at any minute. You always know where you are and where you're going. My mom is more like a corkscrew roller coaster. It can be a blast to go the speed of sound and be upside down and jerked in all directions . . . sometimes. But other times it just makes you want to throw up your churro.

I show the picture of too-tan Mom in her too-small bikini to Mags.

"Having a great time at the beach," I recite.

"I'm sorry, but the purpose of a bathing suit is to *cover things*?" Mags informs me, squeezing her eyes closed and pushing the phone away. "I mean, ew."

"Yeah." I nod.

One thing I know is that a Ferris wheel mom *never* wears thong bottoms.

Mags's mom wears board shorts and a tankini even on

the hottest days when she takes us to the Carmine Street Pool. If my mom took us to the pool in this eye patch, I'd die a hundred deaths of embarrassment and *then* throw up my churro.

"Will you delete that thing already? It's just plain disturbing. And can I just tell you that you should warn a person before showing them something like that. It's like a scarred-for-life kind of thing."

"It's my too-much-skin mom, not yours," I tell her. "I'm the victim here."

"Still." Mags takes another look and then wrinkles her nose up at me. "TMI supreme."

My thumb hovers over the Delete button, but I decide to save it instead.

And on our walk to Fun City, while Mags is going on about Jack the busboy, who was shirtless yet again while he pulled weeds in the garden out in front of the hotel, I can't help but wonder why Mom's text didn't say *Wish you were here* or even *Miss you.*

I mean, is it too much to ask for a gif hug even?

How hard is it to send a smiling dog?

A bursting heart.

Something.

WHAT-IFS

Are you looking for an answer
that doesn't end in five suitcases?

84

At Fun City, Mags calls dibs no less than three million times before lunch alone.

Dibs at the miniature golf.

Dibs at the go-carts.

Dibs at the bungee trampoline.

She even calls dibs at the giant water walking balls, which turn out to be a real metaphor for life. You get inside these clear plastic bubbles and you push and bounce and bumble, butting heads with all the other bubbles while trying to stay upright and afloat on the dirty pond of life.

I fall on my face seven times.

Mags doesn't fall once.

Typical.

"Dibs on him, too." She points to the kid behind the snack bar counter while we wait in line for corn dog baskets.

I roll my eyes. "What will Jack the busboy say when he finds out you're cheating on him?" I ask her.

"Yeah, well . . . we're not exactly exclusive," she says.

"You mean he doesn't even know yet?"

"I feel like he's getting a sense of it," she assures me.

I laugh at that one.

We watch the snack bar boy as he waits on the family of five in front of us. He's tall, with long black hair hanging out of a knit skullcap, and has pale white skin and more eyeliner than the models in Manhattan coming from a photo shoot. He's wearing a long-sleeved Fun City T-shirt pushed up on his elbows, displaying two fake sleeve tattoos. They have to be fake because he can't be much older than I am and everyone knows you can't get a tattoo until you're eighteen.

I'm getting a crescent moon.

It's my signature sign.

Mags is getting the SKIP A STRAW, SAVE A TURTLE slogan.

"He's more my type than yours anyway," I tell her.

"How do you figure that?"

I consider the boy and his eyeliner.

"He's . . . brooding," I say. "Brooding is more my style. Shirtless is more yours."

"Fine, but be cool for once," she warns. "You know how you get."

"What is that supposed to mean?" I ask.

"You know, the weirdness and all."

"Define *weirdness*," I tell her, pushing up my horn-rims at the bridge.

"Ah . . . totally awkward and completely embarrassing," she informs me.

"Next," the boy calls.

She gives me a nudge forward and says, "You're on."

The boy looks at me and our eyes lock.

"Can I take your order?" he asks.

I suck air.

Fear. Panic. Sweat.

WHAT-IFS

Sooooo awkward.

Mags gives me another nudge.

I take a giant step up to the counter, flicking my hair like the girls in the shampoo commercials do. Except my hair isn't shiny and wavy and blond, it's more limp and dull and the same brown as the smiling poop emoji. And instead of the slow-motion bouncing locks, a big clump lands in my mouth instead of all flowy and perfect down my back.

I spit a wad of hair from between my lips, straighten my glasses and say, *"'S up."*

His eyebrows crinkle and he's all, *"Huh?"*

WHAT-IFS

Abort! Abort! Abort!

That's when my heart starts beating behind my eyes and my mouth feels like there's too much saliva inside, creating a serious spit tsunami warning.

WHAT-IFS

WARNING: Spit storm imminent.
Take cover.

Mags to the rescue.

"So yeah, we'll have two corn dog baskets, extra ketchup and . . . um . . . ah, oh, right . . . um, two Fun City Blue Raspberry Slushies. And if I see a plastic straw, we're going to have a serious problem," she warns with a pointer finger. "Get me?"

"Oh . . . um, it's a whole turtle thing," I tell him, pulling dollar bills out of my jeans and handing them to him.

He looks confused.

"The turtles are *dying*," Mags says. "*Dying*. From straws."

His eyes narrow and then he says, "Well, not from *our* straws. We don't even have them."

"Good, then," she says. "We won't have a problem."

I sense an internal eye roll on his part, even though I don't actually see it as he pushes buttons on the register.

"Eleven dollars and fifty-one cents," he tells us.

I hand him the money and watch him count the bills.

His name tag has a piece of masking tape covering where the first name should be, with three letters scribbled in black ink instead.

NYX Brown

"So, is that your actual name?" Mags asks him, with her elbow on the counter and her chin in her hand. "Nyx Brown?"

He stares at her.

She points to his name tag. "That," she says. "I've never heard of anyone named Nyx before. Is it short for something?"

"Here, you gave me too much," he tells me, handing me back two bills.

I feel my cheeks burn and say, "Oh, right . . . sorry," while I shove them back in my pocket.

WHAT IF
forgetting basic math skills is the first sign of early-onset dementia?

"Sooooo, anyway . . . yeah . . . we're with the Netflix crew," Mags goes on. "Out to film the hauntings at the Stanley Hotel."

Nyx is stuffing money into the correct compartments of the register when he freezes mid-stuff and stares at us again.

"*You guys* are with Totally Rad Productions?" he says.

"Yeah," I say. "I mean . . . it's my dad's company and everything, but like yeah. I help and stuff . . . like you know, doing the research and answering phones and whatnot. I mean, I don't sing the hold music or anything like that . . . even though he wanted me to, but I was all like *that's bizarre . . .* and like *who's Barry Manilow anyway—*"

WHAT-IFS
Please stop talking . . .

"What do you know about it?" Mags asks him.

"Are you kidding? Small towns." He shrugs, pulling coins from the different compartments and slamming the drawer with his hip. "There are no secrets in small towns, everyone knows everything and everyone knows every-body. Forty-nine cents is your change."

"So, I suppose you know about the hauntings and all that's going on at the Stanley, then?" Mags asks him.

"Who doesn't?" he says.

"So then you must know all about Mr. Honeycutt?" I ask.

He raises his eyebrows at me and leans closer. So close I can tell you that his breath smells like sweet raspberry Slushie.

"I already know about Mr. Plum and his polka-dot boxers," he whispers.

I suck air. "But that *just* happened."

He shrugs. "I told you."

There is this majorly cool vibe about this kid, and when he looks at you, his brown eyes really see you. I mean *really* see you. Not to mention his eyelashes go on for days.

"Are you going to take our order, son?" the man in line behind us complains.

"Oh, sorry," I say, stepping aside.

"Here." Nyx hands me a plastic card with a big six on the front of it. "I'll call your number when your order is ready." And then in a loud and robotic voice meant more for his manager than for us, he says, "Thank you for choosing Fun City as your family's entertainment center for fun. You can pick up your beverages on the side counter."

"Thanks . . . I mean, you're welcome . . . I mean . . . *six,* it rhymes with *Nyx,* so I'll definitely remember—"

Mags curls an arm around mine and yanks me in the direction of the tables. "We'll be over there," she tells Nyx, and then whispers to me, "What's wrong with you?"

I push my glasses up. "You mean besides the usual?"

"I mean, why are you rhyming?"

"You know how sometimes when you get super nervous you just start rhyming?"

She blinks at me. "No," she says flatly.

"You're saying that's never happened to you?" I ask.

"I'm saying it's never happened to anyone."

She pulls me toward the picnic tables, all of them with big red umbrellas that have the words FUN CITY written on them. I can hear the man who was behind us in line step forward and spout out his order.

"We'll take two chili cheese dogs, two corn dogs, four orders of fries and four churros, please," the man says while Nyx punches the buttons on his cash register.

"Let's just sit here," Mags says, choosing a table close to the counter. "Then you can stare at the freakazoid all you want."

"Did you see his eyelashes?" I breathe.

"Nope," she says, slipping into a red plastic chair. "But I saw his wrists. Fake tattoo sleeves? Check."

"I think he's probably the coolest boy I've ever met," I tell her.

"You would."

"Even cooler than Skyler Cade," I gush. "He's cute, he's smart, and he doesn't seem stuck-up at all."

"He's all yours. I officially retract my infinite dibs for that one."

"What do you think his story is?" I ask, pulling out a chair next to hers.

She wrinkles her nose as she considers him, slurping up sips of her strawless Blue Raspberry.

Slurp.

Swallow.

Consider.

Slurp.

Swallow.

Consider.

"I'm going with divorced parents, misunderstood *annnnnd* . . . middle child syndrome," she says.

"Thank you, Dr. Finkelman Junior," I tell her.

"Well," she says. "Got to be Goth, right? I mean, what's up with the black eyeliner? And I'm sorry, but black fingernail polish? That is *sooo* last year."

"Yeah, but what is Goth . . . really? I mean, what does it mean to be a Goth?"

"It's not *a Goth*, it's just *Goth*," she informs me.

"Are you sure?" I ask.

She slurps again. "Pretty sure," she says.

"Well, what does it mean?" I ask her.

"No clue." She shakes her head. "Ask Siri. She knows everything."

I pull my cell phone from my back pocket. "Siri? What is a Goth?"

Nyx's voice comes over the loudspeaker before Siri has a chance to answer.

"Fun City order number six is ready," he calls into a microphone attached to the counter. "Fun City number six . . . your order is ready."

I hold up my plastic number to show Mags. "That's us," I say.

"Ah . . . I remember." She slurps again. "*Nyx* rhymes with *six*."

I give her a good glare.

She laughs. "Just kidding. Good luck. And just remember . . . be yourself."

I stand and stare at her. "That's the worst advice you've ever given me."

WHAT-IFS
True dat.

"You'll be fine," she says. "Just relax, say as few words as possible, and whatever you do, don't rhyme *anything*. Last time I checked, you're not Dr. Seuss."

"Got it," I tell her, eyeing the long journey to the counter. "I'm going in."

I take a breath and dart in his direction.

Lucky for me, I make it without a single major embarrassing incident. Nyx is standing at the counter waiting for me with a red tray filled with square paper baskets spotted with grease stains. I hand him my plastic number, making sure to keep my mouth closed and curl my fingers around the edge of the tray.

I gaze up at him.

He has light brown freckles on his nose.

"I'm going to give you some advice," he tells me.

WHAT-IFS

I feel a rhyme coming on.

I pull the tray toward me without saying a word, but Nyx doesn't let go. Instead he leans closer toward me over the counter and says something like "You better watch your back."

I glance down at the corn dog baskets overflowing with fries and then back up at him.

"Wiiiiiith . . . the corn dogs?"

Mags hogged all the fries.

You snooze, you lose!

94

"No," he says. "Paranormal investigation isn't a joke. I know this is a first for your film crew. You're clearly not professionals."

"Oh, right, well, that's no big deal," I tell him. "We have a ghost doctor with us. He has a badge and everything, I saw it—"

"I'm being serious."

"So am I," I tell him. "It's a silver one."

"Paranormal investigation must be handled properly or else."

I swallow. "Or else what?"

"You can open yourself up to evil spirits within the space, or they can even attach to you personally."

"A-attach to you personally?" I say.

This can't be good for my what-ifs.

"Just whatever you do, make sure you contact me if you plan on doing some kind of séance. You know, like with a Ouija board. Amateurs can get themselves in real trouble. There are rules with those things."

"T. S. Phoenix didn't say anything about any Ouija boards."

"T. S. Phoenix doesn't normally conduct séances," Nyx tells me. "He's all about the science."

"What about Tally?"

"She never uses a Ouija board either," he says. "She believes they can be dangerous when it comes to unwanted spirits."

"Madame Drusilla said something about evil spirits at the ghostly meet-and-greet."

Nyx nods. "I know."

I put my hands on my hips and sigh. "Is there anything you don't know?" I ask him.

"Yeah," he says. "I don't know whether or not you have a Ouija board. Do you or don't you?"

"Nope," I tell him. "We definitely don't have one of those."

That's when Mags comes up behind me and puts a chin on my arm and holds out her empty Slushie cup toward Nyx. "Do you give free Fun City Blue Raspberry refills?"

"Sorry, I'm officially on my break," he tells her.

"He's talking about a Ouija board," I tell her.

"So, you're saying you can't refill my Slushie if you're on break?" Mags demands.

"Do you have a cell phone?" he asks me, pulling his phone out of his pocket.

"Yeah."

"What's your number?" he says with his thumbs poised over the tiny keyboard.

Mags gives me a kick under the counter.

I tell Nyx my number and watch as he types.

"Let me know if you need help," he tells us. "I can provide you with some backup technical séance support."

"Backup *what*?" I ask, while Mags takes a fry out of a basket and stuffs it in her mouth.

"Séance support," he says again.

I look at Mags. "I told him, we aren't doing anything like that."

"So, what's with all the eyeliner?" Mags asks him with her mouth full of fry. "You Goth or something?"

"No."

"Emo?"

"No," he says. "I'm an illusionist."

Mags and me look at each other and then back at Nyx.

"Pardon me?" Mags says.

"I'm into magic. You know, illusion; endurance or transfiguration tricks . . . that kind of thing. You ever hear of Harry Houdini?"

"Oh, right, that prince who quit and moved to Canada," I say.

"No." Mags shakes her head. "Different Harry."

"Oh, right," I say. "He's that One Direction singer."

Mags nods. "Right," she says. "That's him."

"Wrong again, that's Harry Styles," Nyx says. "Harry Houdini is like the greatest illusionist of all time. He's the actual father of magic."

"So, like *magic* magic?" Mags says. "Like abracadabra pulling-a-rabbit-out-of-a-hat magic?"

"Rabbits are amateur time," Nyx tells us.

"Serious?" Mags asks, grabbing another fry. "So, do something magical."

"Like what?" he asks, reaching behind my ear and pulling out a quarter.

"Whoa!" I say, grinning big. "That's so cool!"

"Keep it." He hands it to me, slipping it into my open palm.

"Thanks!" I say, holding it tight in my hand.

Mags snorts.

"Twenty-five cents?" she says. "I'm sorry, but I'd be way more impressed if you found a twenty back there. It cost seven bucks just to ride the bumper boats."

"Young man? Can we order, please?" a woman calls from the counter on the other side, tapping an angry running shoe on the cement.

"You'd better get back to work," I tell him, picking up the tray from the counter. "We don't want you to get in trouble. Thanks for the . . . um, you know . . . ghost advice and everything."

He nods.

"So, where do we get one of those Ouija boards?" Mags calls after him. "It's that game for spirit contact, right?"

"It's *not* a game," he warns her.

"Don't they sell it in the toy department?" she asks.

"That doesn't mean it's a toy."

"Ah . . . I'm pretty sure it does," she says.

"I'll text you my number later," he tells me. "But I'm telling you . . . don't fool around with evil spirits."

I stare directly into his dreamy eyes and say, "We will definitely heed your warning, Nyx Brown."

"Charlie," the manager calls over to us. "There are people waiting."

"I got to go," Nyx tells us, turning back toward the register.

"Hold up," Mags says with a snort. "Your name is . . . *Charlie Brown?*"

He gives her a glare over his shoulder and snaps, "Oh, so what?"

A Bad-Idea Midnight Séance

O ne thing I know about Mags is that she doesn't heed warnings from anyone.

Not even ones about evil spirits.

Which is the exact reason why she dragged me into Toy Mountain on West Elkhorn Avenue to get a stupid Ouija board on our way home from Fun City.

Minus one plastic bag.

And that was only after an embarrassing confrontation with the store owner about contributing to the death of all the turtles in all the seas.

Save the turtles!

But to her credit, Mags may have saved at least one reptilian life.

Now we're sitting on the floor of room 217.

The room.

Mr. Ozgood Honeycutt's room.

And it's mad creepy, too.

I asked Crystal Mystic if conducting a séance in room 217 to call up the dead ghost of Mr. Honeycutt is the biggest mistake of my life.

CRYSTAL MYSTIC

FORTUNE IS NOT SMILING ON THIS.

But Mags doesn't heed evil spirit Crystal Mystic readings, either.

So here we sit, cross-legged on the floor at midnight with one Ouija board, two flickering candles, and a bag of onion Funyuns she found in the vending machine in the employee break room on the bottom level.

It turns out that ever since Mr. Lozano was promoted to interim manager after Mr. Plum went AWOL, he isn't so big on giving Totally Rad or Lights Out! access to everything in the hotel. But lucky for us, Mr. Lozano is a sound sleeper. Especially when he's sleeping off Chef Raphaël's dessert éclairs.

I ate two and I don't feel the least bit sleepy.

So, while T. S. Phoenix and Totally Rad Productions are filming in room 422, aka Mr. Plum's old room, we are conducting a bad-idea séance in Mr. and Mrs. Honeycutt's room.

It actually looks mostly the same as our room except for

the plain white sheets hanging over each piece of furniture to keep the dust off. It looks like a room of sleeping ghosts waiting for their chance to rise up in a Stanley Hotel ghost revolution. Not to mention we practically had to drag Alfred Hitchcock in here against his will, for reasons I'm sure I don't want to know. Now he's sitting in front of the window and growling a low growl at the closed curtains. Mags and me are sitting on the floor between the beds. She's reading the Ouija board instructions and I'm tapping and counting to stay calm.

WHAT-IFS

Such a bad idea.

WHAT-IFS

You're headed for the fuzz.

WHAT-IFS

The TV people are watching.

"Those Funyuns reek," I tell her, pointing at the bag. "And they look like Styrofoam. Even Alfred Hitchcock turned his nose up at them, and he eats everything."

She ignores me and chomps another crunchy piece while she reads.

I gaze down at the new mood ring on my finger.

Me and Mags each got one out of a gumball machine before we left Fun City.

Google said the rings change color based on your mood by measuring your body temperature and the energy inside you.

Mine's been a muddy brown since I slipped it on my finger.

"Brown means you're nervous or anxious," Mags informed me, and then chucked out a laugh. "That ring's got you pegged," she said, holding out her own hand and marveling at her finger. "Mine's bluer than the sky! That's happy and calm."

"You're such a show-off," I said.

I examine the ring closer.

Still brown as mud.

I sigh and put my elbow on my thigh and my chin in my palm.

Mags lays the instructions down and stares at me. "You know, we really should be doing this in the bathroom, now that I think of it."

"Why?" I ask.

"Because of Bloody Mary."

"I don't think I want to know anything more about that, so you can stop there."

She ignores that, too.

"Bloody Mary is this game," she says. "Where you go into the bathroom, lock the door and shut off all the lights and then turn toward the mirror and say 'Bloody Mary' three times and then this maimed woman is supposed to appear in the mirror. Daisy Chang said they saw her outline in the bathroom at her birthday slumber party two years ago."

WHAT-IFS
Run.

"See . . . this is the exact kind of information I didn't want to know," I say.

"Come on, let's go in the bathroom and do it." Mags gets up on her knees.

WHAT-IFS
Run fast.

"There is no way I'm doing anything in the bathroom ever again," I tell her. "I'm here for one ghost and one ghost only. I don't need a Bloody Mary, too. I'm about two minutes away from running out of this room screaming. Let's either do it or not do it. But hurry up."

"I'm just saying it's possible the bathroom is some kind of portal to the afterlife or something. Like through the plumbing, maybe."

I blink at her. "Television ghosts and toilet plumbing? This is what you bring to the table?"

"Hey, I'm helping with the research," she says. "You're welcome."

"Eighties movies and Daisy Chang are your authorities on ghosts?"

"And YouTube," she adds. "Plus, you don't even get it.

The point is that *Poltergeist* is more than a movie . . . it's a blueprint."

"A *blueprint*?"

"Yes, a blueprint. Like a map."

"A ghost map?"

"Right," she says. "A map by which all paranormal experiences are measured."

I blink at her. "Fine, but you told me that blueprint was through a television, not a toilet."

"You don't think spirits have more than one portal to reach the living?" she asks. "Open your mind, why don't you."

"Let me put it to you like this," I tell her. "There's no way I'm doing a séance in the bathroom if some bloody woman is going to jump out at us. Final answer."

WHAT-IFS

How will we ever pee in peace again?

She considers me then, chomping on another Funyun. "You know who you are?" she asks, crunching.

"Who?"

"You're a Shaggy."

"Of the Scooby-Doo gang?"

"Yeah," she says. "You're definitely a Shaggy."

I put my hands on my hips and snap at her. "No way," I say. "I'm totally a Velma."

"Mmm." She tilts her head. "I don't see it."

"Velma Dinkley has poop emoji hair just like me, has glasses just like me and is especially studious just like me."

Mags considers me again. "Still don't see it."

"Well, at least I'm not a blond Daphne," I tell her. "That's you."

She shrugs. "What's wrong with Daphne?"

"The only things she cares about are how short her skirts are, if her hair is perfect and how close she's standing to Fred. You just know he and she have something going on when no one's looking. Kissing in the Mystery Machine van when the others are risking their very lives hunting for paranormal entities."

"I'd rather kiss Jack the busboy," Mags tells me. "He's like fifty thousand times cuter."

I roll my eyes. "Can we please just do this already? This room gives me the creeps."

"Okay, this is what we do, see all these?" she says, pointing to each one of the signs on the game board on the floor in between us.

I nod.

"These are all ways the spirits can commune with us."

WHAT-IFS
You're doomed.

"There is a sun in one corner and a moon in the other," she goes on. "A *yes* and a *no,* the full alphabet, numbers zero through nine and the words *good bye.*"

I see HASBRO in the center of the board and tell my jumping beans that if Hasbro makes Candy Land, Yahtzee and Hungry Hungry Hippos, how bad can it be?

WHAT-IFS

Dooooomed.

One. Two. Three. Four.

"The spirits will guide this spirit indicator," Mags says, placing her fingertips on a heart-shaped plastic piece in the center of the board.

It has a single round window in the middle of the heart.

"Put the tips of your fingers on the edge of this pointer dealy thing," she tells me. "It's the message indicator. But barely touch it so that the spirits can move it from under our fingertips. Get it? Then the spirit drags the message indicator over the letters it wishes, to spell out a word to answer us. Or it can choose the *yes* or *no* at the top, see? Or even the numbers if the spirit has a need for it." She points.

"Wait . . . what if Mr. Honeycutt is a bad speller like Jordy Meeks?"

She stares at me in the dim light of the candles.

"Being a bad speller isn't Jordy Meeks's problem," she informs me. "It's his addiction to Minecraft."

"What does that mean?" I ask.

"He doesn't study."

"Oh," I say.

"Ready?" she asks.

"I guess," I tell her. "You go first."

"*You* go first," she says. "This is your job, not mine."

"The séance was your stupid idea," I remind her. "I wanted to heed Nyx's warning."

"Fine." She takes a deep breath. "We need to close our eyes."

"No thank you," I tell her.

Sigh. "Can you please not make this one of your things right now?" she asks. "I'm trying to conduct a serious séance here. And anyway, that's how they do it."

"That's how who does it?"

"The YouTube people."

"Wait, what if we're snatched by the TV fuzz while our eyes are closed?"

She blinks at me.

"Well?" I demand.

"I'm not going to lie," she says. "It could happen."

"Oh, man," I mumble. "I want to go on record here and say that Father O'Leary will keep us in confession a month straight for sure. Maybe even longer. I really think this might be a penance-for-life kind of thing."

"We don't have to tell him everything."

"Mmm," I say, shaking my head. "That doesn't sound right."

"Will you just close your eyes already," she demands.

"Fine," I grumble. "But if we get sucked into the in-between, never to be seen again, it'll be all your fault."

I close my eyes while Mags takes a deep breath in and blows it out again, leaving me in a cloud of Funyuns.

"The YouTube people say we have to say *Ouija* three times to open the board to the spirits. On three," she tells me. "One, two, three."

"Ouija. Ouija. Ouija," we call out to the darkness.

"Attention, all paranormal entities," Mags says. "Including the undead, ghosts and the eternally departed. We are here to conjure up the spirit of Mr. Honeycutt."

I open one eye and giggle.

She opens both eyes and glares. "What?" she demands. *"Conjure?"*

"If you know a better way to call Mr. Honeycutt forward? Be my guest."

"Sorry," I say. "Conjure away."

We close our eyes again.

"Like I said, we are here to speak to a Mr. Honeycutt. Ozgood Honeycutt of Cheboygan, Michigan, who died here on May twenty-seventh, 1909, to be exact. If you're here, Mr. Honeycutt, please make yourself known. We would like to commune with your spirit."

Paranormal silence.

We wait some more.

Nothing.

I open one eye. "Nothing's happening," I whisper.

"Shhh," Mags hisses. "Can't you stop blabbing for two minutes?"

"No offense, but this may just be the slowest ghost download ever."

"We aren't *downloading* Mr. Honeycutt," she says. "The board isn't even Wi-Fi compatible."

"Still, we kind of are," I tell her. "If you think about it. Except instead of using the Wi-Fi, it's like a supernatural download. SNi-Fi." I giggle. "Get it? Supernatural Wi-Fi? SNi-Fi? Come on, that's funny."

She gives me her eyes-to-the-sky roll. "Are you going to take this seriously or not?"

"I'm sorry," I tell her. "I'm just nervous."

"You think I'm not? But if you don't close your eyes and keep quiet, we're going to be here all night."

I close my eyes again.

"We are here to commune with Mr. Honeycutt. We don't mean you any harm, sir, we just want to know if you're really still here at the Stanley Hotel searching for your bride—"

"Oh, and also," I interrupt, pulling my phone out of my pocket and holding it in the air for all the ghosts who may have been conjured to see. "If you wouldn't mind . . . we could really use a selfie for our ghost-hunting documentary."

"A selfie, yeah, that's good," Mags tells me. "And we also have to say . . . I mean, I'm sorry to be the one to tell you this, but . . . you're dead . . . deceased . . . *expiiiiired.*"

More paranormal silence.

Rain starts to prick at the window.

A clock under another white sheet ticks and tocks.

A toilet somewhere on the floor above us flushes, and water rushes through pipes inside the walls.

Alfred Hitchcock rolls another slow growl in the direction of the curtains.

"Ow," I say, opening my eyes again.

"What now?" Mags asks.

"What are you poking me for?" I say.

I watch her eyes widen. "I didn't poke you."

"Ha, ha, that's so funny I forgot to laugh."

"I swear to you," she says. "I didn't poke you."

"You're saying you didn't poke me?"

"That's exactly what I'm saying," she tells me.

My mouth falls open and she covers hers with her fingers.

That's when a breeze blows through the room. The same kind of cool breeze that makes chicken skin pop up on your arms on the first cool day of fall when the crispness of the air makes the leaves turn colors and collect into piles on the sidewalk.

"Please tell me the window's open," I say.

"It's him," Mags tells me. "Mr. Honeycutt, if you are present, please let us know by answering on the Ouija board. . . ."

At that exact moment, the message indicator underneath our fingers budges and I lurch back and jump up from my spot on the floor.

"Y-you moved it," I say, pointing an accusing finger in her direction.

"Maybe *you* moved it," she accuses me back.

"You're making all this up," I say.

"I told you I didn't move it, didn't I?" she says.

"You're just trying to scare me, like with the drawers in the wardrobe. And it's not one bit funny."

"I promise you I'm not," she says.

"Swear?"

She swallows and nods. "Swear."

She makes an imaginary cross over her heart.

And then in a gust, both candles are blown out, surrounding us with blackness and filling the air with the smell of smoke.

"M-maybe Mr. Honeycutt thinks it's his birthday," Mags whispers, her voice shaking.

"Mags," I say. "What do the YouTube people say about breezes blowing inside a building?"

"You probably don't want to know."

"Mags?" I demand. "What. Do. They. Say?"

"They're, uh . . ." She clears her throat. "You know, just, ah . . . *disembodied spirits.*"

"I'm out," I say, lunging toward the door.

That's when Alfred Hitchcock starts barking whole-body barks from where he's standing guard at the velvet curtains.

"What is he barking at?" I ask her.

"He's *your* dog."

Mags reaches for the light on the night table between the beds and I point a shaking finger toward the curtains, drawn tight over the windows. "I-is that a-a-a shadow?" I stutter.

But before Mags can even turn her head to look, a piercing alarm screeches through the silence.

This time it's the fire alarm.

"That's it!" she exclaims. "Mr. Honeycutt's ghostly she-nanigans. We did it."

"How do you know?" I ask her.

"Noisy ghost," she informs me. "He's making sure we know he's here. Mr. Honeycutt, is that you?"

One. Two. Three. Four.

The alarm keeps screeching through the halls.

Alfred Hitchcock keeps barking at the curtains.

I keep tapping.

Onetwothreefour.

"Karma," Mags whispers, and points to the board. "Look!"

The message indicator is pointed to the word *YES*.

We wide-eye each other again until suddenly the door to the hall slams open against the wall of room 217 with a bang.

We both scream and Alfred Hitch-cock pees a little.

A hulking male human form stands before us in the darkened doorway, the hall lighting it from behind.

Ghost Log Day 2

1. Made contact?
That's a big-time
affirmative.

And then a voice.

His voice.

Mr. Ozgood Honeycutt straight from the in-between speaks.

"How did you get in here?" the entity demands of us.

As sure as I'm standing here, the ghost of Mr. Ozgood Honeycutt we downloaded on the SNi-Fi is standing before us in the dark. Ready to snatch our souls to the in-between through the television fuzz or toilet plumbing portal.

Never to be seen again.

I wonder if Mom will wear that stupid eye-patch bikini to my funeral, too.

He raises a razor-sharp sword high above his head, ready to put an end to our very lives and maybe even cut our body parts into unrecognizable pieces to hide in the wardrobe, where no one will ever find us.

I swallow hard, letting my quivering fingers find the leather sack of bravery crystals hanging from my neck.

But I get zip.

No vibration. No wave. No bravery power surge of any kind.

I grab Mags's hand and feel her fingers tighten around mine.

"M-Mr. Honeycutt," I say. "Y-y-you have died, sir, and we are here to help you find the light."

Closing Time

So, yeah, if you want to get all technical about it, it isn't Mr. Honeycutt who busts in on our séance.

And it isn't Dad, either.

Just one angry Ubbe Amblebee.

But this is the most embarrassing part of it all—he isn't *actually* swinging a razor-sharp sword to put an end to our very lives.

It's his disgusting plunger.

I know, I know, totally embarrassing.

But I think a very important disclaimer needs to be stated here.

DISCLAIMER: ANYONE COULD HAVE MADE THAT MISTAKE.

And I mean *anyone.*

Because a toilet plunger *in* the middle of the night, *during* a séance, *in* the presence of a Ouija board that moves as if by magic, looks *a lot* like a razor-sharp sword, is all I'm saying. And Mr. Amblebee is still red in the face about the whole deal the very next morning when we find him on the way to breakfast.

Arlo Lozano isn't exactly a big fan either, once he learns about our stealthlike mission to swipe the key card while he was sleeping off his dessert éclairs. But that's only because becoming interim manager has totally gone to his head and he's become weirdly possessive of the key cards.

Despite the disastrous end to our ghostly mission and the sneaky slash semiquestionable activities that led up to them, one very important thing stands true.

We were not alone.

Someone poked me.

Someone blew out those candles.

And most importantly, *someone* moved that message indicator.

Someone . . . on another plane of existence.

I don't know what's disturbing the Stanley Hotel, but whatever or whoever it is has something *very* important to say.

But I'm not sure I want to know what it is.

We just need a ghost selfie to happen and we're out of here. And it can't happen too soon for me. I didn't sleep a wink last night after all was said and done.

My what-ifs have set up a bouncy house on my insides and haven't stopped jumping yet.

"Good morning," I call to Ms. Lettie and Mr. Amblebee.

The pair are huddled together whispering in front of the gift shop door.

Mr. Amblebee with his stupid toilet plunger still in his grasp and Ms. Lettie with her beanstalk hairdo.

And I have to say that in the light of day a toilet plunger doesn't look quite as menacing as it does in the dead of night. But I do have to wonder why he's always carrying it around with him.

Dr. Finkelman might be able to help him out with that one. I'm not positive Dr. Finkelman handles plunger obsessions, but he handles a lot of things.

I wonder if Mr. Amblebee likes playing Uno while he talks about his feelings.

"Hi," I call with a wave.

"Good morning, ladies." Ms. Lettie eyes us through her cat-eye glasses, held across her nose with her thumb and her index finger while her pinky points straight up in the air.

I think her hair is even higher than it was yesterday.

"How are you, Mr. Amblebee?" I ask him.

He shakes his plunger at us. "Toilet's broke in 317," he snaps, and stomps his way up the staircase.

"Oh, ah . . . yeah, right . . . that's, ah, too bad, so . . . well . . . good luck with that," I call after him.

"*Good luck with that*?" Mags asks me.

"It's just something you say."

"About a broken toilet?" she asks.

I shrug. "I don't know."

"At least you didn't rhyme anything this time," she mumbles.

"Nothing rhymes with *toilet* anyway," I tell her.

"Uh-huh," she insists. *"Boil it . . . foil it . . . soil it . . ."* Then she gasps and grabs my arm. "Wait. Oh my gosh, what if it's Bloody Mary?"

"*Bloody Mary* doesn't rhyme with *toilet* at all."

"No, what if she's the one who's stuck in the toilet in room 317?"

"I'm guessing it's more likely a *what* stuck in the toilet and not a *who*," I tell her.

"I bet she totally got stuck in the plumbing as she traveled to our plane of existence last night," Mags whispers to me. "I knew we should have done the séance in the bathroom."

"I thought you said she appears in the mirror."

"She still has to get here somehow," Mags says. "The mirror can't be a portal, but toilet plumbing goes on for infinity."

Paranormal portal plumbing can't be good for my what-ifs.

"Do you think that's who you conjured up last night?" I ask her. "Bloody Mary? I mean, is that a real thing?"

"Daisy Chang says it is," Mags says. "And why would she lie?"

"Yeah," I agree. "Why would she lie?"

"She even said they did Light As a Feather, Stiff As a Board and Destiny Whitaker actually levitated."

I put my hands on my hips. "What is with that birthday slumber party anyway?" I ask. "What's wrong with pillow fights, Truth or Dare and prank phone calls?"

"The thing is . . . ," Mags says, "I don't know for sure who was there with us last night. Even though we asked for Mr. Honeycutt, Nyx said sometimes you get other spirits you don't ask for. The YouTube people say evil spirits can sneak in and lie to you, and you think it's who you're conjuring up when really it isn't."

"How do we really know the YouTube people are reliable?" I ask.

"They don't give just anyone their own YouTube channel."

"Actually, I think they do. The question is, do they have a badge?"

"Mmm . . . no. I didn't see any badges." Mags nods. "But you agree with me, right? Something or someone was there last night. Besides us, I mean."

"Someone totally poked me," I say.

She nods again. "I believe you," she tells me as we make our way across the lobby to the dining hall. "Do you think all Chef Raphaël's meals are French?" she asks. "Because I just want a bowl of Froot Loops."

Mr. Lozano is already at his seat behind the front desk pretending to read a Stephen King book with a scary-looking red staircase on the cover. Except I can see his glaring eyes following us to the dining hall while the rest of his face stays hidden behind the pages.

Clearly, he's still bent out of shape about the whole thing too.

"Good morning, Mr. Lozano," I call.

He just gives a loud *"Humph!"* and then sticks his nose farther behind the cover.

Mags gives me an elbow to my side and whispers in my ear, "That's the book I was telling you about," she says. "*The Shining.* See? Red steps, just like this hotel."

I stop and face her. "Tell me why it's worse than *Poltergeist.*"

"No way," she says, crossing her arms over her chest.

"Please?"

"Nope."

"What if I let you show me five sad pictures of turtles having straws removed from their nose holes."

She blinks at me.

"*Ten* pictures," she says. "*And* I get to tell you about the glaciers melting and what that means for our future on this planet."

"Deal," I say.

We seal it with our fist bump, fanned fingers and a shimmy-shimmy to the floor.

She takes a breath and glances around before she leans in close and whispers in my ear. "Remember your whole deal about serial-murdered hotel managers?" she asks.

"Yeah?" I whisper back.

"You may not be wrong, is all I'm going to say."

I gasp. "Serious?"

"Totally," she says.

"In the first eleven minutes and fifty seconds?"

She nods.

"No wonder you shut it off," I say, glancing at Mr. Lozano.

Still glaring.

My cell phone buzzes and I pull it out of my pocket.

"Oh, man, it's a text from that Nyx kid," I tell her.

"You mean *Charlie Brown,* don't you?"

"Don't call him that," I warn.

"What does he say?" She peeks over my shoulder.

NYX:

Please tell me it wasn't you who
bought the board at Toy Mountain.

I wide-eye Mags. "How does he know?"

She shrugs. "Tell him that, thanks to me, we *definitely* made contact."

I type.

ME:

Yeah and some weird things definitely happened.

"Should I add an emoji here?" I ask Mags.

"Yeah," she says. "Do a heart."

"I'm *not* doing a heart," I say. "I hardly know the kid."

"Hey, you have to put it out there. Boys don't get it otherwise."

"No way," I inform her.

She shrugs. "You asked for my advice and that's it. *Hearts.*"

I type a smiley-face emoji instead and press Send.

"See?" I say. "Smiley face."

"Miiiiistaaaaake," she sings.

Buzz.

NYX:

I hope you at least closed the board.

"Hmm," I say. "What do you think that means?"

Mags wrinkles up her nose as she reads it. "*Closed the board*?" she says. "Like put it in the *box*?"

"Does the dumpster out back count?" I wonder.

"Oh, man, don't tell him we threw it in the dumpster," she says.

"Why not?"

"Because then he'll know he was right." She starts toward the dining hall again.

"So?" I follow after her.

"So . . . that would be awkward," she tells me. "Everyone knows that you never, *ever* tell boys they're right or they'll never let you hear the end of it. That's just the way the world works."

"Oh," I say.

But I'm not so sure she knows what she's talking about.

When we make it inside the dining hall, we find Dad, Big John, The Faz and T. S. Phoenix at their assigned table drinking coffee after a long night of investigating Mr. Plum's hotel room.

Tally must be asleep already. Being a sensitive probably takes a lot out of you. I catch my spirit guide, Luna Shadow, napping on the job all the time when she should be busy telling me which direction to go.

I give Dad a hug around the back of his shoulders, and he pats my arms under his neck.

"Did you get anything on film last night?" I ask him.

"Unfortunately, it was a pretty quiet night," he tells me. "T.S. is going to analyze the audio of the video footage we shot later this morning and delete the background noise to determine if we caught any orbs of light or EVP. But nothing stood out."

"What's EVP again?" I ask.

"Electronic Voice Phenomenon," T.S. explains. "It takes a great deal of energy for spirits to actually reach our plane of existence, so sometimes we have to listen especially close. I can upload the audio to my computer and then remove all background noise to determine if there has been an attempted communication by a spirit."

"Whoa, that's really cool," I say. "So then, if you *hear* a ghost on the audio, is that good enough for the Netflix people?"

Dad shakes his head and yawns a long up-all-night-investigating-ghosts yawn behind his hand.

"No, Snooks," he says. "They want at least one image on film."

"Is an orb of light the same as a ghost?" I ask.

"I'll take an orb of light," Dad says. "I'll take anything if it's on-camera."

"What if you don't get an image or an orb of light?" I wonder.

"We'll get it. You get some sleep after last night's escapade?" he asks me, shaking a sugar packet for his coffee.

"Good work getting access to room 217." Big John gives me the thumbs-up.

Me and Mags exchange glances. "Yeah, so . . . we may not have had official permission," I say. "It was more of a . . . a . . . um . . ." I look to Mags for help.

"A, um . . . a sort of borrowing arrangement where, ah, one party is unaware of the arrangement altogether," she says.

They all sit there blinking at us.

"A *what*?" Dad asks.

"We snuck the key card," I tell him.

"You *stole* it?" he asks.

A big fat *"Ha!"* escapes Big John's lips and then turns into a fake cough after Dad gives him an elbow in the side.

"Not exactly," I tell Dad. "Because we were planning on returning it when we were done, so, *technically* . . . it was a sneak, not a steal."

Big John and The Faz give us another thumbs-up when Dad's not looking.

"That must have been what I overheard Mr. Lozano grumbling about this morning," The Faz tells Big John. "I couldn't figure out what he was so upset about."

Dad sprinkles sugar in his cup, takes a careful sip at the rim and says, "You know what I'm going to say, right?"

I sigh. "Yes," I say. "We didn't get proper permission and that was wrong."

"And?" he asks.

"We owe Father O'Leary a confession over it," I say.

"Don't worry," Mags tells him. "We're making him a list."

Dad smiles. "And an apology wouldn't be out of the question." He takes another sip.

"Okay," I mumble.

"Now that we got that out of the way." He sets his cup down and leans forward. "What'd you find out?"

"Get this," I say. "Some weird stuff *definitely* happened."

"Definitely," Mags adds.

"I mean, before Mr. Amblebee busted in with his plunger and everything, it got legit weird."

"Legit," Mags adds.

"Weird like how?" The Faz asks.

"Ah . . . only a breeze on the *inside* with the window shut."

"Blew the candles right out," Mags adds.

"And there was a freaky shadow on the drapes," I say.

"Alfred Hitchcock barked until he *peed*," Mags adds.

"And somebody poked me and Mags crossed her heart it wasn't her."

"I'd cross it again if I had to," Mags adds.

"And . . . ," I say. "Last but not least . . . the Ouija board *answered* us."

"It totally said *yes,*" Mags adds.

"You used a Ouija board?" T. S. Phoenix asks.

I nod.

"Those can be very dangerous if you don't know what you're doing," he says.

"This kid Nyx at Fun City told us that. But this one"—I throw a thumb in Mags's direction—"doesn't heed any-thing."

"I don't heed," Mags adds.

Dad smiles again. "Well, that's some amazing research," he says. "Wait, um . . . let me say first . . . wrong of you to sneak the key, and, um . . . you know, the whole confession thing . . . but still, awesome job." He throws his arm around my waist and pulls me in for a kiss on my cheek. "I think you might be looking at another promotion soon enough, Snooks."

"What about me?" Mags stands tall. "We wouldn't have made contact if I'd heeded anything."

He laughs. "You too," he says. "Good job to you both. But let's not have any more situations of, what did you call it? A borrowing arrangement where one party is unaware of the arrangement altogether? We need to respect how they want us to do things while we're here."

"I say you do what you have to do," Big John says, crossing his arms over his barrel chest. "Nice investigative work, girls."

"Hey," Dad says to him. "At Totally Rad everything is on the up-and-up. We follow the rules. Deal?" He holds out a fist for me to bump.

Big John groans an exaggerated sigh and The Faz rolls his eyes.

I bump Dad's fist. "Deal," I agree.

"That goes for everyone." Dad points a finger at the guys.

"Yeah, yeah," Big John mumbles.

"Hey, Dad," I say. "Have you ever seen *The Shining*?"

He blows air out of his mouth and leans back in his chair. "How do you know about that?" he asks me.

I point a thumb in Mags's direction.

"Mags," Dad says.

She throws her arms out. "She dragged it out of me," she tells him.

"No more of that." Dad gives her a warning finger.

"What about *Poltergeist*?" I ask him.

Dad gives Mags another look, and that's when she twists an invisible key to lock her lips up tight and then throws it to the wind. But that's just fine by me. Mags's lip lock is an easy one to pick on account of the true blue.

"Petit déjeuner, jeunes filles?" Chef Raphaël sings at us as he floats into the dining hall with a coffeepot to fill cups. "Would you lovely young ladies like some breakfast?" he asks.

127

"Yes," I say. "One Egg on a Roll with a hot Apple Betty, please."

Chef Raphaël tilts his head in confusion. "Egg. On. A. Roll?" he repeats, trying to imitate my American accent.

"I order Egg on a Roll at Toby's every single morning," I tell him. "It's the coffee shop we go to in the West Village. It's my favorite."

"And I usually just have Froot Loops, eighty-six the green ones," Mags tells him. "I don't eat green foods."

Mon Dieu! Non non non non non, mes chéries." He shakes his tall chef hat at us. "This morning I have created a Baked Caramel Brûlée French Toast lightly drizzled with a crème anglaise atop a pour of a fresh strawberry sauce."

"Huh, so you don't have any eggs *or* rolls?" I ask.

"I think you'll be surprised at how good it is," Dad tells me. "It was phenomenal. Chef Raphaël, you're a genius."

"I highly doubt anything is better than Egg on a Roll," I say.

"I accept your challenge, *ma chérie.*" Chef Raphaël nods at me. "I promise to dazzle you away from your Egg and Roll and your Loops of Froot."

"Ah . . . it's Egg *on* a Roll?" I correct him.

"No Apple Jacks, either?" Mags asks.

Mags is just like me and Dad when it comes to being creatures of habit. But it's right then that I realize the haunted spirits stuck in the in-between are too. They don't seem to want to give up their past and move on, and in some ways neither do we. I guess people and ghosts are a lot alike.

Except for the people who pack five suitcases looking for something new and different, but that goes without saying.

Chef Raphaël nods again. "Please, have a seat and I will be back *dans un petit moment* with your brûlée."

Me and Mags find a table of our own and sit down.

Buzz.

"It's *him*." I hold out my phone to show her.

Mags wedges her ear next to mine.

"Okay, answer it," she tells me.

Me: H-hello?

Nyx: How many candles did you use?

Me: Oh, ah . . . two, I think.

Nyx: The number is very important. I need to know exactly.

Me: Two . . . I'm pretty sure.

"Yeah, two," Mags tells me. "The people on YouTube said to create a protective circle."

Nyx: Two candles is not a protective circle. What about salt, did you do that?

Me: There was probably salt on the onion Funyuns.

I look at Mags.

"Yeah," she says. "They were pretty salty."

Nyx: (Sigh.) Did you at least close the board?

I look at Mags again.
This time she just shrugs.
Nyx isn't waiting for my answer anyway.

Nyx: I knew you newbs would leave it open.

"What does that even mean?" Mags mouths to me.
I shrug.

Nyx: This is the exact reason I warned you guys. You need to officially close the board to let the spirits know you are done. If you don't, you leave it open for spirits to flood this plane of existence. Especially the evil ones. Oh, man, you probably opened up the entire hotel to evil disembodied spirits. You thought Mr. Honeycutt was your problem? Well, without closing out the board, who knows how many evil spirits you invited in? What you've got yourselves is one big paranormal problem.

Me: You mean there are wandering evil souls pouring out of the board and flooding the Stanley as we speak?

Nyx: Exactly.

I turn to Mags.

"This information can't be good for my what-ifs," I tell her.

"It's not good for anything," she agrees.

> **Me:** So, what do we do?
>
> **Nyx:** No protective circle? The board left open? We need to smudge the place. And fast.
>
> **Me:** And by smudge you mean . . . ?
>
> **Nyx:** I'll be there tomorrow after work to help you.
>
> **Me:** Okay.

Mags elbows me and whispers, "Ask him about *Poltergeist*."

"You do it," I whisper back, handing her the phone while I wedge my cheek next to hers to listen.

> **Mags:** Hey, Nyx, um, have you ever seen *Poltergeist*? You know, that movie from the eighties?
>
> **Nyx:** Who hasn't? It's only a blueprint by which all hauntings are measured.

I gasp while Mags nods with a sly grin. "Told you," she says.

After we hang up, Chef Raphaël floats out of the kitchen balancing three plates of brûlée.

"Mes chéries!" he calls, setting a plate in front of me and one in front of Mags. "Your breakfast. I hope it is to your liking."

"Thank you, Chef Raphaël," I say. "It actually looks really good."

"It *is* really good," Mags says, her mouth already stuffed full of brûlée.

"Bon appétit," he says, turning toward the back of the room and then back to us. "Oh," he says. "What happened to your friend?"

I freeze and stare up at him. "*Friend?*"

"*Oui,* the fancy woman at the table over there." He points to the very last table by the window.

We all turn to look at the empty table in the very back of the room.

"What do you mean? It's just us," I say.

"But . . . I saw her," he says. "Right there. I figured she was with your group."

I gasp.

Mags chokes.

T. S. Phoenix jumps up with his Geiger counter in his hand and runs over to the empty table.

"Non, non, non," Chef Raphaël says. "It was no ghost, she was clear as day. I saw her. Are you saying you did not see her?"

T. S. Phoenix wipes his hand across the table and we all watch as five dried-up rose petals fall to the floor.

Dad clicks pictures of the petals with his new Nikon D5600.

"Whatever it was is burying the needle!" T.S. exclaims. "Look!" He shows Dad.

"What does that mean?" Mags asks.

"It means something was here," T.S. tells us. "An energy force that is reading on the Geiger counter."

WHAT IF

Bloody Mary made it
through the toilet portal after all?

I touch the leather sack of bravery crystals around my neck and take a deep breath.

One. Two. Three. Four.

I breathe in through my nose and out through my mouth.

Dad gives me an approving nod and that smile. The one that shines a bright ray that bursts through my worry storms every time.

"Chef Raphaël," I say, opening my ghost logbook, my pen poised. "Tell me exactly what she looked like and don't leave a single, solitary thing out."

Vile Cheese and Burnt Strawberries

'm just going to say it. Too much cheese gives me the toots.

Especially the cheddar kind. I loathe cheddar. I despise it. It's the vilest of all the cheeses put together. And it wasn't an allergy or even lactose intolerance that brought me to conclude that cheddar should be banned across all fifty states.

It was the five suitcases.

My mom said it was her spirit guide that led her to the Florida Keys via some app called Tinder, where she swiped right to her new life. A life without us on a houseboat named *I GOT THE CHEDDA BABY* with some creeper named Paul.

Since that despicable day, the mere mention of cheddar makes my stomach feel hot and achy and roll like thunder.

The dude's a perv.

His perviness announces itself in the name.

Pervy Paul is a supreme creeper weirdo. Arms too hairy to be normal, with lumpy man bosoms, a balloon gut that hangs over a man-kini and a weirdly narrow mustache that curls on the ends. He has a neck tattoo of an octopus and a suntan that makes him look more like a wrinkled leather loafer than a man.

Crystal Mystic totally agrees with me.

CRYSTAL MYSTIC
YOU CAN THANK YOUR
LUCKY STARS!

When I showed Mags the octopus she said, "I'm sorry, but who puts an octopus anywhere on their body?"

I actually know a lot more about how things happened than I'm going to tell you. I'll spare you the horrible details. Mostly because you don't want to know. I wish I didn't know. But thanks to the walls of our old-time walk-up circa 1801, I do.

They're paper-thin.

Buzz.

TOO-TAN MOM:

Went snorkeling yesterday.

Picture.

Her and Pervy Paul in the water with snorkel gear.

Tears prick at my eyeballs, and words I'm scared to say out loud clog up my throat.

I show it to Mags while we wait for Madame Drusilla outside her office the next day to do more research on this ghostly woman, who has been spotted twice. First in Mr. Plum's room and now by Chef Raphaël in the dining hall.

Still nothing on film.

And it's day four.

Mags looks up from her phone. She's been Googling *straw deaths in sea turtles* all morning. I just know she's planning on heading back to Toy Mountain with more evidence to support her cause. For Mags, if she can change one mind, she's won a small fight in the battle to save the turtles.

"That"—she points to my screen—"is disturbing."

Mrs. Bogdonavich sent Mags her famous Made-with-Love Chocolate Chip Cookies and FedExed them to the hotel last night.

Their best quality announcing itself in their name.

Love.

Mags had two and I ate seven.

I happen to know that her mom's secret is pudding

mix in the batter. But come to think of it, I crossed-my-heart-hoped-to-die for that. So, again, let's keep that one on the down-low.

I think hard about what to write back while I wish more than anything that my mom were the pudding-in-the-mix mom I want her to be. But I guess being a pudding-in-the-mix mom doesn't make her happy.

Chedda does.

I start to type.

> **ME:**
> Why did you leave us?

Delete.
Delete.
Delete.

> **ME:**
> When are you coming home?

Delete.
Delete.
Delete.

> **ME:**
> I miss you.

No emoji needed.

Send.

I wait.

Buzz.

TOO-TAN MOM:

Aren't you happy for me?

The words are blurry because of the tears.

The kind of tears that scare me.

It's the same kind I cried that first day Mom was gone. The kind that take your breath so long you don't think you'll ever find it again. The kind that make you feel like you might drown. The kind of tears you hope you'll never, ever cry again.

But they're back, threatening to take me over.

And I know if I show the text to Mags and she gives me that look that a true-blue friend is supposed to give you when the worst thing has happened to you, those scary tears will burst out of me.

And maybe this time they'll never stop.

I slip my phone back in my pocket, take a deep breath and squeeze my eyes tight, stuffing it all inside me. Pretending there isn't a hurricane bomb churning and rolling inside my stomach, making me feel like I'm going to explode.

But it's there.

I hear the squeaky-wheeled cart before I actually see

her. Ruby Red in her gray-and-white uniform, pushing her cart at the end of the hall.

I wipe at my eyes with the back of my hand. "Hi, Ruby Red," I say.

"Hello, girls." She smiles a wide smile at us. "Catch any ghosts yet?"

I eye her suspiciously.

"Not exactly," I tell her. "But Chef Raphaël saw a woman in the dining hall yesterday that no one else saw. Probably the same woman Mr. Plum was talking about that night he skipped town in his underwear. Oh, wait, that's right . . . you weren't there for that."

Mags looks up from her phone and we stare at Ruby Red with accusing gazes like a bright bulb on a perp in a police interrogation room.

But she just shrugs.

"You don't seem surprised about that," I inform her.

"I'm not," she says, starting to roll her cart again.

We watch as she goes.

"Good luck catching her," she calls over her shoulder.

Mags gives me a knowing look and whispers, "Phony baloney supreme."

I nod and continue to eye Ruby Red as she wheels the cart away.

"Do you know when Madame Drusilla is coming back?" I call after her.

"It might be a while," she says. "She's out in the garden,

gathering her daily flowers, and that usually takes some time."

"How long does it take to gather flowers?" I call again.

Ruby Red stops and turns to face me. "For Madame Drusilla, it takes a good long time."

"Why is that?" I ask.

"Because she asks the flowers permission to cut them first."

Mags snorts. "Wait . . . ," she says. "She asks who . . . *what* now?"

Ruby Red turns back around and begins to push her cart again.

"You heard me right." She points toward the glass back doors leading to the paved rear courtyard filled with heavy iron chairs and tables. "You'll find her out there."

And she's dead-on, too.

But she isn't the only one. Jack the busboy is on the other side of the yard pulling weeds.

Shirtless, *again.*

"Hi, Jack!" Mags calls in a voice that's far too loud, waving to him.

He just smiles and keeps weeding.

"I'll be over there," Mags tells me, heading in his direction.

I grab her arm. "Oh no you won't," I say. "We're Research."

"No, *you're* Research." She points at me.

"Still," I say. "You have to help. Besties before boy-friends."

"Yeah, *thaaaaat's* not a thing."

"It sure is a thing," I tell her. "It's our thing."

"Fine," she sighs, following me to the garden, but not before flashing Jack the busboy one more smile when he looks up at her.

Madame Drusilla is exactly where Ruby Red said she'd be. Sitting right smack-dab in the middle of the roses like her backside has sprouted roots.

Eyes closed. Palms up.

She's older than my mom but definitely younger than Ms. Lettie. Long, straight gray hair lies flat on her back and a brightly colored scarf is wrapped around her fore-head and tied in the back. Next to her is a brown wicker basket with a whole bunch of freshly cut pink roses piled inside it.

"Excuse me, Madame Drusilla?" I call out.

Silence.

"Hello?" I say again.

"Shhh," she finally says. "I'm busy listening."

I look at Mags and she just shakes her head.

"Listening to what?" I ask.

"To the world around me," Madame Drusilla says.

"Yeah, but there's nothing really out here to listen to," I inform her.

She opens her eyes then.

"The garden is full of somethings," she informs me. "Not nothings."

"Oh, *riiiight,*" I say.

She closes her eyes again.

"You are welcome to listen too, if you wish," she says.

I close my eyes and listen hard.

Birds are singing in the trees.

Water is trickling in the fountain.

A saxophone is playing jazz music from hidden outdoor speakers.

I open my eyes.

"What exactly am I listening for?" I ask her.

She keeps her eyes closed tight and says, "I've asked a question of all the rosebushes in the garden and I'm waiting to hear their answer."

"So, let me get this straight," Mags says. "You really *are* waiting for the rosebushes to talk to you?"

"To answer me, yes," Madame Drusilla says.

Mags's eyebrows go up. "Can you hear them now?"

I give her arm a smack.

Madame Drusilla sighs an exasperated sigh, then opens her eyes again. "We must be respectful of the life of all things. Therefore, doesn't it just make sense that we would ask permission from the lives in this garden to be cut for our vases?"

"Not really," Mags says. "They're *flowers.*"

I shake my head at Mags. "Your channels are so pea soup, it's just plain embarrassing," I tell her.

She gives me her eyes-to-the-sky roll.

I step carefully between the bushes, making sure not to squish any leafy lives under the heels of my Converse, pulling Mags behind me.

"What are the bushes saying to you right now?" I ask Madame Drusilla.

"If you'd like to sit with me and meditate," she says slowly, "you too can hear the answers for yourselves."

I point to the dirt and Mags shakes her head. I point to the dirt harder and Mags shakes her head. I point to the dirt and mouth the word *"Sit!"* That's when she finally blows a puff of air out of her mouth and takes a seat next to Madame Drusilla while I find a patch of ground on the other side.

"Now close your eyes and focus only on the serenity of the garden and the air going in and out of your lungs."

"Actually," I say, "Dr. Finkelman taught me how to do this."

"Dr. Finkelman?" Madame Drusilla asks, her eyes still closed.

"Yeah," I say. "He treats my worries and says meditation can quiet my what-ifs. But the problem is that my jumping beans are way too wiggly and my brain far too busy worrying to just sit there and do nothing . . . it's a vicious cycle, really."

Madame Drusilla takes another deep breath in and out again. "It takes practice," she tells me. "Just listen and breathe. Don't judge yourself for the thoughts that come in and out or the wiggles, either. Just be thankful for everything you are."

"Everything?" I say. "That sure doesn't sound right."

Her lips crack a smile. "If you focus on gratitude for who you are and the gifts you possess, with that mind-set, the what-ifs will quiet."

"That doesn't sound right either," I tell her. "Mine are pretty loud. But I'll give it a shot."

I close my eyes and breathe breaths in and out just like Madame Drusilla does.

In and out.

WHAT-IFS
I'm not going anywhere.

In and out.
And I listen.
Still just birds.
Still just water.
Still just saxophone.

WHAT-IFS
Thankful for me yet?

Somewhere in the distance a leaf blower buzzes.
Probably Jack the busboy.

"Breathe in," Madame Drusilla tells us, taking a big breath. "And out."

"Wait," I say, opening one eye. "I think I hear something."

"Oh, give me a break," Mags mumbles.

Madame Drusilla opens her eyes, snips three more roses from the bush in front of her and places them carefully in the basket.

"See?" I say to Mags. "I knew I heard something."

"Thank you," Madame Drusilla says to her basket, and then pulls herself up, dusts the loose dirt off her backside and heads toward the main building.

We follow after her and her talking flowers through the back door and watch while she unlocks her office door.

She has her very own office just a half flight below the lobby. There is a gold sign that has her name engraved on it in fancy lettering.

Madame Drusilla, Spiritualist

"We were wondering if we could interview you about the stuff that's going on here at the hotel."

"My rate is fifty dollars for a fifteen-minute reading," she tells us.

"But we don't have fifty dollars," I say. "We spent most of our money on the bumper boats."

"*And* the giant water walking balls," Mags adds.

Madame Drusilla turns to face me. "What *do* you have?"

I pull two dollars out of my jeans pocket and Mags pulls out three and some change.

"We have five dollars *annnnnnd* . . . ten, twenty . . . thirty-eight cents."

Madame Drusilla nods and holds out her hand. "I'll take it."

I put the money in her palm and watch her fold up the bills with the coins inside and stuff them in her blouse.

"For five dollars and thirty-eight cents, I will give you six minutes," she tells me, pushing the office door open.

A waft of scorched strawberries hits us like a tropical-fruit-scented tsunami.

"Ooooh!" Mags says, pinching her nose. "Something's very wrong in there."

"Please have a seat." Madame Drusilla turns the lights on and waves a hand in the direction of two chairs set up at a small round table.

"I think your strawberries are done," I tell her.

"That's incense," she says, pointing to a smoking stick in a bowl on a table covered with a black tablecloth.

I sneeze.

"You mean that smell is on purpose?" Mags asks.

"Incense is said to profoundly heighten awareness of mind, body and soul," Madame Drusilla tells us.

I may be more in tune with my woo-woo than Mags is, but in this case, I agree wholeheartedly. Incense just plain stinks. And it makes my nose itch. How could the smell of scorched strawberries help you know anything?

I sneeze again.

Madame Drusilla's room is filled with multicolored

scarves with small gold disks sewn in along the edges. Silky scarves covering the tables, silky scarves lining the walls, and even silky scarves hanging over the window blinds, which makes her office real dark inside.

In addition to the incense burning in a bowl, there are tiny tea light candles lit on every flat surface. In one corner is a small waterfall that's supposed to sound calming but makes me need to pee instead. Dr. Finkelman has one in his office and that one makes me need to pee too. Ever since the whole Bloody Mary theory, I keep the bathroom light on permanently, and just to be safe, I figure it's best just to hold it as long as humanly possible. That cuts down on unnecessary trips to the toilet.

This time is no different.

I cross my legs and pull one of the chairs out from the table while Mags does the same on the other side.

"You have your choice between tarot cards and the crystal ball, or I can read your aura."

Mags sticks a thumb in my direction. "Ask Karma," she says. "She's the woo-woo expert."

"Mmm," I say. "We'll choose tarot cards."

Madame Drusilla nods and places a large deck of cards with a weird sun on them between us and then begins setting different crystals around the cards in a circle.

"What are you doing now?" Mags asks.

"These are crystals. They help to elevate vibrational frequencies and aid in the connection to other planes,"

Madame Drusilla tells us. "Quartz in particular magnifies all the energies around us and also protects us."

"Oh, I'm all about crystals," I tell Madame Drusilla, showing her my leather satchel hanging from my neck. "I brought a collection of bravery ones with me."

"Good thinking." She smiles. "So, I'm guessing you girls came with a specific question for me?"

"Yes," Mags says. "Who is the woman Mr. Plum and now Chef Raphaël have seen in the hotel? Is it Mrs. Honeycutt or are there evil spirits present? We need to know once and for all."

"Wait," I say. "That's not the question. What about—"

"Karma," Mags snaps. "We are *not* asking *that* question."

"Why not?" I ask.

"Because." She subtly juts a chin in Madame Drusilla's direction. "Ee-shay ay-may ee-bay in on the ony-phay aloney-bay."

PIG LATIN TRANSLATION: SHE MAY BE IN ON THE PHONY BALONEY.

I nod.

"Our official question is the one about Mrs. Honeycutt," Mags states firmly.

"Yep," I say. "That's the question."

Madame Drusilla nods and then reaches out to hold my hand and then Mags's. Me and Mags hold hands too while Madame Drusilla closes her eyes and breathes in and out again.

In and out.

In and out.

"Thank you," she says to the ceiling. "Yes, thank you for your guidance. Thank you. Thank you."

I look at Mags and she looks at me.

"Eird-way upreme-say," Mags leans over and whispers in my ear.

PIG LATIN TRANSLATION: WEIRD SUPREME.

I kick her under the table and give her a good glare.

"Thank you for your guidance for these lovely girls, who are searching for answers about Mr. and Mrs. Honeycutt," Madame Drusilla tells the ceiling.

It makes me wonder if she hears the ceiling talk too.

I mean, I'm not judging . . . just wondering.

Then we watch her open her eyes and say, "The cards . . . *are ready.*"

I swallow.

She turns the first card over.

"The death card," she says.

WHAT-IFS

You definitely should have picked the crystal ball.

I swallow. "The d-death card?" I say.

Madame Drusilla touches it with the tips of her fingers. "This card indicates that . . . *someone* is very, very dead—"

Mags scoffs. "That cost us five dollars and thirty-eight cents? I could have told you that for free."

Madame Drusilla places the card back on the deck and leans back in her chair with her arms folded over her chest. "I cannot move forward with such negativity," she says.

"She's talking about you, you know," I tell Mags.

"*I* know she is," Mags says.

Madame Drusilla gives Mags a good eyeballing and then asks her, "Has anyone ever told you of your past life?"

"Ah . . . *no*," Mags tells her.

"Uh-huh," Madame Drusilla says, examining her. "I see a tortured soul."

"Mmm." I nod, leaning back in my chair with my arms crossed too. "That would explain a lot. Especially your aversion to green foods. That's just weird. It's not even an official phobia."

Mags gives me a look and points another thumb in my direction. "Why don't you tell Karma about *her* past life."

"She doesn't have to," I inform her. "I already know it. My name was Betty Lou Wewak and I was a warrior princess."

Mags snorts again. "Where'd you get that?" she asks.

"My spirit guide told me."

"Oh, your invisible friend, Luna Shadow, told you that?"

150

"First of all," I say, "she's not invisible, she's a light being. And secondly, her official title is Almighty Spirit Guide Supreme."

"Uh-huh, and I suppose Crystal Mystic confirmed it."

"Well . . . *duh*," I tell her.

That's when Madame Drusilla looks at her watch, stands up and says, "Our session has concluded," while I give Mags a good glare across the table.

After our five-dollar-and-thirty-eight-cent session, me and Mags head up the grand staircase reeking of charred fruit.

"A total waste of five bucks. Check," Mags is saying.

"Yeah, you and your negativity," I agree. "She should have given us a refund on account of your pea soup channels ruining everything."

"Did you smell that in there?" Mags goes on. "If I had to smell her burnt strawberries five more minutes I would have blown chunks all over her talking roses."

"You know what your problem is?" I ask her. "You are too earthbound. You really need to be in better touch with your woo-woo."

"Yeah well, you are too woo-woo," she tells me. "You need to reel it in."

"*You* need to reel it out," I tell her.

"Yeah . . . that's still not a saying," she tells me.

"Is too."

"Here's the thing," she says. "You don't draw a line at anything. You have no line. You believe everything."

"I *do too* have a line."

She stops and puts her hands on her hips. "So, what is it then? What's your line?"

I think about it.

"My line is the existence of unicorns . . . and fairy portals. Wait, do I believe in fairy portals?" I think about it. "Yes. Yes, I definitely believe in fairy portals. I want to change my line to alien abductees. Unicorns and alien abductees are my line, final answer. I don't believe in those . . . *yet*. But if I actually witness a real live unicorn or alien abduction, I reserve the right to move my line."

She blinks at me.

"What?" I say, throwing out my hands.

"Nothing."

"Why? What's your line?" I ask her.

She shrugs. "It used to be ghosts," she says. "But since the séance, I have to rethink my line."

"Fairy portals?" I ask.

"Nope."

"Abductions?" I ask.

"Nope, my line is definitely before alien abductions, fairy portals, big-haired cowgirl vampires and Bigfoot."

"Oh, Bigfoot is totally real," I say.

"*Hello?* A dude in a suit? Check."

"Watch the videos," I insist.

"The point I'm making here isn't about Bigfoot," she says. "It's about Madame Drusilla being a huckster."

"Okay, maybe some Bigfoot hunters lie," I tell her. "But sensitives don't ever lie. It goes against everything they believe in."

"We're not talking about Bigfoot!"

"You're the one who brought them up," I mumble.

"Can you focus," she says.

"On what?"

Sigh. "We know there have to be multiple spirits here, right?"

"Right," I say.

"There's the woman." She starts the list on her fingers.

"Yep."

"Whoever she is," Mags goes on.

"Probably Mrs. Honeycutt," I say.

"Hopefully," she says. "And there's the whole issue of leaving the board open."

"Yep," I say. "Which means the spirits being experienced in this hotel could be anyone."

"True," she says. "First things first, we need to rid this hotel of the spirits we have invited in by accident. When is Charlie Brown coming over?"

"You'd better not call him that to his face," I remind her. "He's coming over tonight and he's bringing a bunch of stuff with him."

"What stuff?" she asks.

I shrug. "Some sort of Rid o' Ghost Kit."

"Okay," she says. "So that's the plan?"

"I think freeing the Stanley Hotel of unwanted evil spirits is definitely the plan," I agree.

"Then what?" she asks.

"I guess we keep trying to reach the Honeycutts," I say. "But at the same time investigate the phony baloney. I really think Ruby Red is up to something."

"Oh, totally, she is phony baloney big-time," Mags agrees.

We keep walking up the grand staircase past the lobby, past the ancient golden-framed portraits of the Jewel family, and past the second floor. When we're on the last flight of steps just before the third-floor landing, Mags stops and leans against the handrail.

"It's not that I'm saying Madame Drusilla is a liar," she says. "It's just her stuff is obviously, totally random and can apply to anyone. Like fortune cookies—"

"Hold it right there," I say, pointing a stern finger in her direction. "Say what you want about Bigfoot, but never, ever dis the almighty fortune cookie."

How to Rid o' Ghost

After dinner that night, Mags and me watch as Nyx unloads the contents of his backpack on the red steps of the Stanley Hotel. Everything you would ever need to rid a place of ghosts.

RID O' GHOST KIT
1 salt shaker
1 handful of dried leaves
1 get-rid-of-ghosts handbook

"Ghost-Hunting for Dummies," Mags reads off the cover. "There's an actual book about this?"

"There are *lots* of books about it," Nyx informs her.

Mags gives me a look.

"Yeah, open your mind, why don't you," I tell her, which promptly earns an eyes-to-the-sky roll.

"The salt is to form a protective circle," Nyx goes on, holding up the shaker. "It's more potent than candles. A spirit with enough energy can easily blow a flame out."

"That's *exactly* what happened to us," I tell him.

"Yeah," he says. "I figured."

I wide-eye him. "You know *everything.*"

He shrugs with a sly grin, and I come to yet another conclusion about Nyx and his eyelashes that go on for days. He's even cuter when he smiles. He has these straight white teeth and a dimple on his chin that pops in every time he grins.

"The salt makes a protective circle with just a small opening so the spirits can leave once we let them know they're not wanted," he says.

"How about doing a double-layer circle," I suggest. "You know, protection times two? Two is always better than one, right?"

"Yeah . . . it doesn't really work that way," he says. "Plus, you need to have a space for the spirit to leave this plane of existence or you're just going to frustrate the ghost. And I don't have to tell you, we don't need any angry ghosts."

"Maybe we leave *two* spaces?" I say.

He snuffs a laugh out of his nose. "Two is better than one?" he asks.

"Well, isn't it?"

He snuffs again.

I put my hand on his arm. "I'm not kidding."

Mags points to the clump of dried leaves. "What's with that?" she asks.

"This"—he holds it up—"is sage."

I stick my nose in the dried bouquet. "Smells like what my mom adds to the Stove Top stuffing at Thanksgiving time. She always added extra spices to the flavor packet to make it her own." I give it another sniff.

A pervy *I GOT THE CHEDDA BABY* feeling makes my stomach roll just thinking of how me and Dad will spend our second Thanksgiving without her.

No one will set the folding table in the kitchen with the paper plates with leaves on the edges. No one will spread the red vinyl tablecloth with the rip that Mom always hid on the side wedged up against the wall. No one will buy one of those pop-up paper turkey centerpieces from Party Fair on Fifth Avenue. And no one will cook a Marie Callender's still-frozen-in-the-middle pumpkin pie, either. Mom always took it out of the oven too early. But I never complained. Pumpkin pie is good no matter if it's cooked all the way through or in Popsicle form.

At least last Thanksgiving when we went to Denny's for turkey platters, the whole Totally Rad crew came too, including Big John's girlfriend, Gloria, and The Faz's wife, The Fazette—whose real name is Kat but no one ever calls her that.

Even if the pope himself decided to join us for turkey platters at Denny's this year, it wouldn't make it as special as with the red vinyl tablecloth and the pop-up paper turkey.

There's still one person missing.

Maybe Mom will bring her suitcases home for a strip of grass. Then maybe we'll grill the turkey on the barbecue and just pretend this nightmare never happened.

WHAT-IFS

Don't hold your breath.

I swallow down the lump that starts in my throat and focus.

"Burning the sage is called smudging," Nyx tells us. "The process cleans the space of any unwanted evil spirits. So this with the salt should be all we need."

"This is it, then?" I ask. "It's all we need to clear the angry ghosts?"

"I just need you to take me to room 217."

"Uh-oh," I say, eyeing Mags.

"It needs to happen in *that* room?" she asks. "You can't just do it out here?"

"Of course it has to be in the room," he says. "What'd you think?"

"We thought we could do it anywhere," I say.

"If you really want it to work, it should be in the room where you originally conducted the séance," he tells us. "That's where the highest level of activity will be."

"Huh," I say, looking at Mags. "We don't, you know, *technically* have the key card to the room."

"So?" He shrugs. "Just go get it."

"Easier said than done," Mags says.

"What does that even mean?" he asks.

"The first time we got into the room, we got the key card by not . . . so ethical methods," I say.

He blinks at me.

"Like, you know, sort of a covert lending agreement in which one person is not in the know, if you get my drift," I tell him.

He's still blinking at me.

"It's like this," I say. "You know . . . it's . . . we have to . . . um—"

"We have to *sneak* it," Mags says flatly.

"Why can't you just ask for it?" Nyx says. "I mean, what's with all the double-oh-seven?"

"Because Mr. Lozano is weird about his key cards, that's why," Mags informs him.

"Like really weird," I agree. "I think being interim manager has gone to his head."

"So, how are we supposed to do this without getting in the room?" Nyx asks.

Mags turns to me. "Velma? Any ideas?"

159

"Is that your real name or something?" Nyx asks.

"No," I say. "Velma Dinkley is from *Scooby-Doo.*"

"Oh, right." He nods at me and grins again. "I totally see it."

I poke Mags. "See?" I say, giving my glasses a push at the bridge. "I told you I give off a Velma vibe."

"Actually"—Nyx shrugs—"it's the glasses."

Mags's laugh comes out in a burst and I give her a good smack.

"So, do you have an idea or don't you?" she asks me.

I pace the porch and finger my satchel of bravery crystals while I think. I give Mr. Lozano a side-eye peek through the open double doors each time I pass. He's sitting at his post, guarding the key cards with an eagle eye. Well, technically he's reading a book with his eagle eyes, the same stupid one with the red staircase on the cover, but I know he's still guarding the keys big-time.

And then it comes to me.

"I got it," I tell them. "Mags, you go in first. Head to the kitchen through the dining hall. Then come running out and tell Mr. Lozano you saw a mouse run across the floor. He'll leave the desk, and while you're distracting him, I'll grab the key card and then me and Nyx will hurry upstairs. Once you can get away, come meet us up in our room. And if we're lucky, we can replace the key card before he even notices it's gone. Everyone in?" I ask.

Nyx nods.

"Mags?" I ask.

"Yep," Mags pipes up. "Me too."

"Then let's bring it in," I say.

We gather in a circle of three.

I put my hand in the center.

"Operation: Smudge the Stanley is in motion," I say.

Mags puts her hand on mine and Nyx puts his hand on hers.

"On three, everybody, *evil ghosts be gone*," I tell them. "One . . . two . . . three."

And on three we all call out, "Evil ghosts be gone!"

★

At the front desk, I stand there scanning all the colorful postcards stuck neatly into the compartments of a wire carousel.

"Da, da, da," I hum, giving the carousel another push around. "Which one should I choose?" I say, side-eyeing Mr. Lozano.

Still reading.

"Mr. Lozano," I finally ask, "what do you think about the woman Chef Raphaël saw in the dining hall yesterday?"

He sighs, folds the corner of his page and sets down his book.

"Do you really want to know?" he asks.

I stop pushing the postcard carousel. "Yes," I tell him.

He looks toward one end of the lobby and then the other.

Then I do it too and say, "There's no one here, Mr. Lozano."

He raises his eyebrows and says, "Isn't there?"

"Ah . . . no," I say. "There isn't."

That's when he leans forward and tells me something I'll never, *ever* forget.

"This hotel is alive," he tells me in a whisper.

I swallow. "So, like . . . *alive* alive?"

He nods.

"Like it's breathing?"

"It may not be breathing, but it certainly decides who it wants to reveal itself to and who it doesn't," he explains.

I blink at him while my what-ifs process this new information, cataloging worries in order of appearance for later tonight.

The first one is a doozy.

WHAT-IFS

An actual living hotel is watching *me.*

"I—I . . . wh-what . . . ," I stammer. "D-do you think the house actually chewed up the missing managers?"

He picks his book up again. "That's ridiculous," he snorts.

"You were the one who said it was alive, not me," I remind him. "I think that's a very valid follow-up question."

He snorts again and turns a page in the book while I give the postcard carousel another push around.

Every wire compartment is filled with a different picture of Estes Park. And not a single one is of a ghost. But every one has a huge blue sky in it. Rocky Mountains with blue sky, pine trees with blue sky and even romping bear cubs with blue sky. This was actually the very first thing I noticed about Colorado. In New York, it seems like there are so many things attached to the ground all around you, there's no real reason to look up. But in Colorado there's way more open space, so it makes the sky seem a whole lot bigger. There is blue everywhere. In front of you, behind you and above you too.

I pull out a bear cub card and side-eye Mr. Lozano again.

"So, when you say *alive* . . . do you mean like Madame Drusilla's talking roses?" I ask.

He folds the page again and sets the book aside.

"In its heyday, this hotel was full every night. No vacancies," he tells me.

"Not one?" I ask.

"Nope," he says. "And all four buildings were open too."

"Huh," I say.

"But now all this haunting business has been happening and . . . well, everything has changed. It's fishy, if you ask me."

"Like *phony baloney* fishy?" I ask.

"Is there any other kind?"

I nod in agreement. "I suppose not," I say.

"This hotel has been in the Jewel family for over a century, and they're going to lose it. It's just a terrible thing." He shakes his head. "Such a pity."

"It's awful is what it is," I agree.

"I've had my eye on things for a while and I can't quite put my finger on it."

"If you could put your finger on someone or something that's the most phony baloney . . . where would your finger be?" I ask him.

He looks left and then right again. Then he leans forward and opens his mouth, but this time a blaring scream snatches the words before he can even get them out.

It's Mags, right on cue.

"Mr. Lozano! Mr. Lozano!" She runs out the dining hall door and into the lobby. "There's a mouse under one of the tables. I saw it. Come quick!"

Mr. Lozano lurches from his desk, grabs a broom from the corner and darts toward the dining hall.

Mags gives me a nod and I scurry behind the desk and grab the key card for room 217.

"Hurry up," I whisper to Mags.

She nods again and runs back into the dining hall.

"Nyx!" I call to the front porch.

His head pops around the corner of the open double doors.

"Come on!" I tell him.

He throws his backpack over his shoulder and together we run up the grand staircase.

"He went that way," we hear Mags telling Mr. Lozano. "There he is! There . . . no, there he goes. There he is, Mr. Lozano! Over by that table there!"

Moody Ghosts and a Bloody Mary

Up in me and Mags's hotel room, I pace the viney carpet waiting for her to come back. Nyx is busy examining the Ouija board me and Mags pulled out of the back dumpster.

"Why's there dried ketchup all over it?" he asks.

"Oh, that . . . yeah, right . . . so, we had to, ah . . . pull it out of the, you know . . . dumpster," I tell him.

"The dumpster? What was it doing in there?"

I wave away his words from the air between us.

"It's a whole thing," I say.

He just smiles. "Uh-huh," he says.

"What is taking her so long?" I wonder out loud, tapping my fingers on the inside of my sweatshirt pocket.

One. Two. Three. Four.

"She should have been here by now—"

One.Two.Three.Four.

Onetwothreefour.

"What was Mr. Lozano saying to you at the front desk?" Nyx asks.

I stop pacing and face him. "Right," I say. "So, he was saying something like the hotel is alive and there was never a vacancy before the hauntings and also . . . oh, ah, that there's something fishy going on. And that one I totally agree with. I mean seriously, right? There is something phony baloney going on. I mean, you know, in addition to the whole paranormal hubbub. I just haven't figured out what it is yet."

Knock . . . pause . . . knock . . . pause . . . knock . . . pause . . . knock, knock.

"Finally!" I say, running toward the door.

"Wait," Nyx says. "That's not the secret knock. It was 'Knock . . . pause . . . knock, knock, knock . . . pause . . . knock . . . pause . . . knock, knock.'"

"Right," I tell him, and then wedge my ear against the door.

"What's the password?" I call.

"Egg on a Roll," Mags whispers through the wood.

"You got the knock wrong," I say. "How do I know it's really you?"

"Open. The. Door."

I snicker behind my hand.

"No can do," I tell her. "I'm afraid I'm going to need to

hear the proper knock first. I mean, Daphne would have gotten it right the first time."

"My Daphne is going to punch your Velma in the nose if you don't open this door right now."

"So you're admitting, then, that I *am* Velma."

"You'd better open this door."

"Let me hear you say it," I tell her.

"You are Velma," she says. "Okay? You're Velma."

"Mmm," I say. "I'm hearing the words, but they don't feel like you really mean it. Maybe say it again, but this time, you know, with a little more oom-pah to it."

"You *are* Velma, okay?" she says again. "You are more Velma than any Velma who's ever been Velma, okay?"

"You better open the door," Nyx warns me, licking his thumb and wiping at another ketchup stain.

"Better safe than sorry," I tell him, and then turn back to the door. "How do I know it's Mags and not some angry ghost using Mags's voice?" Then I get an idea. "I'll ask you questions of a secretive nature and you answer them, okay? That's how they make sure you are who you say you are for online passwords."

"You couldn't be more annoying right now," Mags informs me.

"Let me think of a good one," I say, tapping my lip with my pointer finger. "Oh, here's one. What favorite deli did the health department close around the corner from our walk-up on Charles Street?"

Exaggerated sigh. "Chester's."

I turn to Nyx. "That's right," I say.

"What does Rhonda Thomas pick during study hall when she thinks no one is looking?"

Exaggerated sigh. "Her right nose hole."

I turn to Nyx. "She got that one too."

"She sounds pretty mad—" he starts.

"Finish this sentence," I call through the door again. "Woo-woo isn't cuckoo and without it . . ."

Groan. "You'll have bad juju."

I fling open the door. "Mags! It's really you!"

She's standing with her hands on her hips giving me the rankest stink eye ever given in the history of stink eyes.

"You're dead," she says, lunging at me.

I race toward the bed with her right behind until we land on the velvet spread together, giggling so hard we fall off one side.

"What is that?" Nyx asks.

"What's what?" I ask, standing up and straightening my sweatshirt.

"The bad juju thing," he says.

"Oh, yeah . . . it's my personal mantra," I tell him. "It goes like this: *Woo-woo isn't cuckoo and without it you'll have bad juju.*"

He raises his chin in the air to consider this and then lowers it again, nodding his head up and down. "I like it."

"Do *you* have a personal mantra?" I ask him.

"Of course," he says. "Who doesn't?"

"Ah . . . everyone else," Mags tells him.

I shake my head at her. "*So* closed."

She throws her palms up. "Am I wrong?"

"What's your mantra?" I ask Nyx.

"You'll laugh," he says.

"I won't," I promise him.

"Let me guess," Mags says. "There's a Snoopy in it."

Nyx points an accusing finger at her. "See?"

"Mags!" I scold. "Mantras are sacred. Never, ever dis the mantra."

"Fine, fine," she says. "I won't laugh."

Nyx looks down at his shoes for a few more seconds.

"It's a German proverb," he tells us.

"Are you German?" Mags asks.

"No."

"So, why—?"

"Shhh," I tell her.

"Fine," she says.

We wait.

Nyx clears his throat.

NYX'S MANTRA: FEAR MAKES THE WOLF BIGGER THAN HE IS.

We both stare at him.

And then Mags wrinkles up her nose and says, "I don't get it."

"I do," I tell him. "I totally get it."

Nyx smiles at me and I smile back and that's the very

moment when I know that Nyx Brown is the one for me. It's a sign sent straight from Luna Shadow, Almighty Spirit Guide Supreme.

And I didn't even need to swipe right on some stupid app, either.

That's because when your spirit guide gives you a sign . . . you just know it all the way inside your bones.

It makes me wonder how Mom got hers so wrong.

★

We make it down to 217 without a hitch and then watch as Nyx gets his whole Rid o' Ghost Kit set up the way he wants it.

One ketchup-stained Ouija board. Check.

One protective salt circle (with an exit for angry ghosts). Check.

One clump of burnt-up sage. Check.

"Okay, so we need to do a closing ceremony with the Ouija board and the salt to ward away unwanted entities."

He takes a lighter out of his backpack and uses it to burn the leaves of the sage so that there's just a thin line of smoke floating out from the top.

"Here." He hands them to me. "Wave this around the room slowly to smudge the place."

I step across the carpet vines, waving the smoking leaves over my head.

"Like this?" I ask.

"Yep," he says while he sets the Ouija board on the floor and sprinkles salt in a circle around it.

"Okay," he tells me. "That's good enough. Now everyone come and sit down around the board within the protective circle."

I sit next to Nyx, and Mags sits next to me.

"Ew . . . what's that?" Mags points.

"Dried ketchup," Nyx tells her.

"Ohhhh" is all she says.

"A hazard of hanging out in a dumpster," he goes on with a grin.

She turns to me and says, "You *told* him?"

I shrug.

"I've never heard of anyone throwing out a Ouija board in an attempt to block its spiritual connection to the in-between," he says, shaking his head.

Seriously, we stuck it way down in there!
←

Covered it in garbage too. (P.S. Save the turtles.)

"It felt like the right thing at the time," Mags tells him.

I nod in agreement. "Definitely," I say.

Then she turns to me and with her hand straight up above her head she says, "Raise your hand if your best friend stinks at keeping secrets."

"I know, I know," I say. "I have a secret-keeping problem."

"Serious," Mags seconds.

"You guys ready?" Nyx asks.

"You never told us how come you know so much about all this stuff," I say.

He nods. "Remember when I told you guys about Harry Houdini?"

"The greatest magician of all time," I say.

"Illusionist," he reminds me.

"I remember," I tell him.

"Well, in addition to magic, he was very interested in spiritualism and the afterlife. For one very important reason."

"What was that?" I ask.

"His mother died."

"That's sad," I say.

Nyx nods. "After she was gone, he had a real hard time getting over it. He started to seek help from mediums and spiritualists who claimed they could make contact with her in the afterlife. But instead of making contact with her, all he found were hoaxers, charlatans and fakes who took his money and lied. The thought of people like that taking advantage of grieving family members made him so angry."

"Tooooold you," Mags sings.

"Don't mind her," I tell Nyx. "Madame Drusilla said she was a tortured soul in her past life."

He nods and considers Mags. "I get that."

Mags just rolls her eyes.

"So, did Houdini ever make contact with his mom?" I ask him.

"He kept trying, making it known that he would pay ten thousand dollars to any spiritualist who could prove to him without a doubt that they'd made contact with her."

"Did anyone get the money?" I ask.

"Nope."

"Not one person could prove it?" Mags asks.

"Nobody," Nyx says.

"So, he never got to talk to his mom again?" I ask.

"Not in this life he didn't," Nyx says. "But the story doesn't end there. Many years later when he was sick and dying himself, he and his wife, Bess, came up with a secret password. He told her to offer that same ten thousand dollars to any spiritualist who could tell her the password once he died."

"Did anyone know it?" Mags asks.

"Bess went from spiritualist to spiritualist who claimed they had made contact with the great Harry Houdini. But no one could tell her the password."

"Mmm-hmm," Mags says knowingly. "No television fuzz. No portal."

"What about the toilet portal?" I ask her.

"There were only outhouses back then," she informs me. "That's not a portal."

"Do I want to know how we got on toilets?" Nyx says.

I wave the words away with my hand. "No," I say. "It's a whole thing."

"Anyway, he died on Halloween," Nyx goes on. "And for ten years afterward, Bess did a séance each Halloween to try to reach him. But no one could ever tell her the password."

"That's horrible," I say. "Did she keep trying?"

"She conducted her last séance on Halloween night 1936. Ten years after his death. And declared it would be the last time she would try. Her last words to him after the séance were 'Good night, Harry.'"

I hold my chin in my hand and stare at him.

"How do you know all this?" I ask.

"There's an actual audiotape of the last séance," he tells me. "You can Google it . . . or, if you want, I can play it for you sometime."

I smile at him. "I'd like that," I say.

"People still conduct séances on Halloween to try to reach him," Nyx tells us. "But no one knows the password. It died with Bess."

"Why don't you think they could reach each other?" I ask him.

"Maybe they didn't have a Ouija board from Toy Mountain." Mags snorts.

I sigh and shake my head at her. "Raise your hand if your best friend's channels are as fogged up as pea soup," I tell her.

"I belong to a group of illusionists from Denver who come up to the Stanley Hotel every year in October to conduct the same séance, trying to make contact with Harry Houdini."

"Why do you do it here?"

"Because this hotel is one of the places he performed," Nyx says. "It was in 1915. Two years after his mother died."

I gasp. "He did his show here?"

He nods. "And Bess even traveled here with him."

"Bess was here too?"

"Yep, that's what makes an actual connection with the great Harry Houdini at the Stanley . . . a *real* possibility."

"Wow," I say. "That's all really interesting. I can see why you're so into magic."

Mags mumbles something under her breath. But I don't even care because me and Nyx are having a moment and as far as I'm concerned, she and her closed channels can just take a flying leap.

"All right," Nyx says. "You guys ready? Cameras on?"

Both me and Mags turn our phones to camera.

"Check," I say.

"Check," says Mags.

"Everyone put your fingertips on the message indica-tor," Nyx tells us.

When I put mine next to Nyx's, the edges of our pinky fingers touch.

It feels electric. Kind of like the spark you can get from a carpet shock in the wintertime.

But, you know . . . in a good way.

"Now let us close our eyes and we will call to the spir-its," Nyx says.

We close our eyes.

"We are here to send any uninvited spirits away from the Stanley Hotel," Nyx calls out. "We believe that the Honeycutts were called forward, and of course the Houdinis are always welcome here, but no one else. If you are an uninvited phantasm or evil entity, please leave the premises immediately."

I peek one eye open.

Nothing is happening.

"Do you think they're leaving?" I whisper.

"Shh," he hisses. "Close your eyes."

I close them.

"If there are unwanted spirits present," Nyx goes on, "please make yourselves known as you depart so that we know you are leaving the premises."

That's when the sound of footsteps races somewhere above us.

I peek another eye open, and Mags does the same.

"Did you hear that?" Nyx asks.

"It's just the dag gum hooligans," I tell him.

He opens his eyes. "The *what*?" he asks.

"Mr. Plum told us there are a bunch of kids who like to sneak into the hotel to race on the fourth floor," I tell him.

"Maybe it's the unwanted spirits letting us know they are departing," Nyx says.

"I suppose it could be," I say.

"Has he ever caught one?" Nyx asks.

"An unwanted spirit?" I ask.

"A hooligan," he says.

"No," I tell him. "He said when he finally makes it up there, they're always gone."

"Hmm" is all Nyx says.

"What?" I ask.

"I've read up on the Stanley Hotel history," he says. "And what I learned is that when guests came in the early 1900s, they stayed in rooms on floors one, two and three and all the children stayed on the fourth floor with teachers, nannies and caregivers."

"So?" I say.

He shrugs. "It's just curious is all," he says. "That he's never caught the kids."

"You mean . . . there are spirits of the children from the early 1900s running around on the fourth floor?" Mags asks, and then she looks at me. *"Whoa."*

"Whoa is right," I say.

Nyx shrugs again. "I told you this place is highly active. It could be . . ." But he doesn't say another word about it.

He doesn't get the chance.

At that very moment the bathroom light starts to flicker.

Mags stands up from the floor, pointing a shaky finger toward the light.

"I knew it," she whispers. "It's Bloody Mary. She's been here all along. She's here, just like Daisy Chang said. Showing herself in the bathroom mirror . . . her energy transported from the in-between to our very plane of existence . . . through the toilet plumbing."

Nyx leans closer to me. "What is it with her and toilets?" he asks.

"She thinks it's a portal to the afterlife," I tell him.

He shakes his head and blows air out of his mouth. "A paranormal plumbing portal?"

I shrug.

"Where'd she get *that*?"

"Daisy Chang," I say.

"Is Daisy Chang some kind of psychic?" he asks.

"Um, not exactly," I say.

"Bloody Mary," Mags is calling out in the doorway of the bathroom. "Are you here with us now?"

Nyx just shakes his head at me and says, "Oh, brother."

Action!

The Ouija board is officially closed.

At least that's what Nyx thinks.

We stayed in room 217 until Nyx was good and sure every last evil phantasm had departed the Stanley Hotel for good.

But I'm not so sure.

And Mags and Nyx may be two peas in a pod when it comes to *Poltergeist* being a blueprint of all things haunted, but the toilet plumbing portal theory is a *whole* different story. It remains the fuel of a raging controversy.

Bloody Mary is mixed somewhere in there too.

The controversy, I mean, not the toilet.

But someone or something flickered the lights in

room 217, no matter where they came from or how they got here.

That's one thing we can all agree on.

As far as the whole Rid o' Ghost salt-and-smudge party, Nyx thought it was a success and the only ghosts that were invited to stay were Mr. and Mrs. Honeycutt.

And of course the Houdinis.

The thing is, I remain unconvinced the dag gum hooligan footsteps were really a herd of mass-exiting uninvited phantasms. But I kept that what-if to myself.

WHAT-IFS

Angry ghost residue is a definite *possibility.*

After Nyx goes home and me and Mags have successfully returned the key card to the front desk in stealthlike, sleuthing fashion, Mags sets up a two-person viewing party of the blueprint itself.

Poltergeist.

And that's only after warning me that Dr. Finkelman wouldn't think it was a very good idea and making me cross-my-heart promise not to blame her for the aftermath of it all. But she still won't tell me what happens at the eleven-minute, fifty-second mark in *The Shining.*

And as it turns out, Mags is right about *everything.*

I mean *everything.*

The television fuzz taking the girl.

The dining hall chairs defying gravity.

The in-between.

All of it.

And now I'm staring at the ceiling tiles instead of sleeping.

The digital alarm clock on the night table between our beds reads 2:05 a.m. and I've just come to the conclusion that there are exactly two hundred thirty-seven square tiles affixed to the ceiling of room 332. Mags is drooling away in the bed she called dibs on by the window, her stupid ring glowing a blue beacon in the night.

Mine is *still* mud.

Nyx even said he didn't know a mood ring could get that brown.

Alfred Hitchcock is snoring at the bottom of the bed, his chin on my right foot. And I'll bet you a million dollars if he had a doggie mood ring, his would be bright blue too.

By three o'clock, I conclude there are two hundred *forty-two* ceiling tiles and not two hundred thirty-seven. But instead of doing it a third time, I turn over and watch the digital numbers on the clock, counting the seconds between the minutes to see how close I can get.

After the seventh time, I reach over and pull Crystal Mystic off the night table and give it a shake.

"Will I ever sleep again?" I whisper to it and wait for the spirits to conjure up an answer.

CRYSTAL MYSTIC
SEEKER, BEWARE! SPIRIT
HAS GRAVE DOUBTS.

At three-thirty, I wake up Alfred Hitchcock and together we sneak out of bed and go looking for Dad and the others to help with their nighttime investigation. Tonight they're supposed to be set up in the Music Room off the lobby. But when I make it down there, the doors to the room are closed and I can hear Dad, Big John and The Faz arguing inside.

I tiptoe toward the doors and wedge my ear against the wood.

> **Dad:** I don't know, okay? I don't know.
> **The Faz:** The Tupperman wedding got called off, so we're going to be short again this month.
> **Dad:** Are you serious? What happened?
> **Big John:** The groom got cold feet. He's MIA.
> **Dad:** (Blowing air out of his mouth) Oh, man. This is bad. Mr. Drago is saying he needs last month's rent for sure by a week from Friday.
> **The Faz:** Last month's rent?
> **Dad:** Yes.
> **The Faz:** So? When is the Netflix check going to come?
> **Dad:** It was a contingent thing.
> **Big John:** *Contingent?*
> **The Faz:** Contingent on what?

Dad: On getting a ghost on film.

The Faz: Dude, that is not cool.

Dad: I know. I know. I just agreed to everything they were saying. I didn't realize it would be such a challenge in a place that's so rampant with paranormal activity.

Big John: Have we got anything? Anything at all?

Dad: Nothing on film. T. S. Phoenix definitely believes the place is highly active, but I haven't captured an image yet.

Big John: Maybe it's time to . . . make it happen. If you know what I mean.

The Faz: Agreed. It'll be our secret. Just get some footage and we'll add our own ghost.

Big John: Right, it's easy enough to do. I'll create some images and sounds and we'll just dub them in.

Dad: I'm not faking anything.

Big John: Do you really have a choice?

Dad: Yes. I'm not doing that. I'll never do that. Totally Rad is a legit documentary company. I will never cave for any contract. It's unethical. I won't do it.

The Faz: Even a contract with Netflix?

Silence.

Dad: No, I can't do it. It goes against everything I believe. Totally Rad does what's right. Period.

Big John: You have to weigh what's worse … swallowing your pride or the reality of you and your daughter getting kicked out of the only home she's ever known.

Silence.

I look down at Alfred Hitchcock and he looks up at me. "This is not good for my what-ifs," I tell him.

He gives me a snuff in agreement.

That's when we hear the voices of T. S. Phoenix and Tally heading down the grand staircase. Me and Hitchy make a beeline across the lobby to the kitchen. I'm not saying it's right to eavesdrop, but one thing I know for sure, if you're going to do it, you'd better not get caught.

★

Ms. Lettie told me that Mrs. Honeycutt used to play the piano for Mr. Honeycutt and other guests in the hotel on the stage in the Music Room. Ms. Lettie also said that sometimes you can still hear her playing. Which is exactly why the crew is set up in the Music Room tonight.

After Alfred Hitchcock and I get a drink of water from the kitchen, I creep back across the lobby and peek my head in the doorway. This time Dad is crouched behind his camera with Big John holding the boom and The Faz directing Tally at the keys of an ancient grand piano that's set on a small stage at the front of the room.

"Okay, we've only got a couple of hours left before the staff comes in for morning shift. Let's get something on film," Dad says.

"Places, people," The Fazz calls out. "*Annnd* action!"

Silence while Dad films Tally busy being sensitive at the grand piano and T. S. Phoenix using his machine to measure the air for ghosts.

Big John holds the boom above Tally. The boom is basically this very fuzzy microphone on a long bar. The microphone picks up the sound better for the camera. And The Faz stands behind Dad, gnawing on his thumbnail.

I watch through the crack from behind the door while Alfred Hitchcock scratches an itch, sniffs his paw and then scratches again in the same exact spot.

Tally's eyes are closed and her hands hover above the yellowing keys as she breathes in and out.

"I'm feeling a tightness in my chest," she says. "There is something here. Unmistakably, there is a presence. And there is heartbreak. Sadness at these keys. In this very spot a heart has felt pain . . . sorrow . . . and loss. It feels it now as well. I sense it . . . I feel it myself. Inside my chest, I can feel the heartbreak—"

Alfred Hitchcock snorts and then woofs.

"Cut!" The Faz shouts.

T. S. Phoenix looks up from his Geiger counter and Tally opens her eyes.

They're all staring at me and Hitchy.

"What are you doing up?" Dad asks. "You should be in bed."

His usual grin is gone.

"I—I couldn't sleep," I say. "I thought maybe I could help you—"

"Yeah, yeah, sure, but we've got to get this shot done, Snooks," he tells me, wiping sweat beads off his temple. "It's the end of day four, and we don't have any kind of image on film or voice on tape yet. If we don't get something in the next six days, the Netflix people will . . . not be happy. So we need to get back to work—"

"I just thought, um, m-maybe I can help with that," I say. "Ms. Lettie told me once that Seraphina Honeycutt played that very piano while she was here."

Tally reaches a hand out toward me. "Come here, dear, and tell us what Ms. Lettie told you," she says.

Dad sighs, looks at his watch and then gives me a nod. "Sure, yeah, go ahead, hon."

He sounds out of breath.

I hurry across the worn floorboards, my bare feet slapping against the wood. I pass all the crisply painted, perfectly lined-up rows of old-fashioned wooden chairs. Upright seats, patiently waiting for an audience to fill them.

"Hello, sweetheart," Tally says, patting the piano bench.

I slip in next to her.

"Put your hands on the keys, like this." She gently places her fingertips on the keys. "Then close your eyes and breathe."

I blink at her and say, "You want me to touch it?"

She nods.

"Okay," I say. "But I don't know how that's going to help anything."

"Try," she says, closing her eyes and taking a deep breath in, just like Madame Drusilla did in the garden.

I close my eyes and breathe in and out too.

In and out.

Listening to the sounds around me.

The lights.

Buzz.

The clock.

Ticks.

Scampering on the grand staircase.

The dag gum hooligans or maybe exiting phantasms. The possibility remains that we left the board open so long we let way more spirits in than we could smudge out.

Then Tally's voice. "Now," she says in almost a whisper. "Open your eyes."

I open them.

"What does your gut tell you?" she asks me.

I concentrate real hard.

Gut: *I got nothing.*

"Ah . . . my gut isn't really . . . what I mean to say is . . . it's not really good at listening per se. It more just churns and feels tight and is especially sensitive to cheddar cheeses."

"Don't judge it," Tally says. "Just listen to it."

I concentrate again.

Gut: *Gurgle.*

"I'm being totally serious right now, it really doesn't have anything important to say," I tell her.

"Tell me more about what Ms. Lettie shared with you."

"Oh, right . . . well, she said Seraphina used to play for the other guests while she was here and . . . what else? Um, they would gather in all these chairs," I say, pointing to the waiting seats. "And . . . um . . . she said Mr. Honeycutt would watch from the sidelines and marvel at her talent and her beauty and also . . . how much he loved her."

Tally glances down at the keys again, and this time, instead of touching the keys, her fingertips hover just above them.

So I hover too.

T. S. Phoenix motions for Dad to start filming, and The Faz calls out, "Action!"

Tally breathes deep, in and then out, in and then out, before she says, "I feel a woman's energy present." She nods her head. "I feel the spirit trying desperately to make herself known by the notes she wants to play at this keyboard. Are you here with us, Seraphina? Are you with us now? We mean you no harm, dear. We are here to join you with your beloved husband, Ozgood, with whom you have shared love and a life on this plane of existence. Are you here with us, Seraphina?"

We wait.

"It is here where Ozgood Honeycutt awaits your music," Tally says. "The heartbreak I feel is also his to share. His pain. His loss. He longs to be with his bride after so many years."

That's when T. S. Phoenix's Geiger counter starts crackling and buzzing and popping like crazy.

"I'm getting something!" he exclaims.

And then one single solitary key plays on the piano.

I jump, but Tally puts a gentle hand on my arm.

"C sharp," she announces with a smile.

Another key plays.

"E," Tally says.

"Does your gut think she's trying to play a song for us?" I whisper.

"No, my dear, I believe she is spelling out a word for us," Tally says.

I suck air.

We wait.

The keys are silent.

"It was just two keys," I say. "*C-E* isn't a word."

"Remember I told you it takes them a great deal of energy to make contact with the living?" T.S. says.

I nod. "Yes, I remember."

"Maybe that's all the energy she had today," he says.

"It's possible next time she'll share more letters," Tally says. "For now, we've made contact with one Mrs. Seraphina Honeycutt."

"Cut!" The Faz calls.

"You know what this is like?" I tell them all. "It's just like with Harry Houdini."

Everyone stares at me again.

"You mean the magician?" Dad says.

"Actually . . . he was an *illusionist*," I correct him. "He performed here in 1915."

Dad turns to T. S. Phoenix and says, "Isn't that the same thing?"

"Not according to Nyx Brown," I say. "Houdini and his wife, Bess, had a password for after he died. She was supposed to go to psychics and spiritualists to try to make contact with him. Maybe Mrs. Honeycutt has a password too."

"What wonderful research you've done," Tally says.

"Yeah," Dad agrees. "How did you learn all that?"

"From this Nyx kid," I say.

Dad's eyebrows go up. "A boy?" he asks.

I shrug.

"What is our agreement?"

I roll my eyes and mumble, "No boys until I'm thirty."

T. S. Phoenix lets out a booming laugh.

"Maybe the Honeycutts *do* have a password," Tally says. "I like the idea of that. I will have to do more reading about Harry Houdini and his wife, Bess. Good job, honey."

"Oh, and his mom, too," I say. "His mom died first and he tried to contact her through mediums and spiritualists but couldn't find a genuine one. I don't know his mom's name, though. Nyx never told us."

Tally nods her head.

"Well, I guess that's a wrap for tonight," Dad says.

"But it was a *good* night, right?" I ask him. "We've got a ghost playing piano on film, right? I mean, a piano-playing ghost? It doesn't get any better than that."

He cracks a weak grin. "It's something," he says. "But Netflix wants an image. They were very specific about that."

"I'm afraid an actual image is pretty rare in this business," T. S. Phoenix tells him. "Most ghost-hunting shows do more reenactments about what's reported and never really catch a live image on film."

Dad locks eyes with Big John.

"Yeah," Dad says. "I'm getting that now. I guess that's why they wanted this one to be different. I didn't realize it would be that difficult. I guess I was pretty naïve . . . or excited . . . or, I don't know . . . arrogant to think I could do something like this. I suppose I would have agreed to just about anything for a shot at my dreams coming true."

"You'll get it," I assure him. "I know you will."

He shakes his head and says, "It's not your job to worry about me, Snooks."

WHAT-IFS

Doesn't he know you at all?

That's when I realize we have an official woo-woo emergency on our hands. And when an official woo-woo emergency is declared, you need one thing and one thing only.

True blue.

"Mags." I jump on top of her in her bed and give her a shake. "Wake up."

The sun still isn't up yet when I make it back up to room 332.

"I hate to state the obvious, but I am sleeping," she says, turning over and pulling the covers over her head.

"I know, but I need to tell you something," I say. "And it needs to be right now. It's mad important and it involves our true-blue-friend pact."

She pokes her head out from under the velvet, rubs her eyes with her knuckle and looks at the digital clock on the nightstand.

"I really don't want to know anything about anything at four-thirty-eight in the morning," she tells me. "Maybe I'll change my mind around say . . . eight or eight-thirty?"

"My dad's in trouble," I tell her. "And it's officially day five. We have to help him."

She peeks an eye out from under the covers.

"We *are* helping," she says. "We're doing the research."

"No, I mean we *really* have to help him," I say. "Mags, if we don't get a ghost on film, grumpy Mr. Drago is going to kick us out of our apartment."

The one eye blinks at me until she emerges from the depths of the covers like a sea monster from a velvet lake, sitting straight up and squinting at me in the light.

"Wait . . . is this your what-ifs talking or is it really real?" she asks.

"*All* my worries are real," I inform her.

"You mean like the time you thought the boogeyman lived in the hall closet?"

"I was six," I remind her.

"What about the time you thought you got a brain-eating amoeba after swimming at the Carmine Street Pool because you thought you swam through a warm patch of pee? That was last year."

"Okay, fine," I say. "Sometimes I get it wrong, okay?"

"What about the time—"

"*Listen,*" I interrupt. "This is legit. I mean, *legit* legit. I overheard my dad and Big John and The Faz talking in the Music Room. The Netflix contract is dependent on us finding a ghost. And even though tonight Tally got Mrs. Honeycutt to play a sharp C on the piano . . ."

"What's a sharp C?"

"It's one of the keys," I explain. "And I guess it's a sharp one."

"It played by itself?" Mags asks.

"Totally by itself," I say. "Just like with the Ouija board that first time we did a séance in room 217."

Mags says, "Whoa."

"Anyway, there's definitely someone here who has something very important to say, and we have to be the ones to lure it out. Because if my dad doesn't get a ghost on film, we're toast."

"What about the phony baloney funny business?" Mags asks.

"We can keep investigating that, too," I tell her. "But we need a ghost and we need one fast. This is a woo-woo emergency."

"Doesn't woo-woo theory say to never interfere with the signs? To just let things happen the way the universe wants to reveal them? Isn't that what you're always saying?"

"Right," I say. "But there is a little-known exception to this rule."

"And what's that?"

"In the case of a destiny emergency," I say. "And this is an emergency if I've ever seen one. We need a serious intervention. Something is obviously blocking Dad's fortune cookie fate."

Mags tilts her head. "Is that really a thing?"

"It is if I say it is," I tell her, grabbing Crystal Mystic off the night table and giving it a good shake. "Is it time for a woo-woo intervention?" I ask it.

CRYSTAL MYSTIC

THE SPIRITS ARE AS SILENT
AS THE GRAVE RIGHT NOW.

"Oh, for crying out loud." I slam it back down on the night table. "Get dressed," I tell Mags. "Today we find ourselves a ghost."

Mags pushes the covers off and heads toward the bathroom. "I guess your crystals are finally kicking in," she calls over her shoulder.

But when I reach up to touch the leather satchel of my garden-variety bravery crystals, I realize I left them on the night table.

Pink Jell-O and Ghost Guts

"**F**or the gazillionth time, *it was not Jell-O,*" Mags tells me.

She's a little crabby after I woke her up at four-thirty this morning, and her mouth is full of toothpaste so it sounds more like *well-o* than *Jell-O,* but I get the gist.

"*You* don't know," I tell her from the doorway.

She spits bubbles in the sink. "I knew I shouldn't have let you watch *Poltergeist,*" she tells me. "I knew this would happen."

WHAT-IFS
She called it.

"I don't know why you let me watch it either," I tell her. "I didn't sleep a wink. Not. One. Wink. All because of you. Did you know there is a total of two hundred forty-two tiles on this ceiling? Do you want to know how I know that?"

She spits more bubbles and then rinses and I follow her out of the bathroom.

"I told you if I showed you the movie, you couldn't blame me, didn't I?" she says. "And the pink goo they were covered in when they returned from the in-between still isn't Jell-O no matter how much you want it to be."

I flop down on top of my unmade bed. "I thought about it all night and decided that was the only conclusion there is. And you want to know what Crystal Mystic said when I asked if I was right?"

"No," she says, getting on her knees and digging through her suitcase for a clean sweatshirt.

CRYSTAL MYSTIC

YOU CAN THANK YOUR LUCKY STARS!

"Why would there be Jell-O randomly floating in the in-between? That's the dumbest thing I've ever heard. Not dumber than talking flowers, but it's up there."

"So, you're saying ghosts can't have Jell-O?"

"I think it's safe to say ghosts can't have Jell-O," she

says. "Not to mention, what flavor of Jell-O is *pink*? There is no pink Jell-O."

I pull my phone out of my pocket. "Siri? What flavor of Jell-O is pink?"

Siri: Here's what I found.

"See?" I hold up my phone. "Red."

"Red's not pink," Mags says.

"Mixed with Cool Whip it is."

"Okay, if you're going to sit there and tell me that there's both Jell-O and Cool Whip floating around the in-between, I can't even talk to you."

"If you're so smart, then what is it?"

"Got to be ghost guts," she says.

"No way," I tell her.

"And why not?" she asks.

"Because ghosts don't have guts," I say. "*Hello . . .* they're see-through? Everybody who's anybody knows that one."

"Still," she says. "It's more likely to be ghost guts than Jell-O. Ask your boyfriend, why don't you."

"He's not my boyfriend," I remind her, dialing Nyx's number.

"Not yet, but it's on the horizon," she sings.

"He'd never *like me* like me."

"After he said that thing about the wolf mantra, your face went all goopy and I definitely think you had a moment."

"Really? Because it felt momenty to me too," I tell her. "Like Luna Shadow was giving me a sign."

"Totally," she agrees.

"But for the record, I *did not* goop."

She snorts and mumbles, "You should have seen it from my angle."

"Voice mail," I tell her.

"Leave him a message."

Nyx's voice mail: Only three people have this number. If you're not one of them, hang up now.

Beep.

"Hey, it's me," I say. "We can't decide if the pink goo in *Poltergeist* is Jell-O or ghost guts. Call me back."

"Maybe he's already at Fun City," Mags says, still digging. "I can't find my sweatshirt . . . the rainbow one . . . have you seen it?"

I shrug. "Maybe Ruby Red hung it up in the wardrobe."

She gets up from the floor and pulls the doors of the wardrobe open and then slams them shut again.

When she turns to face me, all the color in her face is gone and her eyes are as wide as water walking balls.

I shoot up from the bed and point a finger in her direction.

"It's a pinky toe, isn't it?" I demand. "There's a pinky toe in there. I knew it! I knew it!"

"No," she whispers, opening the double doors of the wardrobe wide enough for me to see inside.

A single dress hangs neatly on a hanger.

But not just any dress.

A fancy, elaborate, lacy dress from olden times.

And on the very top shelf above it, a flowery hat with a large brim.

I swallow hard. "Please tell me that's your dress," I whisper.

"Oh, sure," she says. "First off, I haven't worn a dress since I was four years old. And second, I wouldn't wear something this ugly."

"It's not ugly," I inform her. "It's just old-fashioned."

"Still," she mumbles. "Would you walk down the halls of Immaculate Heart of Mary K–8 in that?"

"No comment," I tell her.

"That's all I'm saying."

"I mean, you checked the wardrobe on that first night, right?" I ask, pulling out my phone and aiming my camera at it.

"Mmm-hmm."

"It wasn't there that night, right?" I ask.

"No way," she says. "The closet was empty. That I know for sure."

"Have you checked it since then?" I wonder.

"Nope," she tells me. "You think I want my clothes in the same place a serial killer keeps the missing managers?"

"I knew I'd change your mind!" I exclaim, beaming at her.

"Yeah, yeah," she mumbles.

"So, that's got to be Mrs. Honeycutt's dress, right?" I say. "I mean, last night at the piano and now this?"

"Got to be," Mags agrees. "Why are you taking so many pictures of it? It's not like it's an actual ghost."

"But it belonged to one," I say, aiming again.

"So this woman Mr. Plum saw, and then Chef Raphaël, is Mrs. Honeycutt trying to connect with her husband, right?" she asks.

"It has to be," I say, changing to video mode.

"Wait . . . ," Mags says. "That means sh-she was *in here.*"

"Yeah."

"In *our* room," Mags says.

"Yeah," I agree.

"That's mad creepy."

I nod in agreement and point to the night table. "We should ask Crystal Mystic if this dress belonged to Mrs. Honeycutt."

"That thing doesn't work," Mags tells me.

"Does so," I tell her.

Mags grabs Crystal Mystic and gives it a shake.

"Is this the dress of Seraphina Honeycutt?" she asks, and then waits for the voice from beyond the stars.

CRYSTAL MYSTIC
BOOST YOUR ENERGY AND ASK
AGAIN LATER.

I shake my head. "Even Crystal Mystic knows your channels are blocked."

"Try defective."

I grab it from her and give it another shake. "Is this the dress of Mrs. Honeycutt?" I ask.

CRYSTAL MYSTIC
FORTUNE IS NOT SMILING ON THIS.

"Huh," I say.

"Ha!" Mags says. "Maybe you're the pea soup and not me."

"Doubtful," I tell her.

"And why is that?"

"Because I've been practicing for longer. My mom's been teaching me woo-woo since before I can even remember—"

But the words get stuck up in my throat.

That's when Mags's eyes lock on mine and she doesn't say a word.

That's because no words need to be said.

She just knows.

That's true blue.

I swallow it all down and keep filming.

"Why don't you check if there are any pockets on it." I point to the dress.

"Um . . . not with a ten-foot pole, but thanks for asking," Mags says. "Feel free to check them yourself if you're so curious."

"Me?"

"Be my guest," she says with a wave of her hand.

"Fine," I say. "I will. But I get Velma credit for this one too."

"You touch a dress from the beyond and you'll definitely get Velma credit for it."

I push my glasses up at the bridge, take a deep breath and walk two steps closer to the wardrobe.

The dress rests across a rusted wire hanger that looks as old as the dress itself. The fabric hangs, wilted and drained of its soul, threadbare and fragile. A once-valued treasure, battered by age and waiting . . . longing to be important to someone again.

This time I blow air out in a burst and let my fingers reach slowly toward the sleeve. They are shaking.

Closer.

Closer.

Closer.

The material is sharp and crunchy, the brittle threads barely hanging on. I run my hand down the seams, looking for a pocket of some kind.

"I think I found one," I tell Mags, slipping my hand inside the material.

The tips of my fingers reach deep down inside and touch something.

WHAT-IFS

Please don't be a pinky toe.
Please don't be a pinky toe.
Please don't be a pinky toe.

"There's something in here," I tell her.

"Pull it out," she says.

Whatever is inside is crisp and brittle, even more so than the dress. I take the edge between my fingertips and draw it slowly to the light.

"What is it?" Mags asks, wedging a cheek next to mine.

"A card of some kind," I tell her. "It looks burnt."

"Yeah," she says.

"Did Ms. Lettie say anything about a fire when she was talking about Mr. and Mrs. Honeycutt?"

"I don't think so," Mags says. "I mean, it was a buggy accident, there could have been a fire."

I point to the smudged image on the front of the card.

"This looks like a cake, doesn't it?" I ask.

"Maybe it's an old birthday card," Mags says. "Wait. Maybe it's a wedding invitation."

"Right," I say.

She points a finger. "Take a picture of it."

I place the dusty card on the bed and take a picture.

"Take a bunch," she says. "Just in case. The people on YouTube say that sometimes you don't see the ghosts but they end up in your picture later."

I nod and aim again.

"Can you make out the letters?" She squints.

"That's definitely an *L*." I point. "And maybe that one is an *I*?"

"That one might be an *A*." She points to a third letter. "And is that a three?" She gives it a sniff. "It smells," she says.

I sniff it too. "It smells like fancy perfume at the counters in Macy's in Manhattan," I say.

She gives it another big whiff.

"Yeah," she says. "Like roses. Lots and lots of stinky roses all stuck up in one bottle." That's when the dress slips off the hanger and onto the floor of the wardrobe. And when it does, rose petals float up into the air from somewhere deep inside the dress.

Dried rose petals.

Mags turns to me with wide eyes. "Just like in the dining hall," she breathes behind her hand.

I nod.

"This," she says. "Is getting real."

"Totally real," I agree.

After we brief Totally Rad and Lights Out! at breakfast, we decide to go and find Nyx. We try Fun City first, and when the manager tells us Nyx doesn't have a shift until Thursday, we look him up on Google and map the address to his house.

While we walk, I pummel Mags with more paranormal questions about the official blueprint.

"What about Tweety?" I ask.

"I knew I'd be sorry for showing you that movie, I knew it," Mags mumbles. "You're going to torture me with your questions for life."

"I'm just saying," I go on. "The pet canary had to have something to do with the haunting."

"It was a bird," Mags tells me. "How does a canary have anything to do with anything paranormal?"

"Ah . . . *hello,* it dies at the beginning of the movie."

"So?"

"So, every single thing in a story has a purpose," I tell her. "That's what makes a good story. If something doesn't mean anything, it's edited out. That's what Mr. Cavanaugh says in creative writing class."

"Yeah, well, sometimes the detail can just be a red herring."

"The canary isn't a red herring," I tell her. "First off, it's not red, it's yellow. And second, they made too big a deal about Tweety for him not to mean something major."

"The thing dies in like the second scene," she says.

"Right, but then the little girl sees it before her mom flushes it down the toilet and then they end up having a funeral for it and bury it in the garden. And there's even yet another part where the workmen accidentally dig it up later. Those are all clues."

"Clues for what?"

"That Tweety haunts the family," I tell her.

"I'm sorry, but that's even dumber than the Jell-O." She snorts.

"Says you."

"Sometimes a canary is just a canary," she says.

I stop. "Wait." I look down at my phone and look up again. "I think this is it."

"906?" she asks.

"Yeah."

"Yep, it's this one." She points to a small cabin made of logs and a front porch lined with eight different-colored rocking chairs.

The front door has a copper engraving that reads THE BROWNS.

I ring the doorbell and we stand and wait on a welcome mat that has a cartoon picture of a Bigfoot sitting on top of a mountain.

"See?" I point to it. "Even Nyx believes in Bigfoot."

She gives me her eyes-to-the-sky roll and says, "He would."

The door opens and a girl in an Inkwell & Brew sweatshirt is standing in front of us. She's got long, dark brown hair in waves with these super-cool hot-pink highlights and sparkly gold threads weaved in.

"Yeah?" she says, taking a bite out of an apple.

She has the exact same smile as Nyx and the same color eyes too.

"Um . . . yeah," I stutter. "We are here to see . . . um—"

"Netflix, right?" she exclaims. "I'm right, right? You're Charlie's new friends from the Stanley Hotel? The Netflix crew?"

"Um . . . yeah," I say.

"Come on in." She waves us inside. "Oh, man, all that kid talks about these days is you guys. I'm on my way out, I have class, so just make yourself at home. The fridge is full, so help yourself." She takes another bite of her apple. "Charlie!" she shouts up the steps. "You have company!"

We watch her grab a Colorado State University windbreaker and a blue backpack and shuffle out the door.

"Later!" she says.

"Ah . . . yeah, so, see you! I mean, you know . . . peace out."

She stops chewing and blinks at me and then smiles before slamming the door.

"*Peace out*?" Mags mumbles.

"It's just something you say," I tell her.

"Oh, I know *some* people do," she tells me. "But it doesn't look good on you. I think it was in the delivery."

"Hey," Nyx calls from the top of the stairs. "What are you guys doing here?"

It's the first time I've ever seen him without his skull-cap on or any eyeliner, either. His tattoo sleeves are gone, showing his skinny bare-naked arms, and his long hair is pulled up in a twisted knot and secured with a black band.

"A man bun?" Mags snorts. "*Noooot* a good look, Charlie Brown."

I give her an elbow. "Oh . . . um, we didn't, I mean . . . you didn't call back and, um, we found a dress from the beyond . . ."

"So, who was that girl?" Mags asks.

"My sister," he says, sitting on the very top step.

"Oh," I say. "Aren't your mom and dad home?"

"They died a long time ago," he tells me.

I blink at him. "What? I mean, oh . . . I didn't know . . . sorry," I stammer. "Why didn't you tell us?"

He shrugs. "Didn't come up."

"But . . . it's kind of a big thing," I say. "I mean, don't you think?"

"I guess," he says. "I mean, it happened when I was a baby, so I don't even remember them."

"How did they die?" I ask.

"In a fire," he says. "The house caught on fire and they saved all the kids but didn't make it out themselves."

"Oh," I say. "Sorry. I don't technically have a mom either. I mean, I do, but I don't. She . . . she left us last year." I swallow.

"Mmm." He nods.

"Is that why you're so interested in Harry Houdini's story about his mom?" Mags asks him.

He shrugs again. "Maybe," he says. "I never thought about that."

Nyx's eyes meet mine then and they don't let go.

I guess you could say it counts as another moment . . . but this one doesn't feel like a carpet shock at all. Not even close.

This one hurts . . . and not in a good way.

And in that moment, I know he feels the same.

We share something we shouldn't share.

He pulls his eyes away first, and I let out the breath I've been holding inside my lungs.

"I have four older sisters," he tells us. "And they've all taken turns raising me. Jasmine's the only one left who hasn't moved down to Denver or Boulder. So it's just us now. Marigold, Lily, and Poppy are all married and have kids of their own."

"Your sisters sound like the garden out back at the Stanley," I say.

"Yeah, I guess our mom and dad named them all after flowers."

"But not you?" I say.

"No," he says. "My mom's name was Rose, but I'm Charles Junior after my dad."

"Oh," I say. "Where does Nyx come from?"

He shrugs. "Cool, right?"

"Oh, totally," I agree.

"My mom was into Greek mythology, and *nyx* means 'of the night.' That's why I picked it. A long time ago I found all these books that belonged to her, and they were all on Greek mythology, and on one page she had underlined the name. So ever since then, I go by Nyx."

"I like that," I say. "I mean, really. It's like perfect for you. Like so perfect it's like exactly who you are and everything—"

Mags gives me a kick.

"Come on," he says. "I'll show you my room."

Mags and me follow him upstairs.

"So, what's this about a dress?" he asks over his shoulder.

"We found this ancient dress in the wardrobe in our room," I say.

"Wow," he says. "That's huge. I mean, for the docuseries and everything. That should be some good evidence."

"Yes," I say. "But we still need a ghost on film to secure the contract and get paid. And I looked through all our pictures and didn't see one single paranormal image in any of them."

"Mmm," he says, pushing open his bedroom door. "I've also been thinking about your theory of phony baloney."

"Yeah?" I ask.

"I was thinking . . . you may really be onto something."

"What do you know?" I ask him.

"Nothing," he says. "It's just a feeling."

But I'm not sure I believe him.

"Does that mean you'll help us investigate?" I ask. "We need to find a ghost ASAP. My dad's big break relies on it. Actually, everything does."

Nyx opens the door to his room and we all step inside. The walls are black and completely covered in posters.

"Sick!" Mags calls out. "I love lava lamps but my mom won't let me get one."

She flops down on his bed, watching the pink goo ooze up and back down again in slow motion inside the glass while Nyx fills his backpack.

"Who is this?" I point to the poster above his bed.

"Criss Angel," he tells me. "Another illusionist."

"Oh." I nod. "You actually kind of look like him, you know, with the hair and the skullcap and everything."

He smiles. "He's my second favorite after Harry. He's a modern-day illusionist."

"Look, Karma," Mags says. "I've solved the pink goo mystery. It's not Jell-O or ghost guts, it's lava goo from an in-between lava lamp." She laughs.

"Very funny," I say, squinting to read a news clipping taped to the wall.

It's something about Harry Houdini escaping from a milk can. Actually, every single inch of Nyx's walls is covered in a poster or a picture or news clippings about magic.

"It must have taken you forever to collect so much stuff," I say.

He shrugs. "Yeah, I'm hoping one day I can be a famous illusionist in Las Vegas just like Criss Angel." He zips his backpack and slings it over one shoulder. "Ready?" he asks, securing a black skullcap on his head.

"Wait," Mags says, looking up from the lamp. "First, can you please tell her that the pink goo in *Poltergeist* is not Jell-O."

"Tell her *what*?" Nyx asks.

"That the pink goo in *Poltergeist* isn't Jell-O," Mags says again.

"What Jell-O is pink?" Nyx asks.

"Exactly," Mags agrees.

"Jell-O mixed with Cool Whip," I say.

Nyx blinks at me.

"I don't think it's that much of a stretch to say the un-dead like Jell-O," I say. "I mean, who doesn't, right?"

Still blinking at me.

"It's not Jell-O," he says, heading out the door.

"Well, it's not ghost guts," I say, following after him. "Why don't you tell *her* it's not ghost guts."

"It's not ghost guts, either," he calls over his shoulder.

"Ha ha," I say to her. "You think you're so smart."

"So, what is it, then?" Mags asks.

He stops and turns to face us again.

"It's ectoplasm," he tells us.

"Ecto *what*?" Mags asks.

"Ecto*plasm*," he says again.

"Is that a flavor of Jell-O?" I ask.

"Not even close," he says. "It's supposed to be like the leftover energies of paranormal entities."

"Oh, right, like the energies that T. S. Phoenix measures with the Geiger counter," I say.

"Exactly."

Mags throws her arms up over her head in a V for victory. "Well, that's closer to guts than Jell-O, so I win," she announces.

"Wait . . . they didn't talk about ectoplasm in *Poltergeist,* and that's supposed to be the blueprint of all things haunted," I say. "So where did you get it from?"

He shrugs. "You know . . . *another* blueprint."

"Uh-huh, which *iiiiiiiis*?"

"The other blueprint of all things haunted."

I put my hands on my hips. "Yeah, I got that, but what *is* the other blueprint?" I demand.

He shrugs again. *"Ghostbusters."*

Dry Lips and
a Secret Recon Mission

That night Nyx waits for us in our hotel room for another covert mission while Mags and me eat Chef Raphaël's French croque monsieurs in the dining hall, like we're not up to anything fishy.

After dinner we race back up to the room with some leftover croque monsieurs wrapped in a napkin for Nyx. And if you ask me, *croque monsieurs* is just fancy talk for ham and cheese Hot Pockets, but I don't tell Chef Raphaël that. It might hurt his feelings if I told him his dinner reminded me of something that comes in a box from the frozen section of the Brooklyn Fare grocery store.

By ten-fifteen, me, Nyx and Mags are in a line of three, crouched along the windowsill of me and Mags's hotel room spying on the employee dorm.

I know I'm supposed to be focused on what's happening

outside the window, but all I can think about right this minute is that Nyx's arm is touching mine.

Mags talks all about butterflies in her stomach when Jack the busboy looks her way, but I don't feel light-winged flutters at all. Mine feel way less fluttery and way more like the feeling I got right before I threw up after riding the Cyclone at Coney Island.

But, you know . . . in a good way.

"This is your plan?" Mags asks. "We could have spied on them ourselves."

"Wait, there's more," Nyx says, grabbing his backpack. "Here."

Instead of his Rid o' Ghost Kit, this time Nyx brought his Phony Baloney Funny Business Recon Kit.

PHONY BALONEY FUNNY BUSINESS RECON KIT
Three pairs of Dora the Explorer binoculars

"*Seriously?*" Mags says, holding up her pair. "They're purple."

"They work just the same," Nyx tells her. "And they were the cheapest ones at Toy Mountain."

"Yeah," I say. "They work just the same."

"Still," Mags complains. "Dora is for babies."

"What do you expect? I make minimum wage."

"Yeah," I say. "What do you expect?"

Mags makes a kissy face at me when Nyx isn't looking and I give her a smack.

Then I turn to Nyx and say, "I think it's . . . you know, really nice of you to buy these for us and everything. Thanks for doing that. . . . I mean, Dora's pretty cool. Well, I watched her when I was little and everything, but not anymore. So, yeah . . . it's all good."

WHAT-IFS

Are you still *talking?*

"Anyway," I say. "I guess we better get to work."

He just nods and aims his Dora the Explorers out the window.

Then me and Mags do the same.

We watch and we wait.

Tonight there are three lighted rooms.

"The first one from the right is Ubbe Amblebee," I tell the others. "The second is Madame Drusilla, the third is Ms. Lettie and the fourth is Ruby Red."

"What is your gut feeling telling you?" Nyx asks me.

"My gut says Ruby Red is phony baloney," I say. "There is definitely something not right about her."

"What about Ubbe Amblebee and his stupid plunger?" Mags says.

"Yeah," I agree. "There's something not right there, either."

"And Mr. Lozano?" Mags says. "He's far too paranoid about those key cards."

"*Totally* paranoid," I agree.

"So, basically what you're saying is that the phony baloney you're talking about could be anyone or anything," Nyx says.

Me and Mags look at each other and nod in unison.

"But I feel like we are on the cusp of knowing . . . *something*," I tell him.

"Uh-huh," he says, turning the dial on top of his binoculars to focus on the employee quarters.

I do the same and so does Mags.

"Hey, look at Madame Drusilla!" I exclaim.

We watch as she stands in front of a vase of pink roses, talking and motioning with her hands like she's telling her precious flowers something very important.

"What is she doing?" Nyx asks.

"She's, ah . . . she's, ah . . . ," I start.

"Talking to her roses," Mags finishes.

"Oh, right. She asks their permission to be cut, right?" Nyx says.

I gasp. "How do you know everything?" I ask.

He just shrugs.

"Ubbe Amblebee is just watching television," I say. "Nothing big there except that I don't see his plunger, which is a first. Right?" I ask Mags.

"Definitely," she says, squinting into her lenses. "Oh, hey . . . he's watching an *Avengers*! I like this movie."

"Will you focus, please?" I say.

"But it's *Endgame*."

"What is Ms. Lettie doing?" I ask, watching her pace back and forth in front of her door.

"It looks like she's waiting for something," Nyx says. "Or someone."

"I really don't think there's anything phony baloney about Ms. Lettie. She's like a hundred years old," I say.

"Oh, hey . . . this is where Gamora beats down the Hulk and makes him cry," Mags laughs. "I like this part."

"I don't think we should rule Ms. Lettie out just yet," Nyx says. "At least until we know more."

I nod.

"Wait," Mags says. "I think someone's at her door."

"I'm telling you both, there's no way Ms. Lettie is involved in anything against the law," I say.

We watch her turn the knob, and the door opens.

Mags gasps. "It's Ruby Red," she says. "And she's got the suitcase."

"The one with the leather handle?" I ask, squinting through my Dora the Explorers.

"One and the same," she says. "I knew there was something up with her and her mile-high hair."

"What does her hair have to do with it?" I say.

"Everyone knows the higher your hair, the more you have to hide," Mags tells me.

"Where'd you get that?" I ask.

"It's a thing," she insists.

"I don't think it is," I say.

"Look!" Nyx says. "I think they're going to open it."

We watch as the women talk and Ruby Red places the black suitcase on top of the bed. She fishes a key from her pocket and slips it in the lock of the case.

It opens.

WHAT-IFS

I knew there were pinky toes
hidden somewhere in this hotel.

I close my eyes tight.

One. Two. Three. Four.

"I'm telling you now, if I see dead manager toes in there I'm going to hurl my croque monsieurs all over this viney carpet," I warn them both.

I feel Nyx lower his binoculars and turn to face me. "Dead manager *what*?"

"Don't ask," Mags tells him without taking her eyes off the window. "It's a whole *Dateline* thing."

"*Dateline*?" Nyx says. "You mean the television show? That's random."

"Not if you know her," Mags says.

"I don't get it," Nyx says.

"Karma, we can't even see anything, so you'd better just reel it in," Mags tells me.

I open my eyes and point a stern finger in her direction. "You better reel it out."

"Still not a saying," she tells me.

We all watch Ms. Lettie and Ruby Red standing over the suitcase, staring at the contents without saying a single solitary word before Ms. Lettie gives Ruby Red a nod and she closes it back up again. Ruby Red gives the key a twist to lock it back up tight, then slips the key into her pocket.

"Did either of you see anything?" I ask.

"Not me," Nyx says. "The case wasn't facing the window."

"Mags?" I say.

"Huh?"

"Did you see what was in the suitcase?"

"What? Oh, right, um . . . I was, ah . . . watching *Avengers*." I groan.

"You want to know what I think?" Nyx asks.

"Yeah," I say.

"I bet there is someplace in the hotel that will end up revealing a lot of clues about what's going on here."

"Like where?" I ask.

"Is there any place in the hotel that Mr. Lozano is especially sensitive about besides room 217?"

I think about it.

"He's weird about all the spaces equally, so . . . not one

particular place that is more so than any other," I say. "What do you think, Mags?"

"Huh?"

I sigh. "Never mind."

"Wait!" Nyx says. "Someone must have knocked, because Ms. Lettie is running back to the door."

All three of us focus on Ms. Lettie's door.

The knob turns.

The door opens.

And Mags sucks air until she actually chokes.

"Jack the busboy," I whisper. "I knew there was something off about that kid. At least he finally has a shirt on."

"Oh, like you're the end-all be-all of first impressions," Mags says. "Aren't you the one who thought Ms. Lettie was a purple-haired vampire on the first day?"

Nyx lowers his binoculars and looks at me and says, *"What?"*

"I eventually changed my mind," I say. "I mean, first impressions and everything. She's got a thing about being on film and all."

"Yeah, but she doesn't wear a cape," he says.

Mags throws her hands out. "Exactly what I said."

"Capes aren't standard issue for vampires anymore," I tell him.

"You wouldn't say that if you saw the *Dracula* show on Netflix," Mags says.

My head snaps in her direction.

"You *saw* it?"

She nods, her eyes wide.

"Worse than *Poltergeist*?"

She nods again.

"What's worse about it?"

She just twists her invisible key on her lips and throws it to the wind.

"I saw it," Nyx says. "It wasn't even scary. But she's right about the cape. He definitely still wears one."

"Huh," I say.

Mags sighs then with her chin in her hand and her elbow on the sill. "I can't believe my honey bunny is up to phony baloney," she says.

"That's probably the most sickeningly sweet thing I've ever heard in my lifetime," Nyx mumbles.

Official Research Findings

1. Vampire capes standard issue. Affirmative.

Not a member of the undead squad. ←

"Jack-of-all-trades indeed . . . even the phony baloney kind," I say while Mags keeps mumbling on about betrayals of the heart. "Here's the new plan," I tell her. "You need to do some secret intel to find out what's going on."

"Yep," Nyx agrees. "That's definitely the new plan."

"How do you suppose I do that?" she asks.

"He's *your* boyfriend," Nyx says. "Just get it from him."

"There's one problem with that," I tell him. "He still doesn't know about the relationship."

"How does that work?" Nyx asks.

"I was just getting around to telling him," Mags says. "And now I'll never realize my dream of kissing him in the walk-in cooler."

I roll my eyes. "Number one, that's disgusting, and number two, why are we even having this conversation? He's tainted. Bad news. Phony baloney. Why would you still want to kiss him?"

"The thing is, I've only been kissed that one time by Jeremy Kelly in the school gym during the winter dance, and there was nothing really spectacular about it."

Nyx groans.

"I mean, you know, everyone talks about fireworks going off and everything," Mags goes on.

I turn to look at Nyx and think about the pinky carpet shock and how good it felt.

"It was like all my fireworks were duds when his lips touched mine," Mags says. "And I guess it could've been because his lips were like chapped and all scratchy, but I think the kiss would have dudded out either way."

"Please," Nyx says. "I can't listen to any more of this."

"Raise your hand if you've heard the Jeremy Kelly's dry lips story a million times," I say with my hand in the air.

"Raise your hand if you didn't hear this before but still don't care to listen to another word of it," Nyx says with his arm high above his head.

"Don't act like you don't think about this stuff too," Mags tells him.

"I don't," he says to her. "And I can't believe I'm actually saying these words, but I wish we'd go back to the whole toilet-as-a-portal debate."

17

A Secret Tunnel and a Symbolic Canary

Nyx is dead-on.

And I mean *dead-on.*

Again.

He said there was something about the phony baloney that we had yet to discover and that there was probably some place in the hotel that Mr. Lozano was especially weird about.

And he was so right.

I find all this out the very next day while I'm minding my own business, sitting on the floor outside Madame Drusilla's office door, waiting for her to finish talking to her roses out back. I'm updating my ghost log with the very latest intel when I see Mr. Lozano skulk out from behind an unmarked door across the hall.

But not before he checks to see if the coast is clear. Looking left and then right.

But . . . *hello* . . . I'm sitting here, so when he sees me he jumps and barks at me. "What are you doing down here?"

"I—I'm just waiting for Madame Drusilla," I say.

He slams the door behind him and glares at me. Then he pulls an old-fashioned iron key from his pocket, locks the door, rattles the knob and slips the key back into his pocket again.

WHAT-IFS

I think you finally found your
missing manager body parts.

He turns back to me one more time, eyeing me suspiciously.

"You shouldn't go around sneaking up on people. It's rude," he barks again, giving the doorknob one more rattle before stomping down the hall and up the steps to the lobby without another word.

Once he's gone, I scramble over to the unmarked door and give the knob a good rattle myself.

Locked.

I wedge an ear against it and listen.

Quiet.

I peek under the crack at the bottom.

Dark.

"Mmm," I say to myself.

I've never noticed the door before. Probably because there is no sign on it like all the other doors in the hotel. Every door either has a room number on it or a gold engraved sign that says what's inside.

Except this one.

It doesn't even have a Scotch-taped sign on it like the one hanging on the dead elevator. And the whole no-sign thing totally tweaks my phony baloney radar.

"You're alone today, I see," Madame Drusilla says, coming up behind me.

"Oh," I say, getting up from the floor and brushing the dust off my palms. "Yeah. Mags is trying to find Jack the busboy."

"What are you doing there?" Madame Drusilla wants to know.

"Oh, uh, nothing," I tell her. "I have some more questions for you."

"Well, you are welcome to come on in," she says, unlocking her door and sending a waft of burnt strawberries in my direction.

I follow behind her.

"Madame Drusilla," I say, pinching my nose with one hand and pointing to the unmarked door with the other. "What's that door to?"

"Oh, that's just the underground tunnel system," she tells me, matter-of-fact.

My mouth falls open. "The *tunnel system*?" I say. "What does that even mean?"

She carefully places a bouquet of freshly cut roses into a vase of water.

"Back when the Stanley was built," she says, "they dug a tunnel system underneath the hotel for employees to go between the different buildings in the wintertime."

"Are you serious?" I ask.

"Quite."

"So, you're telling me there are tunnels beneath the entire hotel?" I ask.

"Indeed," she says. "All four buildings, in fact. They are carved out of the quartz rock that is the rock of the mountain the hotel sits upon. Some believe it is the quartz rock that causes the hotel to have the paranormal activity. Quartz can be very powerful indeed."

"So, the tunnels are *all* made of quartz rock? The same rock that enhances higher spiritual receptiveness?" I ask.

"That's right," she says. "But it's also where all the wiring, plumbing and electrical equipment is kept. It's very dark and crudely carved, with dirt floors and rock walls. Not finished and lovely like the rest of the hotel. So, definitely not for guests."

"Have you ever been inside there?"

"Of course," she tells me. "But it's not as stable as it used to be. It's been deemed strictly off-limits for safety purposes."

"Off-limits to *who*?" I ask.

She shrugs. "Everyone."

"Then why isn't there a *tunnel at your own risk* sign like with the elevator?" I ask.

"You'll have to ask Mr. Lozano that one," she says. "He's Keys and Signage."

"So, you're saying that is why the door is locked?" I eye her suspiciously. "For *safety*?"

She turns to look at me and then motions for me to come closer. When I do, she holds out her hand for mine.

"You will come across many locked doors in your life, my dear," she tells me, holding my hand tight. "You need to decide which of those doors hold the answers to your journey and not let them stop you in your quest to know."

I blink a few blinks at her and then finally say, "Know what?"

"Know what you need to know, when you need to know it."

I blink at her again.

"I don't have any more money," I tell her.

She smiles. "That one is on the house."

"Well, thanks, I guess, even though I'm not really sure what you mean."

"Oh!" she says with her finger in the air. "Do tell your friend Mags that her journey is blocked with thoughts of doubt and torment and I can help her to clear her channels for a *meeeeeere* . . . twenty-five dollars a session."

"That's a bargain," I say. "Because those channels are fogged up something awful."

She nods with a wise smile of agreement.

"I think her channels might actually take a *few* sessions," I warn her.

"Agreed," she says, putting her flower bouquet on the round table and examining it with her head tilted to the left and then right. "Are those straight?"

"Huh?" I say. "Oh, yeah, they look fine. So, would it cost the same for me? You know, to clear up my channels. And I think there's something wrong with my gut, too."

She laughs. "You don't need your channels cleared, my dear," she tells me. "You're already clear. You just need to learn to trust what you see and what you feel."

"But look at this." I hold out my hand to show her my ring. "Me and Mags got mood rings at Fun City and mine is always stinky brown. Brown means anxious and scared. Mags's ring has been bright blue since she slipped it on her finger, like she doesn't have a care in the world."

"That's because you are a sensitive and you haven't figured that out yet, my dear."

I point to my front and say, "Me?"

She nods.

"A sensitive? You mean, like you and Tally Phoenix?"

"Everyone has the capability. But only a few choose to learn how to tune in to it. You are tuning as we speak and trying to find what to do with your special energies. When you do, your ring will change color too."

"So . . . Mags has already tuned in?"

She laughs again. "That one doesn't even know where the tuner is."

I click my tongue. "It's her whole tortured-soul thing, right?" I say.

She bobs her head. *"Exactly."*

"I actually came here to ask you about the dress we found in our wardrobe," I tell her. "We think it's Mrs. Honeycutt's dress and she left it for us through her energies as a sign . . . you know, that she's here from the beyond. But I'm wondering if you can tell us if we're right. My Crystal Mystic seems to be . . . out of order."

She takes a deep breath in and closes her eyes.

I watch her breathing in and out and in and out for a long while until she opens up her eyes again while she talks to the ceiling.

"Thank you," she says under her breath. "Thank you, yes."

She focuses on me again. "Were there rose petals?" she asks.

My eyes go wide and I suck air. *"Yes,"* I breathe. "Dried rose petals. They were in the dining hall after Chef Raphaël's sighting, too."

She nods then and smiles. "You are getting closer to your abilities, Karma Moon Vallenari. I suspect you will come to your answer soon."

"So, it *was* Mrs. Honeycutt?" I ask. "Leaving us a clue?"

She just keeps smiling. "What does your gut tell you?" she asks.

I close my eyes and breathe in and out.

In and out.

Listening to the somethings all around me.

Gut: *I've still got nothing.*

When I open my eyes again, Madame Drusilla is still smiling at me.

"It *might be* her?" I say, raising my shoulders up and then letting them down.

"Your gut doesn't sound very sure about that," she tells me.

"Yeah, my gut doesn't have much to say that's worth listening to, except when it's hungry. Maybe you can just tell me what yours says. It's probably way more accurate."

"That's the easy road," she tells me. "Just keep listening."

"Listening for what?"

She places a flat palm on her heart and says, "Answers from deep inside you."

"But I already told you," I say. "My inside's got nothing."

"There are no nothings," she tells me. "Only somethings. Never judge it. Trust it."

★

On my way back up to get Mags in room 332, I stop in the lobby.

"Excuse me, Mr. Lozano?" I say, putting two palms on the front desk.

He folds the corner on the page of his book and sets it aside. Another Stephen King, but this one has an evil cat with red eyes on the cover.

"Yes?" he asks.

"Let's put our cards on the table, shall we?" I say.

He stares at me and says, "What table?"

Sly.

Clearly a stall maneuver.

"You know, this." I knock on the desk. "The desk. Let's put our cards on the desk, shall we?"

He looks at the desk and then back at me.

"It's an expression . . . you know, it's . . . never mind. So, what's the deal with the unmarked door downstairs? And don't try any tricks with me because I know all about it. Madame Drusilla told me. I think the fishiness you were talking about begins and ends right there."

He eyes me some more while he chews at the bottom of his bushy mustache and then finally says, "I have no idea what you are talking about."

"Don't you?" I ask.

"No," he says flatly.

"I know there's a secret tunnel, Mr. Lozano," I say. "How come Totally Rad and Lights Out! weren't told of this tunnel? Clearly it's a prime location to investigate and could be highly active, wouldn't you agree? It could very well be the most active spot in this whole place. It's day six and we still don't have a ghost on film."

He takes a breath and blows it out again. "I'm the

interim manager while the Jewels look for Mr. Plum's replacement," he explains. "It's my job to make sure the people in the hotel are safe. The tunnel is not a secret, it's just off-limits for safety reasons."

"Uh-huh, and yet no sign," I say. "You're Keys and Signage, everyone says so. How do you explain that, sir?"

He shrugs. "It's nobody's business," he tells me.

"And by nobody, you mean *us*?"

"It's nobody's business including your busy body and any other busybodies that don't belong down in that tunnel. And that's all there is to say about it."

He hides his nose back in his book while I stand there watching him. The evil feline on the cover is staring at me with its scary red eyes.

"You like haunted stories, huh?" I ask.

"Mmm . . ."

"Haunted stories," I say again. "Especially about *this* hotel."

Silence.

"I saw you reading *The Shining*," I tell him.

He folds the page he's reading and closes his book, setting it aside. "Stephen King wrote that book in this very hotel," he tells me. "They stayed here during a blizzard, he and his wife. The roads were closed and they couldn't get down the mountain. They were the only guests here. Just like you are now."

I swallow and watch him pick his book back up and start reading again.

"So, I guess I have another question, then," I tell him.

He sighs and looks at me over the top of the book.

"What about the movie *Poltergeist*?" I ask. "Have you seen that one?"

"Of course," he says.

"Do you think Tweety is the cause of the paranormal activity? Because it's the source of a raging controversy between me and Mags."

He folds the page again, leans in closer toward me. "The canary," he says, "is only one of the subliminal parallels of the undead entities hidden under the neighborhood of homes in the film."

I blink at him for a long while and then finally say, "Well, sure . . . yeah . . . everyone knows that one."

He rolls his eyes and picks up his book again. "I'm very busy here," he tells me.

"Reading?"

"It's research," he says.

"For what?" I ask.

Sigh. "Is there anything else?" he asks. "Because I'd like to get back to my book."

"Yeah," I tell him, putting my elbow on the counter and my cheek in my palm. "I've got something else."

"Yes?" he asks.

"I get the whole, you know . . . subliminals and everything you're going on about, because, you know . . . I'm in the film business and whatnot, but . . . did Tweety *start* it? I mean he's in three whole scenes. Four if you want to count the bulldozer digging up his cigar box coffin. Not to mention, all his scenes are in the beginning of the movie, which to me seems like it makes his character way more important. My writing teacher, Mr. Cavanaugh, says everything is in a story for a reason. I think a canary ghost haunting the family is a real possibility."

"No, Tweety didn't start it," Mr. Lozano says. "And yes, he's in the movie for a reason. The canary is symbolic."

I point a single-finger gun in his direction and wink. *"Riiiiight,"* I say. "I've got it now, Mr. Lozano."

"Good," he says, opening his book.

"Wait . . . a symbol of what?" I ask.

He closes his book.

"The afterlife continuing to rise to the surface," he tells me.

"Oh, right, right. Yeah, totally . . . I get that. I mean, that's what I thought you meant," I say. "But I was just double-checking."

He opens his book again and I head toward the grand staircase but turn around one more time.

"So, what about the pink goo subliminals?" I ask. "I'm going with Jell-O. Thoughts about that one?"

He sets his book down and this time takes off his glasses. "I know you're not asking my thoughts on Jell-O in the afterlife."

"It's a completely valid theory," I insist.

His eyebrows go up. *"Jell-O* is a valid theory?" he asks.

"Totally," I say. "I mean, Mags thinks the pink goo is ghost gut residue and Nyx thinks it's echo-something. But I still think Jell-O is a very valid theory and, you know, maybe symbolic and everything. Like with the bird. So? What do you think? Jell-O in the afterlife? Yea or nay?"

Messages from the In-Between

The door of room 332 slams behind me.

"You were supposed to meet me down in Madame Drusilla's office," I remind Mags, flopping down in the cracked leather chair next to the desk.

Hitchy finds a patch of sun on the viney carpet and closes his eyes.

Mags is propped against pillows on the bed thumbing at her phone.

"I was talking to Jack the busboy while he was washing the breakfast dishes," she tells me without even looking up.

"Did you get any intel about the suitcase?"

"I got zip," she says. "If he were my boyfriend, I *know* he'd tell me everything."

"Mags, the kid is tainted," I tell her.

"I know, but he's still cute."

"Your line definitely needs to be drawn at phony baloney," I tell her. "That's just basic line drawing 101."

She sighs. "I guess."

"Well, you missed it big-time," I tell her.

"Mmm," she says, still typing. "Missed what?"

"That sneaky Mr. Lozano," I tell her.

Still typing.

"You'll never guess in a million years what he's done now," I say.

"Well, if you're mad at Mr. Lozano it could be a number of things," she says.

"What do you mean?" I ask.

She sighs and looks at me over her phone. "Did he dis your spirit guide?" she asks.

"No."

"Order moo goo with brown rice?"

"No."

"Mispronounce the word *gyro*? Call your woo-woo flimflam? Pick you dead last for dodgeball?"

"Hey." I point a finger at her. "That one's not fair. You know there's a conspiracy against me in gym."

She goes back to typing.

"This one is really big," I tell her. "I mean huge. Like supreme big, really. It's like the hugest thing since we got here."

Her eyes meet mine and she throws her phone to the side. "Fine," she says. "What is it?"

"Remember what Nyx said about there being some real secret place here at the hotel?"

"Mmmm . . . no."

"Well, if you weren't so busy watching *Avengers*, you would have," I tell her.

"I told you it was *Endgame*, didn't I?"

"Guess what I found out," I say.

"What?"

"There's an actual . . . real live . . . secret underground tunnel system under this very hotel," I tell her.

"For real?"

"Totally real."

"No way," she says.

"Way. I mean, you know, 'secret' may be a judgment call," I go on, "but I think that's a matter of opinion considering we've been here six whole days and not a single person has mentioned it."

She sits up straight on the bed. "Did you see it yourself?" she asks.

"Not exactly," I say.

"Then how do you know?"

"I saw Mr. Lozano coming out of this unmarked door when I was down waiting for Madame Drusilla. I'm like, how did we not notice this door before, right? So, I watch him skulk out of it and lock it up tight and he flipped his gourd when he noticed me watching him. So, when

Madame Drusilla was finally done talking to her roses and I'm all like *what's that* and point to the door? Right? Then she just tells me straight-up . . . it's a tunnel."

"She actually *said* that?" Mags asks.

"Exact words."

"Why didn't they tell us about it?" Mags says.

"That's the question."

"Did you ask her?"

"I actually went right up to Arlo Lozano at the front desk and asked *him*."

She gasps. "Whoa, girl, that's so Velma."

"Nailed it, right?" I say.

"Totally," she agrees. "What did he say when you asked him that?"

"He said some stuff about it being unsafe to use anymore and that's why they keep it locked up. I guess there are all these tunnels under the hotel that the staff used to travel between the different buildings. Since some of the buildings have been closed and no one maintains the tunnels, it's risky to use them, just like with the elevator, except in this case it's more like tunnel at your own risk."

"That's bizarre," she says.

"And the tunnel is all quartz."

"Quartz?"

"The whole mountain is," I say.

"Isn't that the crystal that Madame Drusilla said enhances higher spiritual receptiveness?"

"Exactly," I say. "And when I asked Arlo Lozano if any of the other ghost hunters knew about it, he basically said no. I really think this is it. This is where all the answers can be found."

"Check with the expert." She nods toward Crystal Mystic sitting on the desk.

I grab it and give it a shake.

"Is this the place where we will learn once and for all what's so phony baloney in the Stanley Hotel?"

CRYSTAL MYSTIC
THAT IS DEAD-ON.

"I told you!" I exclaim.

"So, we're going to investigate the creepy crystal tunnel?" she asks me.

"Absolutely."

And it's right at this very moment that the ancient typewriter on the desk next to me starts clicking keys all by itself. Black round keys typing without any fingers pushing them down.

I jump up from my chair and scramble onto the bed next to Mags.

Hitchy jumps up from his sunny spot with a woof.

One key snaps and an arm reaches out to stamp a bold, black letter on a piece of paper wound into the machine.

Click.

Another letter.

Then another.

And another.

Mags grabs my arm. "What's happening?" she whispers.

"Grab your phone!" I tell her. "Get it on video! It's a message from the beyond!"

We both fumble with our phones, but mine falls on the floor.

After the final stamp of the keys, I turn to Mags. "Did you get it?"

"Yeah," she says. "I got it."

"I think it's done." I slip off the bed and take a step forward, stretching my neck to read the letters on the page.

Hitchy stretches his neck and takes a few big whiffs toward the ceiling.

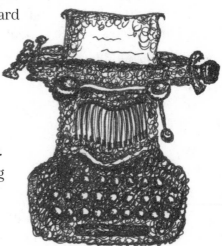

"What does it say?" she asks.

I suck air when I get close enough to see it.

Message: *Leave it alone.*

"Someone is listening to us," I whisper.

"Someone . . . or *something*," she whispers back.

That's when we both know exactly what we need to do, without even having to speak the words.

I make it to the door first, but Mags and Hitchy are right on my heels.

★

"I'm getting nothing," T. S. Phoenix says, running the Geiger counter back and forth over the desk.

It's a no-brainer, really.

When an ancient typewriter types out a message from the in-between right before your very eyes like magic, waking up the paranormal night shift is just plain smart ghost-hunting protocol.

"Nothing at all?" Dad asks, aiming his Nikon D5600 and taking a close-up of the ominous message.

We watch as Dad, who's still in his sweatpants and white T-shirt, and T. S. Phoenix, with another bad case of bedhead, conduct an official investigation at the scene of the disturbance.

Room 332, *our* room.

"The keys just started typing on their own?" Big John asks. "Just like that?"

"That's right," I say.

"All by themselves," Mags adds. "I took video of it too."

"That should make Netflix happy," I tell Dad. "Typewriter keys typing all by themselves?"

"It's good," Dad agrees. "But just like with the piano keys, we still need an image or an orb or something."

I sigh.

T. S. Phoenix continues to float his machine over the desk while Tally is busy being sensitive in the cracked leather armchair with her eyes closed and her palms up.

"What were you talking about at the time of the event?" T. S. Phoenix asks. "What does *leave it alone* refer to? The needle isn't even budging."

"That's the biggest news of all," I tell them. "I found out there's a secret tunnel that runs under the hotel and links all the different buildings together."

Both Dad and T. S. Phoenix stop what they're doing and stare at me. Even Tally opens her eyes.

"Did you say *tunnel*?" The Faz asks.

"That's right," I say, and then rattle off all the details.

Dad looks at T. S. Phoenix. "No one mentioned a tunnel to you?" he asks.

T. S. Phoenix shakes his head. "I think I'd remember something like that." He motions toward the wardrobe. "And this dress? It just appeared here?"

"One day it wasn't here and the next it was," Mags says.

He runs his Geiger counter up and down the wardrobe doors.

"I'm not getting anything here, either," he says. "What about you, Tall?" he calls to Tally. "What do you think about the dress?"

We watch as she slips off the chair and steps toward the wardrobe. She opens the doors, closes her eyes and lets her fingers gently touch the brittle threads of the sleeve.

She closes her eyes again. "I'm seeing more letters," she says. "It's a name. Definitely a name . . . whoever owned this dress. *C . . . l . . .* and an *e*," she says. "It's Cecil . . . no . . . CeCe . . . Clee . . . it's *Cecelia*. It's definitely Cecelia. Yes, and there is a great sadness about her. She has been looking for someone for a very long time and cannot find where they have gone. And . . . I see roses, too."

"Yes!" I exclaim. "There were five rose petals, just like in the dining hall. But what about Mrs. Honeycutt?" I ask. "Her name is Seraphina, not Cecelia. Are you sure you're getting all the letters?"

We wait and watch as Tally's eyeballs flicker underneath her lids, right and left, right and left. Then she opens them again and sighs. "Yeah, I'm just not seeing Seraphina's image . . . it's another woman altogether," she finally says. "A woman with dark hair. But again . . . roses."

"Ms. Lettie told me Mrs. Honeycutt was blond," I say, turning to Mags.

Mags shrugs. "Another mystery," she says. "Just like the dag gum hooligans."

"Oh, right," I say. "Nyx says that in the early 1900s the kids all stayed on the fourth floor while their parents stayed on the lower floors. So I guess it's possible they could be spirits of the children who stayed here at the time and not just local kids causing trouble."

"That's a possibility," T. S. Phoenix says, sitting down on the edge of the desk. "First, tell me more about this tunnel system."

I nod. "Madame Drusilla says the hotel sits on quartz rock, which is what the mountain is made of, and so the tunnel walls are made of that too."

"Mmm," T. S. Phoenix says. "That's a common misconception."

"What is?" Dad asks.

"That the stone on which the Stanley Hotel is built, which is mainly quartz and magnetite, is the main reason for the paranormal activity," T. S. Phoenix says. "But the entire Rocky Mountain area is made up of the same mineralogical content. Which means that the hotel is no different than the Shell station in town. There has to be another reason."

"Madame Drusilla said quartz is powerful enough to enhance higher spiritual receptiveness," I say. "She used quartz and other crystals to zhoosh up our tarot card reading."

"Quartz is known for its power for many things, including receptiveness to spiritual energies," Tally tells us, still grasping the sleeve of the dress like she's holding the hand of Mrs. Honeycutt to reassure her that we're here to help her. "It clears the mind and also works as a magnifier for the powers of all other crystals when used together, adding to their effectiveness."

I point to the satchel around my neck. "I could totally feel my bravery crystals were working extra hard the minute I got here," I say.

She nods.

"But I agree with T.S., it has to be more than that, because all of Estes Park is sitting on the same mountain and the Stanley Hotel is the only highly active spot in the area," she says.

"Definitely," T.S. agrees. "So, why is this place susceptible to residual hauntings more than any other place in the Rocky Mountain National Park?"

"Dr. Phoenix," I ask. "What's a *residual* haunting?"

"That's when the haunting has to do with reenacting a memory in a specific place, such as what is thought to be happening with Mr. and Mrs. Honeycutt," he says. "They are not here to interact, they are here to replay the events of the time, maybe hoping for an alternate outcome."

"But what about the typewriter message?" Mags asks.

He nods. "Then there's intellectual haunting, which is when a spirit is aware of us and is attempting to make contact on this plane of existence."

My mouth goes dry. "I don't know if I really want to know the answer to this question," I say. "But are there any other kinds of hauntings?"

He nods. "Evil spirits," he says.

I look at Mags and mumble, "I knew I didn't want to know the answer to that."

"Then why'd you ask?" she says.

I shrug.

"Evil spirits can appear like a poltergeist . . . at first . . . but their primary goal is to use their energies to cause destruction to something or *someone.*"

That can't be good for my what-ifs.

No one says anything for a real long time.

"First things first," T. S. Phoenix finally says. "We have to gain access to that tunnel." ·

"Agreed," Dad says.

"Tally?" T. S. Phoenix asks.

She nods. "Absolutely."

"After dinner tonight," T.S. goes on. "We'll call an all-staff meeting in the dining hall and get to the bottom of why the information about this tunnel has been withheld until now."

"But what if Mr. Lozano flat-out refuses?" I ask. "Like he did with room 217."

"Well . . . I guess if he's insistent . . . there's nothing we can do," T.S. says, packing his Geiger counter into a black leather bag.

Big John locks eyes with me, giving me one single nod, and I know exactly what needs to happen.

"For now," Dad says, "we need to get some sleep or we won't be good for anything tonight, and we've got some *very important* work to do."

After everyone leaves, I turn to Mags.

"Don't say it," she says. "Don't even think it."

"Too late," I tell her. "You know what we need to do."

"No I don't," she says.

"Part two of our covert operation, where only one party is in the know," I say. "Come on, we have work to do."

"Didn't you hear Dr. Phoenix?" she asks. "Evil spirits? No way I'm going in that tunnel now."

"No way?" I ask.

"No way, nohow." She folds her arms across her chest and sticks her chin in the air like a big fat exclamation point.

"Even if it means my dad doesn't get a ghost on film?"

She shrugs, her chin still in the air.

"He can do more bat mitzvahs," she says.

"Even if it means you're mucking up your own karma by not heeding the signs that the woo-woo is pointing us in this direction?"

Chin still in the air.

"I don't heed," she says.

"Even if it means I will have to move out of apartment 4B and leave Immaculate Heart of Mary K–8, leaving you to fend for yourself through the rest of your middle school years . . . *alone*?"

Silence.

She's still standing there, her chin still high. Then her

foot starts tapping on the viney carpet and she finally lets all the air out of her lungs in an exasperated sigh, throwing her hands out.

"Fine, okay?" she says. "But if my soul becomes possessed by a demonic spirit posing as a noisy shenanigans ghost and Father O'Leary has to perform an actual exorcism on me, it's going to be all your fault."

"Deal," I say.

We seal it with our fist bump, fanned fingers and a shimmy-shimmy to the floor.

A Secret Tunnel and a Warning

Since there is only one key to the tunnel door that I know of and that key is stuffed inside the pocket of Mr. Lozano's pants, Mags and me have to figure out another way to get in.

It's Mags's idea to use a bobby pin.

It may not be very James Bond 007, but it's better than nothing.

"Hurry up!" I whisper that same afternoon. "If we get caught this time it's over. Done. *Finito.* We'll surely be jailed in our rooms for the final four days."

"Don't rush me," she whispers back. "This is my first official breaking and entering. Father O'Leary is going to ban us from Immaculate Heart of Mary K–8 for good after this one for sure."

She stops wiggling the bobby pin and turns to look at me.

"I think this one . . . we keep to ourselves," she says.

I think about that. "Deal," I say. "Now hurry it up."

"Don't rush me."

She wiggles and wiggles and wiggles some more and still nothing happens. Then, just when I'm ready to give up the whole operation, we hear it.

Click.

I gasp. "Was that it?" I ask. "Did you get it?"

She grins big at me. "I got it."

"That was James Bond 007 *girl-style,*" I tell her.

"Girl-style," she agrees, and then we seal it with our fist bump, fanned fingers and a shimmy-shimmy to the floor.

"Here we go," I say, reaching out and turning the knob.

It creaks in protest.

I peek through the crack with Mags's cheek wedged against mine.

"It's pitch black in there," she says. "And it smells."

"Like what?" I say.

WHAT-IFS

Dead managers with a hint of pinky toe.

"Mold." She sneezes. "And a-hundred-year-old dust."

"Shh," I hiss.

"I can't help if I'm allergic to ancient dust," Mags says, rubbing her nose.

"Feel around the corner to see if there's a light switch," I tell her.

"*You* feel around the corner," she says.

"*I* felt the dress," I inform her. "It's your turn to feel something."

"You're the one who wants to be Velma Dinkley, not me."

"Don't be a baby," I tell her.

She blows a blast of air out of her mouth. "Fine," she says.

I pull the door open wider, allowing the light from the hall to shine in, while Mags sticks her hand inside, feeling for a light switch on the wall beyond the door.

"I don't feel anything."

"I'm not going in there with it pitch dark like that," I tell her.

"I know," she says, pulling out her phone. "Let's use the flashlights on our phones. Take yours out too so we'll have both the lights to shine in there."

We get out our phone flashlights and shine them toward the blackness and peer inside once again.

"There." I point. "A light switch. Right there."

Mags reaches in and flips the switch up.

One tiny dim bulb lights a small circle on the dirt floor just below it.

"That's a why-bother bulb if I've ever seen one," I say.

"Why-bother bulb big-time," she agrees.

I shine my phone light as far as it will reach inside the door.

There is one small tunnel leading to another heavy wooden door at the very end of it. And another tunnel connected at the center of the small tunnel like a T. That tunnel looks like it leads deep into the underbelly of the hotel.

"I smell something else," I say.

"One guess. We're standing next to Madame Drusilla's office," Mags mumbles. "It's probably singed strawberry residue."

"No . . ." I sniff again. "It's not strawberries. It's . . . like . . ."

Sniff.

Sniff.

Sniff.

"Like . . ." I gasp. *"Fancy perfume."*

That's when Mags takes two giant steps backward.

"I changed my mind," she tells me, shaking her head back and forth. "I'm not doing it."

I grab her hand and pull her forward.

"You have to," I tell her. "I need my best friend."

She blows more air out.

"What if I do your algebra homework for a whole month?" she asks.

Tempting.

I shake my head. "Nope."

"Okay, okay, how about I let you put my furry beanbag chair in your room for the rest of the school year?"

I just cross my arms this time and I don't say a single word.

She thinks harder.

"Okay, here it is," she says. "I will *give* you my glitter phone case. Just give it to you. No backsies."

"Mags," I say. "I'm calling true blue here. There is nothing that can take the place of that."

"Not even a glitter phone case?"

"Nope."

"*And* my Joe Jonas poster?"

I shake my head. "You know I like Nick better."

"Fine," she grumbles.

"I'll go first," I tell her. "But just make sure you have your camera ready. And even if you can't see anything with your eyes, it doesn't mean the camera lens won't pick up an image or even an orb of light. So just keep snapping. We need a ghost on film. And we need it today."

She takes a breath. "Fine," she says.

"Just keep clicking," I say. "Whatever happens . . . click like you've never clicked before."

"I got it, I got it," she says. "Just go, I'll be right behind you."

I take one step inside and then another, aiming the light from my phone out in front of me.

I breathe.

Then tap.

One. Two. Three. Four.

Behind me, I hear Mags clicking photos on her phone.

My foot slides forward.

One and then the other.

There are no walls, just cavernous rock where walls should be and a dirt floor beneath our feet. There are low beams lining the ceiling above us, interwoven with wires and pipes. As we step in deeper, it's cold and dark and damp and mad creepy.

"What's that?" I shine a light in the direction of a large square object next to the door near the end of tunnel number one.

"It looks like a safe," she says, aiming her phone and taking another picture. "It's massive. What does a hotel need a safe that big for? Especially a hotel with no guests," she adds.

I take a step closer to the safe and then pull on the handle.

"It's locked."

"Umm . . . it's a safe?" she says. "That's its whole job, to be locked."

"Do all businesses have safes that big?" I ask. "I mean, is that a thing?"

"I think it's a thing," she says.

"Totally Rad Productions doesn't have a safe like this," I tell her.

"What would Totally Rad Productions need a safe for?"

I think about the empty rent envelope in the kitchen drawer. "Good point."

We move past the second tunnel as we head toward the heavy wooden door at the end of the first one.

"That tunnel looks like it goes on forever." I point a thumb at it as we go by.

She nods. "Just so you know, there's no way I'm going in there. No way, nohow."

I slide my feet one by one across the dirt floor toward the second door. I can hear Mags's feet dragging behind mine. There is a dim light shining from beneath the door when we finally reach it. I wedge my ear against the wood and listen.

Silence.

I try the knob.

Locked.

"I'm going to get on the ground and peek underneath," I tell her. "Hold my phone and shine the light."

Mags takes my phone now too and shines the light toward the floor. When my cheek touches the dirt floor, I squint through the crack.

"What do you see?" she whispers.

"Um . . . there are piles of clothes . . . a sleeping bag . . . a candlestick from the dining hall . . . onion Funyun wrappers and . . . what is *that*? I can't see—"

That's when the door where we entered the tunnel slams shut.

Mags lets out a scream and I scramble to my feet.

Although it's only a short distance, I run at full speed with Mags on my heels. It feels like it's miles and the door is getting farther and farther away.

When I make it to the door, I rattle the knob.

It doesn't budge.

We're trapped.

My heart is beating so hard, I can feel it pounding in every inch of me. My mouth goes dry and I can feel the sweats starting.

It's a full-on panic attack.

I know because I've had two before this.

Once the day after Mom left us and once in school when we had our first active-shooter drill. And both times, this is exactly how it started, and both times, I thought it was the end of everything. At least that's what my what-ifs told me.

WHAT-IFS

This time is the end for sure.

Bang. Bang. Bang.

I pound on the door with my fists as hard as I can, not even caring one whit if we get in trouble with Mr. Lozano or anyone else, either.

Bang.Bang.Bang.

"Let us out! Let us out!" I shout through the thick wooden door.

Mags is banging now too. Maybe she's having a panic attack of her own.

I try to remember what Nyx said about wolf fear and how most things you worry about don't happen anyway. But this *is* happening and it's happening right this second.

My what-ifs are out of control.

WHAT-IFS

The undead are here to snatch me to
the television fuzz.

WHAT-IFS

Evil phantasms and a living hotel
will be the end of us all.

WHAT-IFS

Bloody Mary is here to extract my soul.

Bangbangbang.

"Let us out!" I shout through the door.

"Hello!" Mags hollers. "We're in here! Hello!"

"I can't breathe." I huff air out of my lungs and back in again. "I can't breathe!"

"But that's all you're doing," she tells me.

That's when the door lock clicks again, the knob turns

and Mags and I fall into the hallway next to Madame Drusilla's office.

"Oh . . . well," says Ruby Red in her gray-and-white uniform with her squeaky-wheeled cart. "Sorry, I thought someone had accidentally left the door open."

"You almost locked us in," I huff out, bending at the waist and trying to catch my breath.

She shrugs, places her hands on the cart and gives it a shove with her hip to get it going.

"I'm sure someone would have found you . . . eventually," she calls over her shoulder. "And you should know that the use of the tunnels under the Stanley Hotel is strictly prohibited."

"Yeah, well . . . maybe you should hang a sign on it saying so," I call after her.

"Mr. Lozano is Keys and Signage" is all she says.

We watch her as she leaves.

"Oh, man," Mags whispers to me, still on her hands and knees on the floor. "I thought we were goners for sure. I mean, really and truly."

"Yeah," I say. "Me too."

"Lucky she heard us," she says.

"It was more than luck," I say, wiping the sweat off my forehead without once taking my eyes off Ruby Red as she stops to dust a marble head statue of Mr. Jewel.

"What do you mean?" Mags whispers. "You don't think it was an accident?"

"No way," I say. "*That* . . . was no accident."

"Then what was it?"

I watch Ruby Red glance back at us one more time, slip her duster back on the cart and give it another shove with her hip.

"That," I whisper, "was a warning."

True Blue

After our tunnel excursion, I stayed up most of the night to draw a map of the whole thing to show to Nyx. At least until my eyelids wouldn't stay open one second longer.

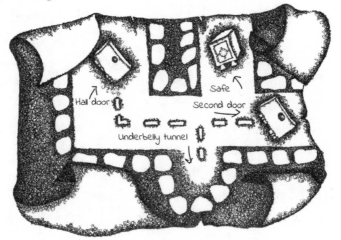

It's day seven.

And even after braving the tunnel of the eternally life-less and going through every single picture on Mags's phone, we haven't found one solitary disembodied soul, orb of light *or* even a severed pinky toe.

How could the fortune cookie have gotten it so wrong?

Its whole purpose is to get the fortunes right.

But when I briefed Dad and the others at breakfast about the tunnel, they agreed there was a definite pos-sibility that it was the most highly active spot in the hotel.

"Karma," Dad said when he heard about our bobby pin 007 maneuver. "We need to get permission."

"We didn't have time for that," I protested. "And today is day seven."

"We have to follow the rules while we're here," he told me.

But following the rules hasn't gotten them anywhere. Last night they were stuck filming in the dining hall hop-ing to spot the ghost Chef Raphaël had seen, and that's only because Mr. Lozano still refuses to give them the key to the tunnel.

By lunchtime, I can barely stay awake.

"Karma!" Mags shouts.

I lift my head up from the dining hall table.

"Huh?"

"You have Chef Raphaël's special *pommes frites* sauce in your hair," she tells me, taking another bite of *frite*.

I yawn and hold my chin up with my palm.

"You can't just *not* sleep," she says. "It had to catch up to you at some point, and I think we're here."

My head is hurting.

My body is aching.

My stomach is churning.

WHAT-IFS

Feels fatal to me.

I wonder if anyone has ever died from not enough sleep. I might be the first.

My eyelids weigh a thousand pounds each. The thing is, when I put on Mom's Journey T-shirt and slip under the velvet covers, the jumping beans won't let me shut my eyelids for more than a few minutes at a time.

"Go upstairs and see if you can sleep awhile," Mags tells me. "I'll wake you up in an hour and we can start again. You look horrible."

I nod and drag my worn-out body from my chair and up the grand staircase. I can hear trampling footsteps on the floor above me.

Alfred Hitchcock woofs.

"Dag gum hooligans," I tell him. "They're going to keep us up."

He gives me another woof to tell me he agrees with me.

When I make it to room 332, I put my hand on the doorknob, but something stops me.

It's Dad's voice.

It's loud and booming, but not the jovial kind of booming like when he's talking to clients on the old-fashioned dial phone in the kitchen of apartment 4B. This time he sounds . . . mad.

I stand there and gnaw on my bottom lip.

I don't even want to know what Big John and The Faz have to say on day seven with no ghost on film. It'll just get me to counting ceiling tiles again.

"Hitchy," I say. "Eavesdropping is wrong."

He tilts his head to the side and stares at me.

"But you still think I should do it?" I ask him.

He tilts his head to the other side and keeps on staring.

"I mean, if you think I should do it anyway . . . then I will, but you need to give me a sign so I'll know for sure."

He gags up a couple of *frites* onto the viney carpet and then re-eats them.

"That's a sign if I've ever seen one," I say. "But it's your fault if I get in trouble, okay?"

He just licks the carpet.

I tiptoe toward Dad's door and wedge my ear up against it.

He's still yelling.

He's not just mad, he's real mad. I know that for sure because I hear words that I don't usually hear Dad say. The thing is, this time it's not Big John or The Faz that I hear on the speakerphone.

It's Mom.

Dad: How can you do this, Lara?

Mom: I had to follow my dreams, why can't you just be happy for me? Your energy is very negative right now.

Dad: *My* energy? *My* energy? What about *your* energy? This is your daughter. If you don't come home for me, come back for her. What do the signs say about that? What could the signs possibly say that make it okay to leave your daughter?

Silence.

Mom: They say it's my turn.

Dad: That sure is convenient.

Mom: They say that I took care of her for eleven years and now it's *your* turn.

Dad: I'm following my dreams too, you know? *Me.* It's just so easy for you to walk away and leave me with everything. The bills. The responsibilities . . . *Karma.*

When I hear my name, I pull my head away from the door and run toward room 332. My hands are shaking and I drop my key card three times before I get the small green light and push the door open. Tears well at the rims of my eyes and my what-ifs are shouting at me at top volume.

WHAT-IFS

He wants to leave you too.

I feel like a balloon that's lost its knot and is leaking air, blowing and darting around out of control. Inside the room, I grab my phone out of my pocket and delete every single solitary picture of Mom. I've always hated looking at my photo album anyway. There was an obvious line, a before and after, and I hated having to see it all the time—but I couldn't stop looking. The pictures before the five suitcases and the ones that came after. I delete them all. Even the befores. The ones where I thought we were happy. The ones when I thought everything was okay. The ones where I had no idea that moms could leave.

The tears start down my face, and that sadness, the one that makes you feel like you're drowning and will never make it to the top again, hits me.

Delete.

Delete.

Delete.

After all the pictures are gone, I pick up the stupid Crystal Mystic, and it spouts an answer to a question I didn't even ask.

CRYSTAL MYSTIC

YOUR SPIRIT GUIDES ARE ON A LUNCH BREAK. TRY AGAIN LATER.

"Hunk of junk!" I shout, and hurl it at the door of the room.

Alfred Hitchcock woofs whole-body barks at the ceiling.

Then the door opens and Mags is standing in the doorway looking at me.

"What's going on in here?" she asks me.

"What's going on?" I holler back at her. "My mom isn't coming back and my dad doesn't want me. How about that?"

My jumping beans are using my insides as a trampoline, my brain is racing, my heart is pounding and air is rushing inside my lungs and out again.

It feels like I'm running a relay and I can't catch my breath.

Air rushes.

Jumping beans hop.

My head spins.

My heart drums.

"What's the matter with you?" Mags asks me.

"I—I can't . . . catch . . . my breath," I say.

"Well, sit down or something," she says. "I mean, just stop it."

That's when my stomach starts to roll like thunder and the explosion I've been stuffing down is coming and I can't stop it. I run past Mags and jump over Alfred Hitchcock, making it to the toilet just in time to throw up all of Chef Raphaël's *pommes frites* and his special sauce.

I gag again and more *frites* come out of me.

Mags is on the floor with me, her hand on my back.

Because that's how it is with true blue.

When I don't have any *pommes frites* left to hurl, Mags reaches up and flushes while I lay my cheek on the cool porcelain seat. I don't even care that it's gross or that Bloody Mary might reach out from that little hole in the bottom of the toilet and snatch me to the in-between, right this minute. It feels good on my hot cheek.

"Come on." Mags pulls on my arm. "Get into bed."

I feel like the Raggedy Ann rag doll I got at a stoop sale in first grade, with nothing to hold me upright.

Mags pulls the covers down. "Get in and sleep already," she tells me. "You can't just not sleep."

I burst into tears and throw myself face-first on the pillows and cry the painful heaving cries that come out from the depths of you. The kind that feel like they'll never stop. The kind that take your breath and all your strength, too.

"News flash!" I shout into the pillows. "My dad hates me and doesn't want me either."

"Where did you get that?"

I turn my head to face her. "I can read between the lines."

"What lines?" Mags asks.

"I overheard him talking on the phone in his room," I tell her. "Mom isn't coming home and he doesn't want me either and Netflix isn't getting their ghost and it's all because of me. Why can't I just be normal like everyone else? Then no one would leave me."

Mags sits down next to me on the bed and puts a hand on my arm and says, "I would die a thousand deaths if you weren't you. You're my best friend. I wouldn't want you to be anyone else."

"Everyone hates me," I sob.

"That's not true."

"Darby Woods hates me."

"Yeah, well, Darby Woods hates everybody."

I sit up and wipe my face with my sleeve. "Why can't I just be normal?" I ask her.

"What's normal?"

"Everyone else but me," I say.

"That's ridiculous," she says. "Maybe you're a little different—but that's what I like about you. You're like no one else I know—and there's nothing wrong with that."

"Still," I say. "Where am I going to live now?"

"I really think you're wrong about your dad," she says. "But if you really had no place to live, you'd come live with us. My mom likes you better than me anyway."

I snort a laugh and so does Mags.

"That's not true," I say. "She calls you all the time and baked you cookies because she missed you so much."

"First off, she always asks how you are too, and second, half the cookies were for you."

"The Made-with-Love Cookies?"

She nods. "I just didn't tell you so because I didn't want you to hog them all, but you did anyway, so . . ."

I laugh again.

"That's the thing," she tells me. "You're already part of the family. You'll never not have a family. No matter what. She already canceled our trip to Ohio for Thanksgiving this year so we can have all you guys over. Big John and Gloria and The Faz and The Fazette, too."

"She did that?"

Mags nods.

"What if I do something that makes you want to leave me too?" I ask her.

"Like what?"

I shrug. "I don't know."

"That would never happen in a million years," she tells me. "I'm here playing superspy with you, aren't I? Chasing ghosts? Only true blue does that. And I've never told you this before, but everyone knows that your mom leaving has nothing to do with you and everything to do with her. *Real* moms don't leave. And that's the truth of it."

"Really?"

"Totally."

There's a knock on the door and Mags gets up from the bed.

"But what about my dad?" I call after her.

"All I can say about that," she tells me over her shoulder, "is that you must have heard it wrong."

The lock clicks and she pulls the door open.

It's Dad.

"What's going on in here?" he asks. "I heard crying."

First there's whispering and then he comes over to the bed while Mags slips out the door.

"What's going on, Snooks?" he asks.

"What do *you* care?" I demand.

"Of course I care," he says. "What do you mean? Why are you crying?"

I sit up and fold my arms over my chest and give him a good glare. "I heard you."

His eyebrows crinkle. "Heard what?"

"The phone call with Mom," I tell him, standing up. "I heard it all. And I know she doesn't want me and neither do you. But just so you know, Mags does. That's how it works with true blue, so here's the new plan: I'm moving in with the Bogdonaviches the second we get back to the Village." I turn on my heel and head toward the door. "At least *they* want me."

He grabs my arms and pulls me close, his nose almost touching mine.

"Don't ever say that again," he tells me. "You are everything to me. Yes, I was devastated your mom decided to leave, but you want to know what I would have been if she took you with her?"

"What?"

"There isn't a word," he tells me. "You are my whole entire heart and will always be. We are a team, you and me. There is no one I'd rather have with me than you. Everything I do is for us. All that I want to accomplish is for us. And that's the way I want it. So please don't ever say that again. It's not true and it never will be. You want to know what true blue is? This," he says, his voice cracking. "Us. We are true blue. We are family and that's *forever.*"

Tears bubbling up at the rims of my eyes burst over and line my cheeks with two thick wet stripes. Mags and Dad are the only ones who've ever been able to catch me when I'm a bursting balloon. But Dad is the only one who can fill me back up with air again.

"Swear?" I say.

"I swear it," he tells me. "I wish I could say Mom's coming back . . . but she's not and I can't change that." He clears his throat again. "I know you don't understand it . . . but I'm afraid neither do I."

More tears fall.

Him too.

"I know she's not," I tell him. "I've always known."

He nods.

"Five suitcases," I say.

He nods again.

"But I was always just too scared to ask the question," I say. "Too scared to hear the answer."

He blows air out of his mouth. "Yeah, me too," he says. "But we know it now and we're going to be okay. You and me. We are going to get through it together just fine. Don't you worry about that."

"We are?"

"Absolutely," he says, giving me a squeeze.

"Promise?" I say, snuggling in under his chin.

"I promise."

It feels good to have Dad's arms around me like this. Even if grumpy Mr. Drago is demanding his money and Dad's Netflix big break wasn't what the fortune cookie said it was, somehow he'll make everything okay. He'll fill our balloon with air again. He always has and he always will.

"But aren't we in trouble?" I ask.

"It'll be fine," he whispers into my hair. "I'll pick up some more wedding and bat mitzvah gigs to make the rent and all will be fine. We always are. So it wasn't my big break. Something will come our way eventually."

"Dad?" I say.

"Yeah?"

I pull away from him and my eyes meet his. "I'm actually kind of glad we're not moving to Connecticut or Jersey or wherever."

"You are?" he asks.

"Uh-huh."

"And why's that?"

"It's not us," I tell him. "We're creatures of habit. We don't change. We're the West Village through and through and always will be. I love it there. I love everything about it. Even the bad things."

"Like what?" he asks.

"The old-fashioned dial phone," I say. "For one."

He laughs.

"The linoleum coming up in the corners of the kitchen," I say.

He laughs again.

"And the fact that the windows don't open on rainy days," I say.

"You know what I love about the West Village?" he asks.

"What?"

"The moo goo at the Noodle King of New York City."

"Definitely," I agree. "And the Carmine Street Pool too."

"The kitchen folding table that no one ever sits at," he says. "And the dishwasher that's always broken."

"Grumpy Mr. Drago drinking coffee in nothing but his ratty old bathrobe on the front stoop in the morning," I say. "And trips to Books of Wonder bookstore."

And then at the very same time we say, "Toby's!"

Because that's how it is with true blue, and me and Dad are true blue to the end. I know it now for sure, and so do my what-ifs.

With or without a ghost or a strip of grass.

"Ah . . . Toby's," he says, nodding. "There's no place like Toby's."

"I love Chef Raphaël's cooking, but I can't wait for an Egg on a Roll and a hot Apple Betty."

"The first morning we're home," he says, holding out his fist for me to bump. "It's a date, okay?"

I bump it and nod.

"See? I wouldn't want to move," I tell him. "Not for a

barbecue, not for anything. I like our life, even if it's a more simple kind of life. It's ours and I don't want it to change."

He wraps his arms around me again. "Thank you," he says.

"For what?" I ask.

His eyes meet mine again and he bends down so we're nose to nose. "For letting me be exactly who I am and for being who you are and who you are meant to be," he tells me. "Even when things don't always go the way we want them to. The whole thing about life is . . . it's a gift that we are always unwrapping. Who wants to know what's inside the gift before you've opened the box?"

"Dad," I say.

"Yeah."

"Tell me again why you call me Snooks."

He smiles. "When you were born, I remember holding you for the very first time," he starts, his eyes filling with tears again. "You were the sweetest thing I'd ever seen. I didn't know if you were as sweet as the frostiest snow cone in the middle of the hottest summer or hot baked cookies straight from the oven. So I called you Snookie, a combination of both." He wraps his arms around me again.

"I'll never get tired of hearing that story," I say into his shoulder.

He squeezes me even tighter and says, "And I'll never get tired of telling it."

The Eyes Have It

I t's day eight and we've got squat as far as a ghost on film goes.

And we leave in two days.

That being said, we're fairly doomed as far as the Netflix contract is concerned.

But here we are.

Dad assures me that Big John and The Faz have some new weddings and bat mitzvahs on the calendar and grumpy Mr. Drago has given us an extension on the rent, so we're going to be okay.

That puts my what-ifs at ease.

For now.

And my jumping beans even let me sleep all night last night, which makes my whole body feel a lot better today.

At breakfast Dad decides that me and Mags should take another mental health day after a tough eight days at the Stanley Hotel. He even gives us extra money to spend the day in town.

We call Nyx and he meets me and Mags at Inkwell & Brew, the coffee shop where his sister works. It has this supercool loft that has long shag carpet and an old-fashioned record player and old board games. We spend the day playing Monopoly, Battleship and Clue while we listen to old records from the seventies like KC and the Sunshine Band, the Village People and the Bee Gees, and sip hot chocolates. Hannah, the coffee shop manager, even teaches us some funky dances—one called the Hustle and another one called the Chicken Dance.

Sipping hot chocolates and dancing like a chicken make me forget all about my worries for a while. This makes me wonder why Dr. Finkelman didn't write that on his prescription Post-it pad.

Before me, Mags and Nyx make our way back to the hotel we stop at Purple Mountain Taffy Company and fill an entire paper sack with different flavors of taffy.

Bing Cherry Vanilla, Birthday Cake, Cotton Candy, Huckleberry and even Strawberry Lemonade.

Nyx eats all the Bing Cherry Vanilla by the time we make it back to the Stanley, which is fine by me. I like the Huckleberry ones best.

"I hope Chef Raphaël doesn't take it personal if we don't eat dinner tonight," Mags says as we make it up the red front steps. "I'm so stuffed full of taffy, my ectoplasm guts might explode if I eat one more bite."

But by the time we make it into the lobby of the hotel, the last thing anyone is thinking about is dinner because of what we see when we step through the open double doors. Poor Ms. Lettie is sprawled out on the floor at the bottom of the grand staircase. Madame Drusilla is cradling Ms. Lettie's head in her lap and Chef Raphaël in his tall white hat is sitting on Ms. Lettie's other side, holding her hand. Ms. Lettie's face is whiter than a sheet and she's shaking so badly that her mile-high hair is actually vibrating.

At first I thought maybe Ms. Lettie had swirled her beanstalk hair so tall that it knocked her right over. But it turns out that wasn't it at all.

"*Où est son eau?*" Chef Raphaël is shouting toward the dining hall.

"Coming!" Mr. Lozano says, crossing the lobby with a glass of water in his hand that's dripping all over the carpet as he darts by us.

They all help her sit up.

"Here you go, Ms. Lettie." Mr. Lozano hands the glass to Chef Raphaël.

"*Ma chère,* please take a sip of this."

I rush to Ms. Lettie's feet, with Mags and Nyx right behind me.

"What happened?" I ask. "Is Ms. Lettie okay?"

"She saw something," Madame Drusilla tells us.

"What do you mean?" I say. "She's seen lots of things and she's never been freaked out by them before."

"I don't know," Madame Drusilla says. "I just heard her scream and came running and found her like this."

Ms. Lettie points to the grand staircase with a single shaking finger.

"Up there," she says, taking a gulp of water.

"On the staircase, Lettie?" Mr. Lozano asks her.

She nods while gulping more water, then takes an even shakier breath and says, "The eyes, the eyes. They *moved*."

"Whose eyes?" Madame Drusilla says.

"Was it a woman?" Mags asks.

"No," Ms. Lettie says. "The pictures."

"You mean the portraits on the wall?" I say. "Are you talking about the Jewel family portraits along the staircase?"

"Yes, the eyes followed me," she whispers. "They *moved*."

That's when Ubbe Amblebee comes running in with his plunger.

"What happened?" he asks, rushing to Ms. Lettie's side.

We all gaze up the grand staircase in unison.

"Which one?" Mr. Lozano asks. "Which portrait was it?"

We watch as Ms. Lettie points one more time.

"Honeycutt," she whispers.

"Honeycutt?" I ask, examining the many golden-framed Jewel portraits lined up on the wall of the staircase, from the baseboard all the way up to the ceiling. "I thought all these paintings were of the Jewel family."

"The Jewels put one portrait of the Honeycutts up there as well," Mr. Lozano tells us. "As a tribute."

"There's an actual picture of the Honeycutts?" I ask, scanning the frames. "Where?"

Mr. Lozano points to the smallest portrait on the wall.

"The only one without an elaborate golden frame," he tells me.

Me, Mags and Nyx scurry up the steps to examine the picture. It's high up on the wall, so Nyx gives me a ten-finger hoist so I can get a better look, holding myself straight by placing my palms flat against the wall.

And I realize this is the first time my worries didn't stop me once.

I'm Research for Totally Rad.

Me.

A real-life James Bond 007, but even better on account of the *girl-style* part.

My name is Moon. Karma Moon.

"What are you doing there?" Ubbe Amblebee calls out to me. "Stop that. You get down from there this instant."

"Mr. Honeycutt's eyes are gone!" I exclaim.

"Didn't you hear me?" Ubbe Amblebee stands up now, waving his plunger. "I said get down."

"What do you mean *gone*?" Mr. Lozano demands.

I turn to face everyone below me.

They are all watching.

Waiting.

"The eyes are actually cut out," I tell them, poking my fingers through the holes on the canvas. "See? *Gone.*"

That's when Mr. Amblebee blows a gasket and storms out the front double doors mumbling something about meddlesome kids, which is the exact same thing every single villain says when they are finally nabbed as the culprit in every single episode of *Scooby-Doo.*

And I know Mags is thinking the very same thing because when I look down at her and she looks back at me, we don't have to even say the words out loud.

Best-friend telepathy: *Phony baloney supreme.*

★

After Mr. Lozano and the others get Ms. Lettie on the couch in front of one of the fireplaces in the lobby, Dad, Big John, The Faz and Lights Out! get the equipment ready to interview Ms. Lettie on-camera.

I guess when actual eyes follow you from a portrait on the grand staircase, you don't care as much if the camera lens steals your soul.

Since everyone is distracted, me, Mags and Nyx take the opportunity to sneak down to the lower level when we think no one will notice.

"What are we doing?" Mags whispers behind me.

"Shush," I tell her. "Someone or something has been watching everything and everybody all along."

"So?" she says.

"So we are going to get to the bottom of this once and for all," I tell her.

"Don't you think we should leave this to the night crew?" she says. "They were going to have a sit-down with Mr. Lozano to get access to the tunnel."

"You heard them," I say. "If Mr. Lozano refuses, that's it. Done. *Finito.* No ghost and no Netflix contract."

She sighs and drags her feet behind me.

"This is it," I tell Nyx, waving a hand in front of the unmarked door to the tunnel. "You were right. You said there was some place in the hotel that Mr. Lozano was particularly weird about, and this is it. The door to the tunnel system that runs underneath all the buildings. I'm surprised you didn't know about it."

"Hey . . . yeah," Mags says then, giving him a suspicious eyeballing. "What's up with that?"

"What's that supposed to mean?" he wants to know.

"Oh, nothing," she says. "Just something ony-phay aloney-bay, Arlie-Chay Rown-Bay."

PIG LATIN TRANSLATION: PHONY BALONEY, CHARLIE BROWN.

I give her a smack while Nyx rattles the doorknob.

"Locked," he says.

"Yeah, that's *some* detective work you've got going there," Mags tells him.

"Mr. Lozano keeps it locked up tight," I tell Nyx, pulling the folded map out of my back pocket to show him.

"So how'd you get in?" he asks, looking over the map. "There's no key card access."

"Mr. Lozano is the only one I know who has a key, and I saw him put it in his pocket," I tell him. "So we had to resort to more creative methods of access."

"Oh, man." He rolls his eyes. "This again?"

"I picked the lock with a bobby pin so we could get in there and look around," Mags tells him.

"Ahhh . . . I believe law enforcement personnel might refer to that as breaking and entering," Nyx says.

Mags gives me a smack and says, "See? I told you so."

"First of all, there was no breaking," I tell him. "Just entering. And second, it's our only option."

Nyx waves a hand in front of the door and steps to the side.

"Be my guest," he tells her.

"But be quicker about it this time," I say. "We've only got a short window of opportunity here."

Since this is officially Mags's second unauthorized unlocking, the process goes much faster and we're inside the door in a matter of minutes. We prop the door open this time with a big rock we found on the back patio and enter.

I reach around and flip on the why-bother bulb first and then me and Nyx shine a path with our phone lights on the dirt floor.

"Mags," I say. "You film it."

She nods.

"Ready?" I ask them.

We stand there staring into the dark abyss beyond where our light reaches.

My heart is racing and my fingers tapping while I try to count my worries away.

One. Two. Three. Four.

WHAT-IFS

Still here.

I breathe in and out and think about something. Anything. Just to keep my what-ifs from taking over.

Chicken dancing.

Pinkies touching.

Dad smiling.

I breathe in and then out, taking each step forward.

"There is a door at the end of the hall, past the big safe," I whisper to Nyx, pointing to the drawing. "And a dark tunnel at the top of the T that leads to the underbelly of the rest of the hotel."

He nods, folds the map back up and says, "Lead the way."

I swallow and take one step forward and then another. Thinking about all the eyes that may be hiding in the blackness outside the reach of the light leading our way.

WHAT-IFS

A hotel manager serial killer.

WHAT-IFS

An evil canary rises up from the dead.

WHAT-IFS

Jell-O straight from the in-between.

"There," I whisper to Nyx. "See that door at the end?"

"Yeah," he whispers back. "There's light coming from underneath it. Where does that door lead?"

"I don't know," I say. "But last time I peeked underneath it and it almost seemed like someone was living here."

"It's probably just another employee dorm room," he says.

"I don't think so," I say. "Everyone has a room inside the employee quarters except Jack the busboy."

"He lives in town with his mom," Mags says.

"And Mr. Plum, of course," I say. "He stayed up on the fourth floor above us."

We step closer toward the door until we're right outside it.

Nyx wedges an ear against the wood.

"I hear a television or something," he says.

"A *television*?" I gulp and look at Mags.

WHAT-IFS

The television fuzz is here to snatch your soul.

I finger the satchel of bravery crystals around my neck.

Nyx presses his nose against the door.

"It stinks," he says.

"Strawberries, right?" Mags whispers.

"No." He sniffs again.

"Toilet plumbing?" I ask.

"No," he says, giving it one more sniff. "BO."

"Ew," Mags says. "Ernie Porter has mad BO at Immaculate Heart of Mary K-8 and on the days we have gym class I can't even stand next to the kid."

I turn to face her.

"Will you focus, please?" I say. "I don't want to hear another dry lip story."

"You couldn't make me kiss Ernie Porter for any money, so I wouldn't know if he has dry lips or not," she says. "His armpits smell like Peter Piper Pizza."

Nyx's leather military boot is tapping the floor.

"Are you done?" he asks us. "Because if I have to listen to one more kissing story between the two of you, I'm tendering my resignation to this whole operation."

I turn to Mags. "Yeah," I tell her. "You need to reel it in."

"Yeah well, you need to reel it out," she says.

"That doesn't even make sense."

"That's what I've been telling you."

"Are we doing this?" Nyx demands.

"Yeah," I say.

"Someone needs to look under the door," he says.

"I will," I offer. "I did it last time."

He nods and takes my phone while I get down on my hands and knees, pressing my cheek to the dirt floor.

"What do you see?" he whispers down to me.

"Same thing as before," I whisper back. "Crumpled bags of Funyuns, a stack of newspapers, empty cans of soda and . . . ew . . . hairy legs."

Mags sucks air. *"What?"* she breathes.

"Hairy legs," I say again. "Do ghosts have hairy legs?"

"Not in the blueprint," Mags tells me.

"What about at the eleven-minute, fifty-second mark of *The Shining*?"

"Nope," she says. "No hairy legs there, either."

I swallow. "*Dracula*?"

She shakes her head.

"What else do you see?" Nyx asks me.

"Um . . . I see . . . I see . . . *polka dots.*"

"Who's out there?" a voice booms from behind the door.

I suck air and scramble to my feet.

WHAT-IFS
Run.

Maybe Nyx's theory about the wolf making things worse than they really are makes sense sometimes, but I think my what-ifs make sense too.

Because right now they are dead-on.

WHAT-IFS
Run fast.

A Clue and a Candlestick

Maybe Nyx was the one who flung open the door at the end of the first tunnel. And maybe it was Mags who got it all on film.

But it was me who figured out there was phony baloney to begin with.

Even if I was wrong about Ms. Lettie being a tiny, purple-haired vampire, I was right about everything else.

There was way more going on at the Stanley Hotel than ghostly mayhem.

Polka-dot boxers and matching socks, to be exact.

"Mr. Plum!" I exclaim in the doorway of the tiny room at the end of the tunnel. "What are you doing in here?"

He's standing in front of us with one of the candelabras from the dining hall held out in front of him.

"I'll tell you exactly what he's doing here," a voice from the abyss calls out from the second tunnel.

Nyx spins around and flashes light into the darkness behind us. Its light bobs and weaves at first until it finds the culprit.

Ruby Red.

"I knew it! I knew you were part of the phony baloney this whole entire time. And just so you know, we know about the suitcase, too, so don't even."

I watch as she steps into the light. Except she's not wearing her gray-and-white housekeeper uniform this time either, just jeans and a blazer. And hanging from a chain around her neck is something silver and shiny and gleaming in the light.

I gasp.

A *badge.*

A real live badge.

"Wait . . . what are you doing with that?" I ask her, pointing at the silver shield.

"I'm Detective Ruby Red with the Estes Park Police Department," she tells us. "And, Mr. Plum, you're under arrest."

We watch as she steps toward him with handcuffs in her hand.

"This is all just one big mistake," Mr. Plum says, backing toward his room and shaking his head from side to side.

"Do not resist," Ruby Red tells him, grabbing his right hand and locking it in with a click.

"You don't understand," Mr. Plum goes on. "I was here to help. I was helping—"

That's when Mr. Lozano bursts through the door from the hall with a badge hanging from his neck too.

"You good?" he asks Ruby Red.

"Yep," she says, taking Mr. Plum's other hand and locking that one in too.

"Mr. Lozano!" I exclaim. "You too?"

He grabs a radio off his belt and holds it up to his mouth. "Larimer County badge number 4432."

"4432 Larimer County, go ahead," a voice calls from the speaker.

"Subject in custody," he says. "I'm out with 6314, looking for a patrol unit for transport to county jail."

"I don't understand," I say. "What's going on?"

"Mr. Plum has been behind the hauntings," Detective Ruby Red tells us.

I suck air. "This whole time?" I ask.

She nods. "That's right."

"And you're a detective?" I ask her.

She nods.

"You too, Mr. Lozano?"

"That's right," he says.

I turn to Mr. Plum, who is still standing in his polka-dot underwear, but now he has sparking silver bracelets, too.

And not in a good way.

"Mr. Plum," I say. "You did all of it?"

"I've done nothing wrong," he protests again. "This is all just a big misunderstanding."

"What about the eyes in the portrait?" Mags asks. "Those were yours?"

He doesn't say a word.

"You know Ms. Lettie took a header in the lobby because of that one," I tell him.

Silence.

"What about the warning on the typewriter?" Mags asks.

He gives us a wide smile. "You can attach a remote control to just about anything nowadays," he says.

"Wait . . . what about the chairs defying gravity that first night?" I say.

He shrugs. "I made that one up."

Mags grins with a finger pointed in his direction. "You got it from *Poltergeist,* didn't you?" she asks.

"Of course," he says. "It's a blueprint for all things haunted."

I gasp again and Mags gives me a grin. "Told you," she says. "Everyone who's anyone knows it. Even Mr. Plum, and he's a crook."

"But why, Mr. Plum?" Nyx asks. "Why do all this? I mean, what was your end game?"

But Detective Ruby Red answers for him instead.

"The constant hauntings were keeping guests away," she says. "Isn't that right, Mr. Plum?"

"I have the right to remain silent," he says.

"Why in the world would he want to keep the guests away?" I ask.

"The Plum family has been trying to buy the property for years from the Jewels, but the Jewels didn't want to sell it," Ruby Red explains. "So Mr. Plum devised this scheme so that the Jewel family would lose money and have to sell the hotel at a very low price."

"That's pretty bad, Mr. Plum," I tell him. "Even worse than bobby pin infractions. Father O'Leary would charge you big for that one."

"A lifetime of Hail Marys for sure," Mags adds. "Not to mention a mess of Our Fathers."

Mr. Plum just rolls his eyes.

"Detective Ruby Red," I say. "What was in the suitcase? The one with the leather handle."

She raises her eyebrows at me. "Evidence," she says. "You've been digging deeper than we thought you were."

"I'm Research for Totally Rad," I tell her, pointing to myself. "And I take that *very* seriously. *Very* seriously."

She nods with a slow-spreading grin. "You're good, you know that?"

I don't say anything, but I can't help but grin back real big.

"Wait . . . what about the dag gum hooligans?" I ask Mr. Plum. "Did you fake that, too?"

"That wasn't me," he says. "I swear it wasn't."

I wide-eye Mags and she wide-eyes me right back.

That's when Dad, Big John, The Faz and T. S. Phoenix come bursting through the first door from the main hallway.

"What's happening?" Dad's all out of breath. "Karma? You're okay? Mags? You good? Everybody's okay? Wh- what's going on in here?"

I stand tall and clear my throat and give him the skinny.

"It happened just like on *Dateline*," I say. "First the mystery unveils itself and then bam . . . the culprit is exposed. The perp lambasted. The hooligan nabbed."

They stand there staring at me.

"*What* does that mean?" T. S. Phoenix asks.

"It means this," I say, pointing an accusing finger at Mr. Plum. "It was Mr. Plum, in the tunnel, with the candlestick."

"*What?*" Dad says.

"Let's go," Detective Ruby Red tells Mr. Plum, ushering him toward the door to the hall. "You're being charged with disorderly conduct, trespassing, burglary, damage to property and, of course"—she clears her throat—"*obscenity.*"

And that's when she stops next to me and whispers, "Once you see polka-dot boxers paired with matching socks on some old guy, you can't unsee it."

297

A Shining Aura and the Greenest of Green

It's day nine.

We fly out tomorrow, but T. S. Phoenix and Tally are driving back to Denver today.

With not even a glimpse of a ghost on film during our trip to the Stanley Hotel, there is no Netflix contract, season one or season two. Dad decided to wait until he gets back to New York to make the actual call and takes the last day to finally get some sleep after all those late-night investigations. And even though Dad promised every which way but Sunday that he wasn't mad at me for ruining his big break, a part of me still feels like it's all my fault.

And I bet you can guess which part of me it is, too.

WHAT-IFS

It's your fault.

I'm Research.

It was my job to help Dad get a ghost on film, and it didn't happen.

"Good detective work, Karma," T. S. Phoenix is saying while he pumps my hand up and down in a hearty handshake. "You have quite the nose for investigation."

"Not quite good enough," I say.

"Well, if this place isn't haunted, it isn't haunted, right?" he says. "Science first. Always science first, but keeping an open mind to all other possibilities—"

"Without being pareidolic," I add with a pointer finger in the air.

"Exactly." He nods and grins. "We must follow the evidence."

Ghost Log Day 9

1. Totally Rad has diddly squat?
Zip?
Nada?
A big, fat, hairy goose egg?

That's a big-time affirmative.

"We still haven't figured out the dress or the dag gum hooligans," I remind him.

He nods again, with another gigantic grin. "Karma, I think you may have a future in the paranormal business if that's what you choose."

Tally grabs my hands then and smiles a warm smile at

me, her bracelets jingling. "She has talent in many areas," she tells him, and then bends down so we are eye to eye. "I don't know if you know this, but you have something very special inside you, Karma," she says. "Don't shy away from it or condemn it. Your sensitivity is a gift. Don't ever wish it away."

My mouth falls open.

"How did you—"

"Because I know . . . and also because . . . I was just like you when I was your age," she tells me.

"You were?" I breathe. "The what-ifs and everything?"

She nods. "Still have them," she tells me.

"No way."

She nods again. "But now I use them to understand the world better. To understand people. To understand the different experiences we all have and to respect everyone for those differences. With that in mind, I'm grateful for all my thoughts, because they allow me to put myself in the shoes of others with compassion and love. And I am happy for them mostly because they make me special. And they're what make you special too."

"Me?" I point to my front.

"You," she says. "Your aura shines, sweetheart. Don't ever let anyone blow the light out on your brightness just because they don't shine themselves."

Her words float in the air between us. I breathe them in.

In and then out.

Trying to get them to stick inside me somewhere.

My aura light.

It makes me wonder why Mom never said anything about it. Maybe she's not as woo-woo as she thinks she is. I mean, how can she be? She got everything wrong and she can't even see it. Maybe she's the dull light Tally is talking about.

"You really think I'm a bright light?" I ask Tally.

"I don't think it," she tells me. "I see it. I feel it. And I *know* it."

It's at that very moment that tears find the back of my throat and lodge in a big mess. Except this time is different. This time it's not the kind of tears that make you feel like you're dying to breathe. Not even close. This time they are tears that make my shoulders straighter and my back grow longer as I stand tall in front of her. Like her words made it inside me and I can actually *feel* the light Tally is talking about.

Me.

Karma Moon Vallenari.

I wrap my arms around Tally, squeezing her way too tight, but she doesn't even complain either, she just hugs me back.

"Thank you" is all I can think to say in her arms, even though I wish more than anything that I knew how to tell her just how much her words made me feel on the inside.

She holds my hand as we walk down the red front steps and watch as T. S. Phoenix loads all the bags into the back of their black SUV with a sign on the passenger-side door that reads,

LIGHTS OUT!

After everyone says their goodbyes, me, Dad and Mags wave as they pull away and T. S. Phoenix toots the horn three times. It's when they roll down East Wonderview and turn onto Steamer Parkway and the SUV is finally out of sight that I notice it.

"Whoa! Look!" I hold my hand out to show Mags my ring.

"Whoa!" she agrees, grabbing my finger and examining it. "When did that happen? That's the greenest green I've ever seen!"

"What does green stand for?" I ask her.

She pulls out her phone and starts typing.

"Green," she says. "Calm and together."

"I found my tuner!" I exclaim.

"I don't even know what that means," she says.

"You'd have to be a Velma to get it and you're *waaaaay* too Daphne." I throw an arm around her shoulders and we head back inside.

★

That night, our very last night at the Stanley Hotel, Mags and me decide to binge-watch *Scooby-Doo* episodes on her laptop in front of the fireplace in the lobby. Chef Raphaël popped us real popcorn in a pot instead of the microwave kind and right this minute we're sunk down deep into the leather couch with our feet on the coffee table and the laptop between us.

"It's the manager," Mags tells me with her mouth full of popcorn.

"No way," I tell her. "It's the caretaker. It's almost always the caretaker."

"Almost isn't always," she says. "In the last one, it was the shop owner. And in the one before that, it was the maintenance man."

"I will bet you a million dollars it's the caretaker," I say.

"You don't have a million dollars," Mags reminds me.

"It's not really a million dollars, it's figurative."

"It's what?" she asks.

"Don't you remember *any* of the vocabulary words?"

"Not on spring break I don't." She shoves in another mouthful. "My brain is on vacation. Ha!" she exclaims then. "See? It's the manager! I win! I'll take that money in small bills, please." She holds out her hand.

I give it a smack.

"What's the next one?" I ask her.

She squints at the screen and says, "'Jeepers, It's the Creeper.'"

I snort and shake my head. "Classic," I say.

"I'm going to go out on a limb and say the manager did it," she tells me.

"It's the museum owner," someone calls out from behind us.

We turn around to see Jack the busboy.

He's taken over for Mr. Lozano as interim manager, and instead of a T-shirt or no shirt, he's wearing a blue button-down and a bright yellow tie.

"Oh, hey," Mags breathes at him. "If you're done for the evening, you can join us for a *Scooby-Doo* binge marathon. I mean, if you want to you can."

"So," I say. "I guess you knew about the whole Ruby Red deal, huh?"

"Mr. and Mrs. Jewel let Gran and me know about it because they needed some trusted employees to help. No one is more trustworthy than Gran," he tells us, slipping on his jacket.

"So, you want to stay and watch, then?" Mags asks.

"Nah," he says. "I'm meeting my girlfriend at Fun City for miniature golf."

Mags's mouth falls open, but no words come out of it.

"Later," he calls to us with a wave.

We watch him over the top of the couch as he pushes open the front double doors and whistles down the red steps.

"Now that I get a real good look at him," Mags says, sinking deeper into the leather after Jack heads out, "he's not even cute. Plus he probably uses straws too. He just looks like the type who wouldn't care two hoots about saving the turtles."

"I thought you wanted to kiss him in the cooler," I tease her.

"I'd rather kiss Fred," she mumbles. "Did you see his lips? Could they *be* more chapped? Fireworks kiss dud supreme."

"Uh-huh," I say with a grin.

"I'm going to get another soda." Mags passes the laptop to me and jumps up from the couch. "So push Pause and don't start it until I get back."

I watch her head across the lobby.

"The museum owner," she grumbles. "Like he really knows."

"Get me another Snapple too," I call after her. "A Fruit Punch one."

She doesn't answer me because she's already singing a Taylor Swift song about never getting back together.

"Fruit Punch," I holler again.

I type in *baby monkeys playing* on YouTube while I wait for her, but I don't even get through the first video because in about twenty seconds, she is full-on sprinting back across the lobby.

"Karma!" she exclaims.

"I told you Fruit Punch, didn't I?" I say, holding up two fingers. "Twice I said it."

"I—I—I," she stammers.

"Is it all gone? You drank the last one, didn't you? You know they're my favorite. It's payback for me hogging the Made-with-Love Cookies, isn't it?"

"No," she says, pointing back toward the dining hall. "It's just . . . I—I think . . . I mean, there was . . . um—"

"What's wrong with you?" I ask her. "Spit it out already."

"Mr. Plum," she says. "He's arrested, right?"

"Yeah," I say.

"And the doors are locked up, right?"

"Yeah," I say again.

"And the Ouija board is in the dumpster, right?"

"Will you spit it out already?" I demand.

"If I said I saw something or heard something, it'd be real, right?" she asks.

I push the laptop aside and scramble up off the couch. "What are you saying?" I ask her.

"I'm saying I *s-saw* her," she tells me. "And I *heard* her too."

"Who?" I say.

"The woman."

"But Mr. Plum said he made everything up," I tell her.

"Not the dag gum hooligans," she says. "And not the dress, either."

"So you heard the dag gum hooligans?" I ask. "Is that what you're saying?"

"No," she says. "This was a woman. *The* woman."

"*The* woman?"

"Maybe you were right all along," she says. "Maybe there was a paranormal disturbance and phony baloney all at the same time."

I gasp, grabbing her by her arms and giving her a shake. "Was it Mrs. Honeycutt?" I demand. "It was, wasn't it?"

"No," she says.

"Please say it wasn't Bloody Mary," I say. "Was it Bloody Mary?"

"No," she says again. "It was *her*, her."

"Her *who*?"

"*Cecelia.*"

I suck air. "How do you know?" I ask.

"She *said* it. She actually told me her name and I *heard* it."

"You *heard* her say her name?"

She nods. "But that's not all I heard either."

"What else did she say?"

She swallows and whispers, *"Tunnel."*

"Whoa!" I exclaim. "That's huge."

"It's gigantic," she agrees. "Better call Charlie Brown for this one, because there's no way you're dragging me in the tunnel for a paranormal investigation for a third time."

I'm already dialing.

"Voice mail," I tell her.

"Leave a message," she tells me.

Nyx's voice mail: Only three people have this number. If you're not one of them, hang up now.

"Nyx!" I exclaim into the speaker. "Operation: Ghost Selfie is on! This time we get an image on film. Call me back."

A Football Hail Mary Ghost

Knock . . . pause . . . knock, knock, knock . . . pause . . . knock . . . pause . . . knock, knock.

I rush to the door of room 332.

"What's the password?" I call, and then wedge my ear up against the wood.

Mags looks up from her phone. "Are we still doing that?" she asks.

"It makes things more interesting, don't you think?" I say.

"I just saw a ghost in the kitchen," she tells me. "I think things are plenty interesting."

"What's the password?" I call through the door again.

"Choose woo-woo over bad juju," Nyx calls.

"Oh my good God, you've got Charlie Brown saying that now too?" Mags asks.

I grin real big at her and pull open the door and Nyx is standing there with his backpack and black skullcap.

"It's important to have a mantra in life, right?" I ask Nyx.

"Real important," he agrees, slipping in past me.

"But he already has his own," she tells me. "He doesn't need to adopt yours."

"Yeah, but we made a pact that he's going to adopt mine as his surefire mantra and I'm going to adopt his for mine. *Fear makes the wolf bigger than he is.*"

"Are double mantras totally weird? Check," she says.

Nyx shakes his head at her. "So pea soup," he says.

I laugh while Mags gives him an eyes-to-the-sky roll.

"So, what did you bring for our tunnel excursion?" I ask Nyx.

He unloads his backpack one item at a time.

"First off," he says, "I agree with you. Since the entity said the word *tunnel,* we're better off investigating there instead of the kitchen. Even though that's where the spirit showed herself."

"Agreed," I say.

"I also think that with the quartz enhancing the receptivity of our contact, that will be our best chance at getting something on film. But . . ."

"But what?" Mags asks.

"Where's the map?" he asks.

I pull it out of the night table drawer and show it to him.

He unfolds it. "Here." He points to the second tunnel. "It needs to be this one."

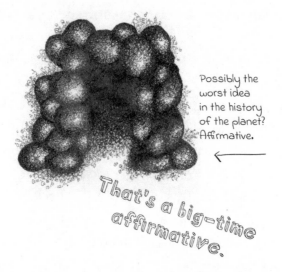

Possibly the worst idea in the history of the planet? Affirmative.

←

That's a big-time affirmative.

"The deep dark tunnel that leads to the underbelly of the entire hotel?" I ask.

He nods.

I swallow. "You're *sure* it needs to be that tunnel?"

I turn to Mags.

"I'm out," she says.

I give her a pointer finger. "Don't be a baby."

"I'm going to be a baby," she says.

"Mags, we need you to bobby-pin the lock."

"Fine," she says. "I'll bobby-pin it, but I'm not going in there this time. Not after what I just went through."

I look at Nyx and he shrugs. "We can do it and she can be the lookout."

"Fine," I say. "Will you be the lookout at least?"

"As long as I don't have to go in," she says.

I turn back to Nyx. "So, what is all this stuff?"

"My Hail Mary Ghost on Film Kit," he says.

"You mean, like the Father O'Leary kind of Hail Marys?" I ask him.

"No, like a football kind."

"What's the football kind?" she asks.

"It's like a last-ditch effort at the very last second when there's no time left on the clock. You gotta just hurl the ball down the field to get the touchdown. Or in this case, to get the ghost. Get it? A Hail Mary Ghost on Film Kit."

I nod. "It's definitely time for a football Hail Mary," I tell him.

HAIL MARY GHOST ON FILM KIT
1 GhostPro Night Vision Camera
1 laptop
1 PX

"With Infrared Illuminator," Mags reads off the package.

"Better night vision perception," Nyx tells her.

"Yeah, Mags." I grin. "You gotta illuminate. Open your mind, why don't you."

She snorts. "Oh, like you know," she says.

"What about this?" I ask, holding up a small box a little bigger than a deck of cards with some buttons, a speaker and a small screen on it. "What's a PX?"

"It's this somewhat controversial device ghost hunters

use to detect energies and then translate it into language. Like a tool to transcribe the language from the in-between. It has a vocabulary of over two thousand words. A lot of ghost hunters say it's a joke, but in this case, being a Hail Mary and all, better not rule anything out."

"Yep," I agree.

"Definitely," Mags says.

"What about the Ouija board?" I ask.

"The ghost is already here and has been this whole time," Nyx says. "We don't need to conjure her up. We just need to make contact."

"Sounds good," I say, putting my hand in the center of our circle. "Everybody bring it in."

Nyx puts his hand on mine and Mags puts her hand on his.

"Tonight," I say. "We find a ghost! On three, Operation: Football Hail Mary Ghost!"

We sneak our way down to the tunnel door, snaking down the stairs in stealthlike fashion to avoid all detection.

Our mission is a success.

Once we make it, Mags expertly bobby-pins the lock. She's so good now, it doesn't hardly take any time at all.

When I hear the lock click, she turns to me and says, "We're in."

I nod and take one giant breath.

"Our mission to find a ghost and save Totally Rad begins now," I say to Nyx. "Are you ready?"

"Ready," Nyx says.

"Good luck and Godspeed," Mags tells us, and we step inside. First me and then Nyx. He turns on the flashlight so there is a round spot of light straight out in front of me.

It's only a few steps to get to the second tunnel.

Nyx shines his light inside.

But it's windy, so the light bounces back off the quartz rock.

"Ready?" I ask, selecting the camera app on my phone.

"If you are," he says.

I duck and take a step into the second tunnel.

Today it smells even more damp after it rained earlier in the day. There's a trickle of water coming from somewhere and we hear a dripping sound.

A machine kicks on, causing a loud buzzing noise.

That's when I remember I've been so worried about ghosts that I forgot about my other phobia.

WHAT-IFS

GOOGLE: An average of 6.8 people die each year from venomous spider bites.

I'd rather see ten linty belly buttons and do algebra problems until the end of time than see even one spider.

They're the worst.

Another step forward and then another.

The light shines on rock and on the dirt floor where my feet are stepping. Around a bend and then another.

"Are you here?" Nyx calls out into the darkness. "We don't mean you any harm. We are here to help you."

The PX box crackles in his hand.

"What's that?" I ask.

"It's picking up energy," he tells me.

"But no words?"

"Not yet," he says. "Maybe—"

That's when we hear something and we both stop in our tracks.

"Did you make that out?" he asks.

"Uh-huh," I say.

"Keep listening," he tells me.

I nod.

Then PX Siri says it again.

PX Siri: Searching.

"She said *searching*!" I exclaim. "I'm sure of it."

"You are searching?" Nyx calls out to the entity again. "What are you searching for?"

The box crackles again.

"Keep going," Nyx tells me.

My feet feel heavy and my chest hurts.

I squint and strain my eyes, trying to see into the abyss of the tunnel, attempting to make out anything other than the darkness that is engulfing us as we move deeper and deeper beneath the hotel.

Rocks crumble down the side of the wall above us and we stop again.

"Did you hear that?" I ask Nyx. "That can't be good."

WHAT-IFS

I wonder if anyone has ever
been buried alive by quartz.

"Mr. Lozano said the tunnel was off-limits because it wasn't safe," I tell him.

"Do you want to turn back?" Nyx asks me.

I don't say anything.

"This is your thing, so if you want to turn back, we'll turn back," he says. "But you told me this was an emergency."

"It is."

"You needed a ghost on film."

"We do."

"It's your call," he says.

I bite on my lip and turn back toward the abyss.

"Let's keep going," I say.

He nods.

I take one careful footstep and then another. Sliding my Converse in case there's a drop-off into the in-between. Slowly, I make my way around each bend in the tunnel, never able to see farther than a few feet in front of us at one time.

"Are you here with us?" Nyx calls again.

PX Siri: Yes.

I gasp.

"We need you to make your-self visible to us," Nyx tells her. "Can you do that?"

Electricity soars through the box in Nyx's hand.

Crackle.

Pop.

Buzz.

"We know you are here with us," I call out to the entity now. "Please let us see you."

We make our way around another bend and then Nyx's flashlight goes out.

"What are you doing?" I demand. "Turn it back on."

"I didn't do it," he tells me.

More rocks fall and scatter, but this time it's behind us.

I spin around, the camera still filming, and that's when I see a blur of fog flutter across the lens.

My breath comes fast and my stomach feels sick. I can feel spiders crawling on me, down my shirt and up my arms, even though I can't see any. Sweat prickles under my arms, below my bottom lip and across my scalp.

Focus.

Breathe.

In and then out. In and then out.

I wait, listening to my own lungs and the trickle of water and the mechanical buzzing.

But all we hear is paranormal silence.

"Hey, what's this?" Nyx says. "I'm stepping on something."

WHAT-IFS

Please don't be spiders.
Please don't be spiders.
Please don't be spiders.

All I hear is some shuffling, and then he turns on the light from his phone.

"It's dried-up old rose petals."

I suck air.

"She's here," I say. "I knew it!"

"M-maybe we've got enough," he says. "Should we turn back?"

I turn to face him.

It's the first time I've seen Nyx scared. I guess everyone has their what-ifs, Dad and Nyx, too. Even Mags has them.

Maybe I'm more normal than I even thought.

"Fear makes the wolf bigger than he is," I tell him, and then I take the satchel of bravery crystals from around my neck and pass them to him.

"Here," I say. "Maybe you need these more than I do. Because one thing is for sure. We aren't leaving until we get a ghost."

Velma Dinkley Indeed

Knock . . . pause . . . knock, knock, knock . . . pause . . . knock . . . pause . . . knock, knock.

Mags flings open the unmarked door for us.

"Well?" she demands. "What did you get?"

"We got her voice on the PX and more dried-up rose petals," I tell her.

She gasps. "Rose petals?" she exclaims.

"Yep," I say. "She was definitely there, but I didn't see her. Nyx's flashlight just went out. Like that." I snap my fingers. "We were in there in total darkness until he pulled out his phone."

"You just know she interrupted the electrical current in the tunnel with her energies," Mags says.

"Totally," I agree.

"Remember, just because we didn't see anything with our eyes doesn't mean that the camera didn't pick up an image," Nyx tells us. "Let's review the video."

"But why did Mags see her with her own eyes in the kitchen and we didn't?"

He shrugs. "I don't know everything there is to know about ghosts," he says. "All I can say is that sometimes you see them, sometimes you hear them and sometimes you just sense them. But still, the camera eye can pick up things we don't always see with ours."

Nyx sits down in the middle of the downstairs hall in front of the unmarked door and we crouch down to get a look over his shoulders. He plugs the camera into his laptop with a short, skinny cord and taps the keys on the keyboard until an image of the tunnel comes up.

"The screen is all green," I say.

"That's the night vision scope," he tells me. "So even though we couldn't see into the darkness, the camera could."

He pushes the triangle-shaped Play button in the middle of the screen.

We watch what we just recorded inside the tunnel. It looks a whole lot different than it did with my eyes. Now I can see what I could only hear inside the abyss.

Rocks tumbling down the walls in front of me.

Water trickling from cracks in the quartz.

Spiderwebs woven across the ceiling.

Rusted pipes and loose wires hanging.

And then . . . a *dress.*

An ancient dress, just like the one in our closet.

"That's her!" I exclaim. "That's her!"

Mags grabs my hand and squeezes it tight.

We all watch as the image whisks by the camera and back again, and behind it . . . hundreds of orbs of light.

Thousands.

"You didn't see any of this?" Mags asks.

"No," I breathe. "We felt it, though. Didn't we?" I ask Nyx.

"Definitely," he says without taking his eyes off the screen.

"What is that?"

"In *Poltergeist,*" Nyx says, "they showed the orbs as people all stuck in the in-between for some reason or other."

"Why are they stuck?" I ask.

"Just like I said on the first day," Mags says. "Some don't know they are dead. Some have unfinished business. And some are just afraid of the unknown."

"It's sad," I say, staring at the screen.

"Yeah," Mags agrees.

"To be stuck in your very own prison because you're afraid of what might happen, instead of seeing the surprise of the gift you haven't opened yet," I say, watching the bobbing lights.

Mags turns to look at me.

"That sounds like a good mantra," she says.

"Yeah," I say.

"You did it, Karma Moon!" she exclaims. "You got a ghost on film just like you said you would!"

I feel my shoulders push back as I stand tall again. The aura light that Tally talked about wraps its arms around me.

"Dad is going to wig out," I tell her.

"Totally," she agrees.

"Totally Rad Productions is on the map," I say. "It happened just like the fortune cookie said it would."

Mags's hand shoots up high in the air at that very moment and she says, "Raise your hand if your very best friend in the whole wide world is more Velma than anyone else on the planet!"

I can feel the grin spread slowly across my face. A wide smile that feels a lot like my very own ray of light. One that might even have the power to shine away a worry storm all on my own.

Ghost Log Day 9

1. Ghost on film?
   Nailed it.

A Netflix Original
Season Premiere

I t all started with the moo goo gai pan.

On that very fateful day last winter, while we just sat there, eating takeout leftovers like it was any other Tuesday afternoon.

And then the old-fashioned yellow phone rang and changed our lives forever.

Just like the cookie knew it would.

FORTUNE COOKIE

A heavy burden will be lifted with a single phone call.

And that cookie was dead-on too.

Just like I knew it would be.

Even if it happened with a football Hail Mary big break.

In the end, it all happened just the way it was supposed to. Even though I worried the whole time that it wouldn't.

I let my fears make my wolf too big.

But I'm working on that.

Especially because after all that worrying for nothing, Dad's big break is happening right now, just like the cookie said it would.

And I'm still not sure if I am tuned in the way Tally and Madame Drusilla say I am, but I'm paying a lot more attention to my gut these days just in case.

Tonight, only six short months after me and Nyx captured an actual ghost on film, we are having an official private showing of our docuseries in apartment 4B.

Brought to you by Netflix.

Dad even ordered a red mat for the front door outside our apartment to make it an *official red carpet* premiere.

A PARANORMAL DISTURBANCE AT THE STANLEY HOTEL

Not to brag or anything, but the title was totally my idea.

Dad wanted to call it *A Ghost at the Stanley,* but I convinced him to change it.

And when I saw it on the computer screen while Big John was editing and adding the scary music, all I can say is . . . *nailed it.*

All the A-listers and bigwigs are gathered for the big event in our living room right this minute. Bigwigs being T. S. Phoenix; Tally; Mags; Mr. and Mrs. Bogdonavich; Big John and his girlfriend, Gloria; The Faz and The Fazette; and grumpy Mr. Drago—and Dad even flew Nyx out to surprise me.

And was I surprised.

Side note: Nyx is totally sitting next to me on the couch right now and it feels like we may be having another moment.

Nothing's touching or anything like that, but it's a definite carpet shock kind of feeling anyway.

But, you know . . . in a good way.

Sitting next to Mags is Jeremy Kelly. It turns out that once he got his chapped lips in check, Mags gave him another shot, and the fireworks didn't dud out the second time.

The only person who should be here and isn't is Mom.

But it's her choice to live her other life without us. And as much as it still hurts my heart when I let myself really think about it, I try to focus on other things instead.

Like Dad, for one.

Me and him are solid as concrete. Nothing will ever break that. I know that now and so do my what-ifs.

Dad and I have even been busy fixing up our place a bit too. After getting special permission from the owner, Dad laid a new floor in the kitchen, and grumpy Mr. Drago helped him do it, too. I oiled the windows, which now open even when it rains, and there's a new coat of paint in all the rooms. I chose bright green for my room to match my mood ring, which has never turned mud brown again. As long as we paint everything white again if we ever move out, we could pick any colors we wanted. And when Dad said we should order something special for our spaces to make them our own, I chose a new poster for above my bed.

Criss Angel.

Dad chose a spanking-new seventy-two-inch flat-screen with Dolby Surround Sound for the living room. He said for a proper premiere you always need Dolby Surround Sound.

There *is* one big thing that hasn't changed.

Huge, really.

The old-fashioned yellow phone.

We were in total agreement about that one.

It's a part of our story (even though it doesn't have Wi-Fi).

Oh, and get this one . . . on the credits of our docu-series, Dad promoted me to full-on editor. That's my exact title, too. So it actually looks like this *while* the credits roll on the screen . . .

Karma Moon Vallenari, Editor

How cool is that?

I'm definitely walking a little taller because of that one. I even got involved in the video production group at Immaculate Heart of Mary K-8, and everyone in the group thinks it's the coolest thing ever that me and my dad make documentaries together.

I've officially decided I'm going to be just like Dad when I grow up. With the exception of a little woo-woo mixed in. Because I will always stand by my mantra.

KARMA'S MANTRA: WOO-WOO ISN'T CUCKOO AND WITHOUT IT YOU'LL HAVE BAD JUJU.

With all the footage we got on film in the ten days we were at the Stanley Hotel, we were able to edit the show into ten full episodes. The Netflix people were beyond thrilled in the end, especially because of the footage me and Nyx got in the tunnel on that very last day.

Still no confirmation about a season two yet.

But I'm keeping my eye out for a sign to tell us it's coming. And I know Dad is too—even if he won't admit it—because ever since we got back from Estes Park, he actually *reads* the fortunes in his cookies.

But tonight? Tonight is all about celebration, friends

(new and old) and of course takeout food from Noodle King of New York City.

Dad even let Alfred Hitch-cock have some moo goo in his bowl, the one I painted for him at Color Me Mine in Tribeca  moo goo ⟵ three years ago. I drew his full name on it. And even though there's a chip on the *A* from when Mom dropped it on the peeling linoleum floor, you can still read it just fine. Hitchy's out cold right now in a moo goo coma underneath the glass coffee table, and I bet if he had a doggie mood ring, it would surely be a satisfying green.

I watch Dad while I nibble on an egg roll and he chats it up with everyone, making good and sure that each per-son has something to drink or enough food on their plate. He's happier than I've ever seen him.

And I am too, in a way.

If I had to put my finger on it, I'm not sure where my finger would be. Maybe it's because we've finally accepted something we hadn't wanted to accept, just like the ghosts stuck in the in-between need to do. Maybe we learned through the lost spirits that sometimes things don't go our way but we still have to keep on the road that's ours. And find ways to be happy about it.

And we definitely have.

I've actually learned to think rather than worry so much lately. Ever since we got home, me and Dr. Finkelman haven't played Uno once. Maybe he took a class at the Institute of Paranormal Studies and Professional Ghost Investigation of Boulder, Colorado, after all (although I haven't seen any badge pinned to his front). Or maybe it's me being open to new things. But whatever it is, it's working way better than Uno ever has. We do activities now that help me see things differently to calm my what-ifs way better than ever before. Dr. Finkelman has even helped me feel better about Mom and her leaving us the way she did.

Not great, but better.

And like Dr. Finkelman, MD, PhD, LP, says, sometimes that's enough.

And for now . . . I guess it is.

I also learned you can't predict what will happen, no matter what woo-woo you use, and you also can't change your fate, no matter how hard you try.

And I'd like to add . . . never . . . *ever* . . . doubt the almighty fortune cookie.

It's *never* wrong.

Crystal Mystic isn't either, it's just off-line sometimes.

CRYSTAL MYSTIC
YES, ALL YOUR STARS ARE
ALIGNED!

Dad is setting up the television for our Netflix premiere party right this minute while I'm cracking open my fortune cookie.

Mags puts her chin on my arm. "Mine said, *Doing your best at this moment puts you in place to do your best in the next moment*," she says. "I decided that's going to be my new mantra."

"I knew I would change your mind," I tell her.

I pull the tiny slip of paper out of my cookie pieces and turn it upright.

"What does yours say?" she asks.

FORTUNE COOKIE

**The best road to a happy future . . .
eat more Chinese food.**

She laughs and so do I.

"Didn't I tell you?" I say. "Everyone who's anyone knows that the almighty fortune cookie is *never* wrong."

"I think that might be the *rightest* fortune ever," Mags agrees.

I show Nyx and he nods, chewing on a mound of pan-fried noodles trying to escape between his lips.

"Okay," Dad calls out. "Is everyone ready for *A Paranormal Disturbance at the Stanley Hotel* to start?"

"Yes!" everyone shouts, settling into their spots for the viewing.

T. S. Phoenix and Tally are on the kitchen chairs set around the television, Mr. Drago brought his own ratty lawn chair that he uses out on the front stoop, and Mr. and Mrs. Bogdonavich are on the floor right in front.

Everyone is here to celebrate with us.

"Here we go," Dad says, aiming the clicker and pushing Play from his spanking-new La-Z-Boy leather recliner.

We all watch as the fancy-dancy new intro plays. Big John chose this really cool, plinky music that's both scary and exciting at the same time, with images of Dad and T. S. Phoenix, and Tally and even me, Mags and Nyx with serious faces as we search for ghosts.

"I totally feel like a movie star right now," Mags gushes. "I can't wait until Darby Woods sees this. She's going to be so jealous."

Dad turns to me and gives me a big grin. "I wonder if Cecelia is here with us," he says, his chin on his hand.

"She has to be," I say. "This is her premiere too."

"Cecelia?" Nyx asks.

"Yeah." I take another bite of cookie. "That's the name of the ghost," I tell him.

His eyebrows go up. "How do you know that?" he asks.

I point in Mags's direction. "Mags said she heard the ghost say her name during the kitchen sighting."

"You *heard* Cecelia?" Nyx says.

"Yep," she tells him.

"We knew it because she was trying to spell it out to Tally, first on the piano in the Music Room and then in room 332 with the dress. We think it was the woman Chef Raphaël saw in the dining hall, too," I say.

"You never told me her name," Nyx says.

"Oh." I shrug. "I guess I forgot. Why?"

"So you're telling me that Cecelia was the spirit we were chasing in the tunnel on that last night?" Nyx says.

"Yeah," I say.

"And that's who we got on film?" he asks.

"Yeah," I say again. "Why? What's the big deal?"

"The big deal is . . . you never told me her name," he says.

"Do you know her or something?" I snort.

That's when Dad pushes Pause on the clicker and I notice everyone's eyes are on Nyx.

And so are mine.

"I—I think I do," he tells us.

I wide-eye him and say, "What do you mean? How can you know Cecelia?"

"Do you remember when I told you about Harry Houdini?" he asks.

"Yeah," I say.

"Remember when I told you he performed there and that people still do Halloween séances every year to try to make contact at the hotel? Even me?"

"Yeah," I say again. "After his wife stopped trying, many years after his death . . . oh," I gasp. "Cecelia is Houdini's wife? No . . . wait, her name was Bess, not Cecelia."

"Right," he says. "Bess *was* his wife. But Cecelia Weisz"—he swallows—"was the name of Harry Houdini's mother."

Mags lets out a *"Whoa."* I throw my hand over my

mouth, Big John chokes on his moo goo and Dad drops the remote.

"Houdini's *mother*?" I say. "Her name was Cecelia?"

Nyx nods a slow nod.

"So the séances you've been doing at the Stanley on Halloween all this time to bring up the spirit of Harry Houdini have brought up his mother instead?"

"It's possible," Nyx says. "And maybe she's not the only one. What if Houdini and Bess are there too and we haven't made contact yet?"

"And they're all looking for each other," I breathe. "An actual intellectual haunting, just like you said, Dr. Phoenix, attempting to make contact on this plane of existence from the beyond."

"It could have been the Houdinis all along," T. S. Phoenix says.

"It was Ms. Lettie who said it was the Honeycutts," Dad says. "I guess we just went with that theory."

"Wow," Nyx says to no one in particular. "The Houdinis' spirits in the Stanley Hotel. That would be epic."

I turn to Dad and watch the slow grin spread over his face. That grin. The one that says everything is going to be okay. But this grin says something else, too. And he doesn't even have to tell me what he's thinking, either, because when our eyes meet, I already know.

This is our sign.

The one we've been waiting for. And we didn't need a cookie or Crystal Mystic to find it, either.

It turns out we needed a Charlie Brown.

Even Dad knows it's true, and I know that for sure, because at that very moment he reaches to grab a fortune cookie off the coffee table.

He cracks it open and lifts out the message.

First he reads it to himself.

Then our eyes lock.

And then his grin spreads even wider.

"Well?" I demand. "What does it say?"

He reads each word aloud, slow and sure.

FORTUNE COOKIE

An extraordinary opportunity is on the horizon.

I can feel my eyes grow as wide as water walking balls, and Dad is grinning bigger than I've ever seen him grin, and then, at the very same time, we say it. Because that's how it is with true blue.

I point to him and he points to me and together we shout, "Season two!"

Illustrations by: Karma Moon Vallenari

And Mags too!

Acknowledgments

I am incredibly fortunate to have worked with the same talented team at Penguin Random House's Crown Books for Young Readers for my fourth book, *Karma Moon— Ghost Hunter.* What a supportive group you have been! Thank you, Emily Easton, for continuing to be my editor, my writing coach, the perfect word finder in the eleventh hour and so much more. There are many other people who have worked on my books that I don't get the pleasure of meeting, but having you behind me has made this experience more amazing than I ever could have imagined. My name may be on the front of each book, but it's only because of you and everything you do to make it happen. Thanks also to my agent at Fuse Literary, Laurie McLean, who is always in my corner.

To all the wonderful teachers and librarians who have graciously shared my stories with your students, it's an incredible privilege to have my words be part of your lesson—I cannot thank you enough for that honor. And to my readers of every age, thank you for all your kind words—and for choosing to read the stories I write. I hope you love Karma Moon, Mags and Nyx, too.

To my friends and family for sharing in my excitement at every juncture of the process—thank you for celebrating my victories and lending a shoulder when it gets difficult. I couldn't do it without you. I love you all. A special thank-you to Alaina Hayes, my junior consultant and editor for this story. I appreciate your expertise in all things Catholic and explaining why you would never, *ever* use a Ouija board.

For those who also struggle with a bad case of the what-ifs, don't give up. The voice may continue, but there are ways to turn down the volume. Reach out for help; it's there waiting for you.

I wish to express my gratitude to the historic Stanley Hotel for the amazing tours and fascinating stories of the many families who delighted in spending time there. A special thanks to Aiden Sinclair (aidensinclair.net), paranormal illusionist extraordinaire, for enlightening me on very important Houdini facts and for sharing your deep passion for the human experiences of the *passed*. Everyone deserves to have their story told and forever treasured. There will never be a time I walk through the double doors of the Stanley Hotel that I won't think of Lillian. It was an honor getting to know her. Thank you for introducing her to us all.

And finally, Tobin Scott, you are my heart and my inspiration in every story I write and every adventure I dream. They are stories we live together on the pages of each book. You are in the mix as usual, T. S. Phoenix—and you always will be.

Your story . . . forever treasured.

ABOUT THE AUTHOR

Melissa Savage is the author of *Lemons, The Truth About Martians,* and *Nessie Quest.* She is also a child and family therapist. Although the idea of a ghost being defined as a cryptid remains the fuel of a raging controversy, Melissa loves writing crypto-zoological mysteries of any kind for kids—including the paranormal kind. She lives in Phoenix, Arizona. To learn about the real mysteries of the historic Stanley Hotel, visit stanleyhotel.com. You can follow Melissa on Twitter at @melissadsavage or visit her at melissadsavage.com.